"I wanted to make sure we all understood what we're about here. There are leaders in other countries who have the same specific objectives we do, although for different and often diametrically opposed reasons. The program that Admiral Bergen will coordinate should be dedicated to benefiting from such unusual confluences of interests, reflecting the old saying that the enemy of mine enemy is my friend. However, we must be very careful that in winning our war we don't piss off every Muslim in the world."

Mason Kitteridge
President of the United States
The Drone Paradigm

Also by Frederick Harrison

An Opaque War

A Course To Stay

The RCI

Her Eyes Were Filled With Tears

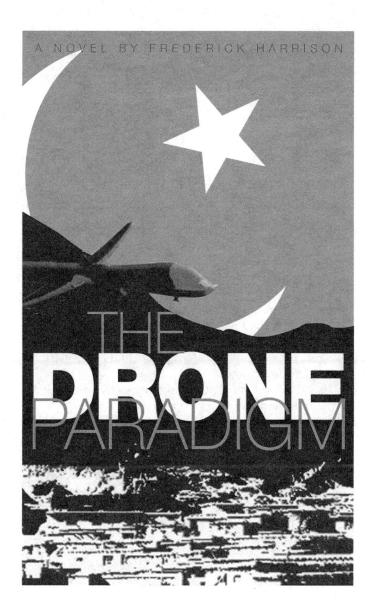

A NOVEL BY FREDERICK HARRISON

THE DRONE PARADIGM

March 2012
FHE Trade Paperback Edition
Copyright 2012 by Frederick Harrison
Registered Writers' Guild of America – East
All rights reserved under International and Pan-American Copyright Conventions.
Published in the United States of America by Frederick Harrison Enterprises (fhentp@aol.com)
ISBN 978-1-4276-5356-7

Cover: Cindy Wokas
Formatting: Peggy Irvine
Printing: Automated Graphic Systems, White Plains, MD

The Drone Paradigm

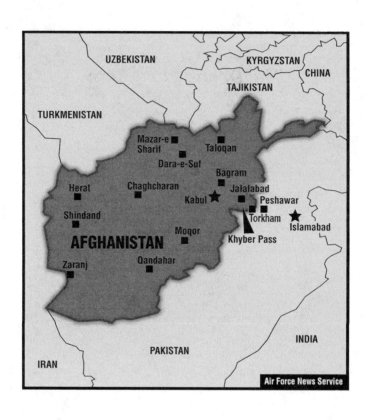

CHAPTER ONE

The house had but a single room and a shed attached at the back to serve as a kitchen. Its few windows covered with heavy cloth, the room was illuminated by hanging kerosene lanterns, which left deep shadows in the corners. The only furnishings were a Persian rug at the end opposite the door on which sat a low table surrounded by brocaded cushions of varied, unmatched hues and patterns. At the table, his back to the wall, sat a bearded man wearing the robe and turban common to the populace of the area. They had once been white, but were now colored by the red oxide dust that permeated the arid hills of northwest Pakistan in summer. The man, Mir Batani Khan, who had been sitting there for more than two hours with eyes fixed on the door opposite, was the self-proclaimed new leader of the Taliban in Afghanistan, his predecessor having been killed two weeks earlier by a CIA drone-launched missile. The house, owned by the Pakistani Inter-Services Intelligence Directorate, the ISI, was a well-guarded meeting place where people otherwise on opposite sides could get together to discuss and agree on matters of mutual interest.

An hour later, two men came through the front door and crossed the room. They wore robes and turbans similar to Batani's, but theirs were pristine and being worn apparently on top of western trousers. One of the men, tall and powerfully built, was General Pervez Orkamzi, Chief of the ISI, the other Mahmud al-Fasal, emissary of Abdul Rashid, a legend among the hard bitten fighters of the Islamic jihad. Batani had never met Abdul Rashid, but knew he was located in Europe, and was the source of the seemingly endless supply of money and materiel that reached Islamic warriors in the far off mountains of central Asia and elsewhere in the world. He could tell from the metal suitcase that al-Fasal was carrying that this occasion would be no different.

As soon as the newcomers seated themselves on the cushions surrounding the table, a woman appeared from the kitchen carrying first a steaming samovar, then cups and plates of sweetmeats and tiny pastries. She was covered head to toe in a dun colored birqa with full face covering, a slit in which permitted her to see what she was about. After serving the men, she backed into a shadowy corner of the room to await their further needs. General Orkamzi spoke first--- in English, their only common language.

"We welcome you, Mir Batani Khan, and Your Excellency Mahmud al-Fasal to our humble meeting place. The Government of Pakistan and its military establishment are anxious to assist in the successful conclusion of your business and, in doing so, advance the interests of a resurgent Islam."

His listeners nodded impatiently, anxious to get on with business. With a hand resting on the suitcase beside him, al-Fasal spoke immediately to the issues at hand:

"My brothers! So that we are able to leave this depressing room as rapidly as possible, let me go directly to the questions Abdul Rashid wishes me to raise. As you know, for a number of years he has been providing substantial resources to achieve the triumph of Islam in Pakistan and Afghanistan, and is prepared to continue doing so." His listeners waited for the other shoe to drop.

"However," al-Fasal continued, "conditions have changed significantly of late, and we wish to have your appraisal of these new developments and hear of the actions you are planning to take in response."

"To what developments are you referring, Excellency?" Orkamzi asked disingenuously, looking at Batani who said nothing.

"I am referring to the great difficulties our friends in the mountains of both your countries are experiencing as a result of the continuing CIA success in striking them with missiles launched from drone aircraft. There is also the offensive undertaken by your army in the border territories, General Orkamzi, as well as the improved capabilities and greater combat effectiveness of the Americans and their allies. The net result has been that many surviving Taliban fighters have been fleeing to the cities and more have begun to leave this area entirely. I know this because Abdul Rashid has been forced to underwrite their evacuation, and is greatly concerned that the jihad in your countries may be failing."

Neither of al-Fasal's companions replied directly, recognizing that he too was being disingenuous. Mir Batani Khan knew that the American drone attacks owed their success, in significant measure, to intelligence provided by the Pakistani ISI with the approval and support of Abdul Rashid. Both he and Orkamzi were also aware that the Islamic fighters "rescued" by Abdul Rashid and al-Fasal were, in fact, being recruited and redeployed for service in other insurgencies, particularly in Yemen and Somalia. The ISI chief had exacted a substantial facilitation fee to assist this movement. Pausing to add emphasis to his next words, al-Fasal continued:

"Most importantly of all, Abdul Rashid fails to perceive the virtue in terror-like attacks by our brothers on the innocent residents of Pakistan's cities. Great damage is being done to our cause, even when the targets are soldiers and policemen. Should the Taliban persist in its present course, the situation will certainly become much worse, and it may become impossible for Abdul Rashid to continue his support."

Batani did not show alarm at al-Fasal's words, nor did he bother to search Orkamzi's face for signs of support. Rather, he calmly took a sip of tea and made an elaborate show of selecting a fig from a plate on the table.

"We of the Taliban in Afghanistan," he replied finally, "greatly appreciate your advice and the assistance given us by Abdul Rashid. We also acknowledge the truth of your criticism regarding the attacks in Pakistan's cities, which hopefully will shortly cease. There is a belief in the West that the Taliban is a single, unified organization in which all members obey the orders of a single leader. This is, unfortunately, not true---at least not yet. The attacks in Pakistan are being carried out independently by a number of elements, commonly out of frustration with their inability to deal effectively with the American drone operations, which are known to be facilitated by the ISI. My brothers seek to cause the Pakistani government to end such assistance and to send the Americans home. The actual result, however, has been total disaster: the people are blaming us along with the government and the Americans, the Army is angry because we embarrass them with our attacks and kill their soldiers, and now Abdul Rashid threatens to leave us penniless. Clearly, we must have a new strategy."

Orkamzi and al-Fasal exchanged surprised looks. Their task was, perhaps, going to be less difficult than expected.

"There is general agreement that our primary objective is to get America and NATO out of Pakistan and Afghanistan," Batani continued, "and there would be little objection to including foreign, Islamist zealots among those to be ejected. There is little support among our people for the jihadi fanatics who have brought us nothing but pain and destruction.

"Unfortunately, however, most of our leaders believe that reaching our goal requires continually attacking the infidels and inflicting upon them casualties sufficient to make them leave, as the Americans left Vietnam. But, this approach is not proving successful, first because the infidels are a lot stronger and more numerous than we and, second, because the United States Government leadership must have some basis on which to declare victory before it can withdraw from Afghanistan without gravely jeopardizing its political future at home. The success of the drone campaign is, unfortunately, encouraging the Americans, just as it emphasizes to us the hopelessness of our current strategy."

Mir Batani Khan paused at this point while he searched out another fig.

"In considering our dilemma," he continued finally, "we came to the realization that both the American concept of victory and ours are meaningless. Just as we will never be strong enough to decisively defeat the invaders and their allies, they will never be able to create in their own image a regime and social order that will not begin to disintegrate the day after they leave. The root of this dilemma is to be found in the mosques and madrassas where those who claim to speak for God instruct the common people what to believe and how to act, including to kill themselves and many others in the name of God. Unless the most extreme of them can be eliminated and the rest controlled, there will be little hope for peace, both within Islam as well as between Islam and the West. We do not believe the Americans and their friends alone are up to that task."

Batani paused to gage the effect of his words, and saw that his listeners were eagerly awaiting his peroration.

"Our conclusion is that we should devote our best efforts to helping the infidels convince one another that they have succeeded in Afghanistan, and can now safely go home. If, in doing so, we can reduce the number of our brothers killed and rebuild my country's economic infrastructure, so much the better. In the future, gentlemen, you will find us transformed from insurgents into dedicated international entrepreneurs, although it may be difficult at times to tell the difference."

His hosts were already lost in wondering how their superiors would greet Batani's revelation, and what it would mean for their own places in the byzantine world in which they operated. Al-Fasal pulled forward the suitcase he had brought with him.

"I have here the funds that Abdul Rashid has sent to support your operations. In light of your new strategy, I am curious to know what you plan to do with the money?" Mir Batani Khan smiled.

"It is critical that we be prepared to fill the vacuum created by the Americans' departure, lest there be chaos. The funds provided by Abdul Rashid---and more---will be devoted to creation of a cadre of experts and officials able to assume operational control of the country in the cause of a just and merciful Islam. Such people must be paid at a rate sufficient to assure they will not be lured away by the ultra extremists or the CIA. We must also be prepared to fund whatever facilitations are necessary to assure that our people and organizations are not hindered in their missions."

At the conclusion of the meeting, Batani was escorted by General Orkamzi to the army truck that would take him, concealed among its cargo, back to Quetta. Mahmud al-Fasal, also preparing to leave, turned to the serving woman still standing quietly in a corner of the room:

"Were you able to hear and understand everything, Miss Crossman?"

"Yes, thank you, sir!"

Hannah Crossman had also been able to record the conversation in the room on a highly sensitive device concealed under her birqa. Since the recording was digital, it was sent that evening to Washington as an encrypted email attachment. Two days later, when she reappeared at CIA Headquarters in Washington, the conversation had already been transcribed, and was being discussed in the Director's seventh floor suite.

"I've been waiting to talk with you, Hannah, before briefing the President on this very bizarre meeting." The speaker was Admiral Philip Bergen, Director of National Intelligence, who had come over from his nearby headquarters; Hannah was his immediate assistant and sometime representative in unlikely places. She was also a member of the National Clandestine Service and a career employee of the CIA. Contrary to the common belief that the best intelligence agents are unobtrusive, Hannah was remarkable for her beauty, which had given rise to the counter belief that no one would suspect of being a spook a woman noticed by everyone.

"Batani's sudden rise to the top was totally unexpected, since he was not considered a member of the inner circle. What do we know about him?"

"Assuming we have the right man," Hannah responded, "Batani is in his mid-thirties, born and raised in Kandahar. He reportedly left Afghanistan in his late teens and ended up in Egypt, where he enrolled at Cairo University to study business administration. While a student, he was recruited into the Muslim Brotherhood and presumably radicalized. The file is essentially bare for the next ten years, with only low-level reports of Batani showing up in Lebanon and Yemen. He reappears back in Afghanistan two and a half years ago, first with the Northern Alliance and then with the Taliban. There is no photograph in the file."

"It's odd that he's made no effort to proclaim his ascendance, as though he doesn't care whether or not anyone knows about his claim to be in charge," CIA Director James Detwiler noted. "I suspect the only reason he showed up at your meeting was to collect al-Fasal's money,"

"More than likely, he's being quiet about it because a substantial number of his Taliban brothers have not yet accepted his claim to leadership," Bergen responded.

"The whole business is very strange," Detwiler's deputy, Sam Glover, added. "Why did al-Fasal and Orkamzi invite us to send someone to eavesdrop on this meeting?"

Bergen shrugged. "I can be persuaded that it was done so we would have incontrovertible evidence that the meeting actually took place and that what was recorded was, in fact, said. What is not clear is whether the whole thing was real or staged for our benefit. However, I find it difficult to believe that either Orkamzi or al-Fasal thinks so little of us that he could believe we would fall for a charade."

"What could they have hoped to gain from faking it?" Glover wondered.

"I have almost the same question, even if what Hannah saw and heard was real," Detwiler added. "What is it that these two very astute and experienced players want us so badly to believe that they would go to such lengths?"

"And, remember," Glover added, "Orkamzi and al-Fasal are not principals. There are more senior people behind them. It's not difficult to suspect the clever hand of Abdul Rashid in this."

"Taken at face value, Batani's revelation of the Taliban's new strategy is a blockbuster," Admiral Bergen acknowledged. "He claims that, no matter what we do in Afghanistan---and presumably elsewhere in the Muslim world---to create the basis for a more modern and democratic society, it will ultimately be undone by the sermons of radical imams calling the faithful back to the 15th Century. What do you think?"

"It could be a persuasive argument," Detwiler allowed. "Americans have grown increasingly tired of the war, which we have already said the Afghans must resolve for themselves. With the assistance of Batani and his associates, it might be very possible to help us convince ourselves that the end is at hand. It would be very difficult for an American President to forego what would appear to be a golden opportunity to bring the troops home."

"What I would like to know," Bergen grumbled, still unsatisfied, "is why Orkamzi and al-Fasal felt we needed to know about this first hand and in such a dramatic way? You were there, Hannah. What were your impressions?"

"From the corner in which I was standing, Orkamzi's back was to me, but I could see the faces of Batani and al-Fasal very well. When the Taliban revealed his new strategy, the look on al-Fasal's face and Orkamzi's body language told me that both were taken by surprise. I couldn't accurately tell whether their shock was pleasant or unpleasant, but they clearly listened more intently thereafter. If I had to bet, I would commit to Batani's revelation not being what they brought me all the way to Pakistan to hear.

"My strong impression is that Batani waylaid them, principally to get al-Fasal's suitcase full of money, but also to amuse himself at their expense. I could tell from the fleeting expressions on Batani's face that he was enjoying himself immensely, particularly when Orkamzi and al-Fasal realized---as he knew they would--- that they had no choice but to continue supporting him. Batani appears to have a wry sense of humor, and the way he talks leads me to believe that he's not your usual Islamist zealot."

"That helps a lot, Hannah," the Admiral responded. "But, now I'm wondering what it was that your hosts thought Batani was going to say that rated an on-scene witness like yourself."

"We've been working covertly with Orkamzi and al-Fasal's boss, Abdul Rashid, for several years now," James Detwiler noted. "We know their primary objectives are contrary to ours, but that there are certain areas in which our interests coincide and where we can help one another. With Abdul Rashid's influence and money, we've gotten Orkamzi's intelligence people to provide targeting information for our drones, since both sides want to prevent the Islamist extremists from capturing Pakistan and the jihad. Perhaps, Orkamzi and al-Fasal wanted to bring to our attention what they thought was a serious, new threat or requirement."

"That's possible, Jim," Bergen responded, "but I suspect that explanation won't satisfy the President. You know what an intelligence junkie he is, always asking questions and demanding more details. He wants to see me about something tomorrow afternoon, and I will need to brief him on this development. When the President asks a serious question, it is never satisfactory for a Director of National Intelligence to answer: 'Beats the hell out of me!'

Mahud al-Fasal, back in Paris, lowered himself with a sigh to the cushions in front of the low tea table, covered as usual with newspapers and correspondence from around the world. This was the sanctum sanctorum of Abdul Rashid from which al-Fasal had never known him to stray, at least not willingly. His large house, surrounded by a high wall, was the subject of continuing neighborhood curiosity because of the stream of limousines with dark-tinted windows that passed through its guarded gate. No one had ever seen a person on foot, other than servants, enter or leave the premises. People wanting to do business with Abdul Rashid invariably came to him, either in person or via the state-of-the-art communications center installed in the house.

However, the business affairs of Abdul Rashid had been in eclipse for almost two years, and the trend was not encouraging. A brilliant strategist, his principal occupation was to usefully deploy enormous funds donated to the international jihad by Islamic political and business interests out of religious conviction or to protect their national and personal equities (or all of the above). Of late, however, the movement was being buffeted by an increasingly strong divergence between fundamentalists and relative moderates, the former seeking to wage unrelenting warfare against those standing in the way of their extremist aspirations, whether they be infidels or fellow Muslims, while the latter sought to preserve relationships necessary to the international businesses and political accommodations upon which their interests and fortunes depended.

Abdul Rashid, the ultimate middleman, realized that he could not successfully promote the interests of both sides simultaneously. Victory by the extremists would come at the expense of the moderates who were the primary source of the very generous fees that supported the Paris household to which he was confined by the premature explosion of a bomb that cost him his legs during a less than successful career as a terrorist more than twenty years earlier. More significantly, he believed the extremists would destroy international order, along with themselves and thousands of innocent people, in an ultimately vain pursuit of their quest.

Mahmud al-Fasal, an Arab businessman and political operative with French citizenship, served as Abdul Rashid's emissary to the outside world, racing from region to region in his private jet to set up operations, solve problems, and dispense large amounts of cash. He also managed to trade for his own account in a number of international markets for desirable commodities like low-sulfur crude oil, gold, and rare earths, while dabbling also in munitions. Success had rewarded him with a large, permanent suite in one of Paris's finest hotels, where he could be at Abdul Rashid's call while enjoying the amenities of the French capital. Al-Fasal's preference, however, was his villa on a bluff overlooking the Mediterranean in the South of France, to which he repaired at the slightest provocation. It was also enjoyed, as a discreetly private meeting place, by senior intelligence officers from countries throughout the Middle East and Central Asia, most of whom were in the pay of Abdul Rashid to one extent or another.

Al-Fasal agreed with his employer's view of the extremists and their ultimate threat to the Islamic cause. At Abdul Rashid's direction, he had established contact with Philip Bergen, proposing a covert meeting to discuss possible arrangements of mutual benefit. The meeting, which had taken place in Paris two years earlier, established the basis for a cooperative arrangement between otherwise existential enemies that had yielded benefits to both sides in areas where their interests coincided.

Operationally, their plan was simple and focused initially on Pakistan, which at the time offered the fundamentalists the best prospect of success. Principal targets were the foreign jihadis who were employing their greater expertise, experience, and religious zeal to guide and stimulate international and local insurgent activities. Many had been operating for years from the safety of the mountainous region on the border with Afghanistan, and considered themselves invulnerable. American and Pakistani intelligence services often knew where they were, but were unable to get to them. While directed by his masters to support their cause, Abdul Rashid was gravely concerned that, if successful in establishing a fundamentalist state in Pakistan, the extremists would ultimately deal the Islamic cause a fatal blow by uniting the rest of the world against it in a dedicated battle to the death that neither side could completely win.

The American weapon of choice was the missile-launching Predator drone aircraft operated principally by the CIA. Able to lurk unseen and unheard at high altitude for a long period of time, the aircraft's sensors scanning for a target that could be still or moving, the Predator's remote controllers could direct a relatively small Hellfire missile with almost unerring accuracy at individuals riding in a vehicle or seemingly safe indoors. Under Abdul Rashid's agreement with Admiral Bergen, al-Fasal arranged for General Orkamzi's ISI to provide the Americans tactical intelligence critical to making the drones operationally effective: clear identification of the individuals to be targeted and timely tip off as to where they could be found.

The cooperative venture succeeded well beyond expectations, and the United States poured additional resources into expanding the drones' numbers and capabilities, in addition to boosting intelligence collection and processing. Eventually, extremist leaders who had been unassailable in their mountain hideouts found themselves at serious risk of being suddenly killed while riding on a back road or lying in bed, their principal vulnerability being the mobile telephone, which permitted them to conduct business from remote, otherwise unreachable locations, but was also exploitable by American intelligence agencies.

Abdul Rashid had succeeded in preventing the extreme fundamentalists from capturing the jihadist movement in Pakistan, but at the cost of perhaps the best opportunity to establish in that country an Islamist regime to spur the revival of the fabled caliphate that once ruled much of the civilized world. To recoup, he quickly shifted the focus of his and al-Fasal's efforts to the Horn of Africa, specifically Yemen and Somalia, which offered perhaps the best such opportunity on the near horizon. The new targets, however, were problematic, insofar as they were geographically much closer to the region from which the bulk of Abdul Rashid's funding came, donations that were intended, in great measure, to buy peace and deter interference from the very people he was importing into the area. Abdul Rashid sighed and, as Mahmud al-Fasal watched with concern, began to knead the stumps of his absent legs.

"What was the result of your meeting with Mir Batani Khan?" he asked. "Hopefully, Orkamzi appreciated our assistance in getting the Americans to send a trusted representative to hear, first hand, the strategic intentions of the Afghan Taliban, so that Washington would agree to increase military and financial aid to Pakistan. Of course, as an added benefit, that would enhance the General's reputation among his colleagues."

"A great shock, Excellency. Orkamzi was concerned that Batani Khan, who is not well known, would scare Bergen's representative to death. But, it turned out that we were the ones scared. The new Taliban strategy under Batani will be the virtual opposite of the old one that Orkamzi depended upon and the Americans expected. Instead of waging an all-out campaign to the death to drive the infidels out, Batani intends to turn the other cheek, contriving to appear peaceable and accommodating, so that the Americans and NATO will seize the opportunity to declare victory and go home."

"Do you believe that approach will work?"

"Putting myself in the Taliban's position, I believe it is worth trying, since it is both low cost and low risk. They can always start again to blow things up, should it fail. I suspect that American domestic politics will be the critical element. The war in Afghanistan appears to be dragging on with no end in sight and little concrete evidence that it can be won, assuming there would be an agreed definition of "win," which is unlikely."

"Did you give Batani our funds?"

"I did, primarily because I could think of no reason not to do so. It is possible that his new strategy might be made to benefit our own objectives. On the other hand, however, it may introduce entirely new elements of competition and struggle into the jihad and our relationships with the West. We need to remember that Batani has not adopted his new strategy because he believes himself defeated, but rather because he sees a more promising path to success."

In Islamabad, General Pervez Orkamzi was puzzling the same questions, while attempting, with limited success, to explain the significance of Batani's pronouncements to his General Staff colleagues.

"It is not yet apparent what Mir Batani Khan is up to, but I am not happy with the prospect of him leading an independent Afghan Taliban movement. Pakistan's critical interests and long term general strategy demand that we prevent the emergence of an Afghanistan that is not closely tied to us, whether it comes under fundamentalist rule or not. Failure in this would complete our encirclement by states larger and much better endowed than we, further reducing our already limited leverage. In the end, we may need to kill Batani or, better yet, get someone to do it for us."

CHAPTER TWO

Charlotte Bergen looked up in surprise as her husband came through the front door of their home, located in a Virginia community just across the Potomac from Washington.

"What are you doing home so early, Phil? I thought you had a late meeting at the White House. Is something wrong?"

If her husband had been late, Charlotte Bergen knew from long experience not to ask the reason, because she generally could not be told. But, especially early was another matter entirely, so she could not resist asking.

"My meeting with President Kitteridge lasted only a few minutes," her husband replied somberly. "I didn't feel like going back to the office afterward, so I came home." The brief explanation was unsatisfying, but his wife could not ask for more, the Admiral having immediately left the room to deposit his briefcase in the safe concealed behind a bookcase in his study.

"The President wants me to become his National Security Advisor," Philip Bergen announced without emotion when he reentered the living room. "Tom Brooks, who's

there now, is going to be named Ambassador to Turkey."
Charlotte Bergen responded more to the apparent lack of
enthusiasm in her husband's voice than to the import of
the announcement itself, which she could not determine.

"Do you want the job, Phil?"

Bergen shrugged. "It doesn't make much difference
whether I want it or not. If I were not already a member of
Kitteridge's administration, I could say no thank you. But,
I can't very well reply that I would prefer not to join him
in the White House. In any event, I've spent more than
forty years saluting smartly, then marching off to do what
I've been told. I'm not about to start now refusing what
amounts to an order, particularly when it comes from the
President of the United States. As to whether the switch
would be good for me, I don't know. I have precious little
operational authority as Director of National Intelligence,
but I would have none as National Security Advisor, where
the emphasis is on the last word of the title. As to influence, being in the White House and having daily access to
the President could provide interesting opportunities. It
would be up to him."

"The President must like and respect you to have offered the job."

"We do get on well together. But Kitteridge is a very
complex man. He's not making this move just because he
likes me. Nor is he unhappy with Tom Brooks, who has
done a very good job. Unless I've misjudged him, the President has got initiatives in mind that he will want me to
front for him. And, don't forget, he's up for reelection next
year, and the campaign will be starting shortly."

Jim Detwiler and Sam Glover agreed with Bergen's
assessment when he told them the next day of the Presi-

dent's proposal, which would directly affect them as well. Kitteridge wanted Detwiler, currently Director of the CIA, to succeed Bergen as Director of National Intelligence while Glover, currently his deputy, would rise to direct the Agency. Highly experienced in Washington bureaucratic life, Detwiler was already wondering reflexively how he was going to cope with an immediate predecessor now risen to the White House, however friendly and cooperative their relationship.

"I wonder what Kitteridge has up his sleeve?" he muttered, looking speculatively at the Admiral, whom he suspected of knowing more than he was telling. Bergen noticed.

"My meeting with the President, as I've told you, lasted no more than ten minutes. First, he told me about the job switches. Then, he said that he didn't plan to spend the next year maximizing his chances of being reelected, that it was not certain that he would even run. He assured me that the view from the penthouse of his skyscraper in New York City is a lot better than that from the Oval Office. The enormous business information empire he built before running for the Presidency is still there waiting for him. Kitteridge believes the country may be headed into big trouble. He plans to devote the remainder of his Presidency to bucking the trend."

"That's unlike the President," Detwiler noted. "He's usually pretty upbeat. What's brought this about?"

"My guess is that it was the results of the mid-term elections."

"But, virtually every sitting President's party loses Congressonal seats in midterm elections."

"I know. But, he obviously sees something deeper. I'm sure we'll be hearing a lot more about it. He's wants a follow-up meeting later in the week. "

"What do you think he plans to do?" Detwiler and Glover demanded simultaneously, their brows well furrowed.

"Beats the hell out of me," Bergen replied.

Hannah Crossman and Naomi Benson were having lunch in a suburban Virginia restaurant, something they had done every couple of months since meeting almost two years earlier. Hannah, a year earlier, had been detailed to enlist Naomi Benson's help in a sensitive matter that involved Sam Glover, with whom she was romantically involved. The two women, evenly matched in age, intelligence, and physical attractiveness quickly decided that they liked each other and had kept in touch, meeting periodically for a meal or cocktails.

"Sam has decided that, since he's going to be Director of the Agency, he has to marry me," Naomi revealed, as the waitress departed with their orders.

"Damned decent of him!" Hannah responded, laughing to cover her dismay. "One can always count on Sam Glover to do the right thing...eventually."

"Please don't misunderstand. Sam began asking me to marry him two months after we met. I'm the one who's been saying no. When we got together, he had just bailed out of the CIA because Kitteridge's predecessor was using the Agency for political purposes. I was working for a company that soon went belly-up, leaving us both out of work with time to enjoy life. Then, the Admiral brought Sam back to the Agency to back up Jim Detwiler, and I was stuck. If I must say so myself, I am one of the world's great software peddlers, and was itching to start again making the big bucks. But, Sam and I were living together by then, and there would have been an apparent conflict-of-interest, since Government agencies—Intelligence Community members especially—would have been my biggest customers. So, we've coasted along at an impasse, which has now got to be resolved. No one pays much attention to deputy directors, but the director of a big government agency, particularly one like the CIA, lives in a fishbowl. Sam believes our living together unmarried would be an invitation to embarrassment for the White House."

"So, you've either got to love him or leave him. Is that the idea?"

"This time, I've agreed to marry him, and would appreciate your coming to the wedding to help make sure I go through with it. You won't need to come armed or anything. My daughter, Nancy, will carry the shotgun."

"That's marvelous, Naomi! Of course, I'll come. Maybe I'll wear the burqa I brought back from Pakistan."

Naomi laughed, but the joke was significantly less humorous to Hannah, bringing to mind something she had been pondering repeatedly of late, particularly during long plane flights to or from some unromantic location. She and Naomi were about the same age: young for a thus far successful career woman, but becoming chancy for a prospective wife and mother. Moreover, unlike her friend, Hannah had no Sam to say Yes to, and there was no one on the horizon. Clandestine service unavoidably described one's personal as well as professional life, and did not contribute to stable and lasting relationships. Hannah couldn't see how it could ever be otherwise and, every time she was forced to contemplate a change in her daily life, thought again about getting out.

"What about you, Hannah? Are you planning to move to the White House with Bergen?" Naomi asked. "Sam tells me that the Admiral will support whatever choice you make. Detwiler would love to have you stay where you are and work for him, while Sam would die to have you back at CIA. Isn't it great to be wanted?"

Hannah had been pondering that decision ever since the Admiral had told her of his impending move. A position on the White House staff, where she would be listed as a Special Assistant to the President, sounded appealing but very restrictive. It was not that she craved being sent to far off locations to be shot at or dumped into the sea, but neither was she willing to risk falling victim to terminal boredom and bureaucratic frustration. In particular, it bothered Hannah that Bergen did not seem enthusiastic about his new position.

"I haven't decided yet," she replied. "My inclination is to stick with what I've been doing. I get along very well with Jim Detwiler, and someone knowledgeable has got to stay around to make sure Sam doesn't become drunk with power."

"I've got that one," Naomi responded. Their laughter attracted the attention of other diners to two beautiful women actually enjoying each other's company.

Mir Batani Khan's guests did not arrive until after dark, not wishing to be visible on the narrow road leading into the small valley. The rendezvous location was a modest dwelling from which the residents had been temporarily evicted so that insurgent leaders in the district could assemble covertly in a place they were not known to frequent. The reason for these elaborate security precautions was the belief that darkness and subterfuge would help protect against detection and attack by American drones; prospective attendees were cautioned not to use their mobile phones during the twenty-four hours preceding the meeting. There were eighteen men in the room when Batani called the meeting to order, many of whom had not come willingly. Not only was the gathering a tempting target for the enemy, but the right of Batani to summon them was far from universally accepted.

"I have asked you here, my brothers, so that I may assist you in our fight against the infidel invaders." He pointed to long, flat cases with Russian markings stacked against a wall and wooden crates painted in olive drab with stenciling in other languages. Seeing the prospective largesse had changed the expression on the faces of most of the attendees when they entered house.

"I have arranged for a continuing supply of such materiel, as well as food rations and medical supplies. These come from very powerful friends, whom I have convinced that our strategy for victory over the invader and the apostate blasphemers in Kabul and Islamabad will succeed." Batani had, in fact, purchased the weapons and munitions on the black market in Kyrgyzstan with some of the funds given him by Mahmud al-Fasal several weeks earlier.

"For us to succeed, my brothers, we must act together with a single plan, concentrate our strength, and recognize our true enemies. We cannot afford to take up arms

24

against people simply because they do not believe exactly as we do. Should we continue to do so, there will be endless war, our families will suffer, and we will continue to be victimized by foreigners, whether they come in military uniform or business suits."

Batani's words resonated with some in the room, but caused others to begin shouting accusations and threats. A small group from Gardez was particularly vociferous in condemnation, its leader waving his AK-47 and attempting to rally the others in opposition. Realizing he was in danger of losing control, Batani Khan backed off, plying the leaders present with flattery and assurances that cooperation and coordination would not mean loss of independence. After refreshments, he watched them load their shares of the supplies into pickups and SUVs and drive off slowly, lights out, into the darkness.

He made a particular point of talking with the group from Gardez, chatting respectfully with its leader as he and his followers climbed aboard their van. With a final expression of praise and appreciation, Batani rapped twice on the vehicle's roof with the flat of his hand as a signal for the driver to proceed, leaving behind a small, magnetized disc. About twenty minutes later, the valley was lit up by a sudden explosion. Batani, who had been waiting in the dark, smiled and returned to the house.

The George Washington Memorial Parkway runs along the Virginia bank of the Potomac River past The Pentagon, the city of Washington on the opposite bank, and through historic Alexandria before ending downriver at Mount Vernon. It is by far the fastest route into the city from the DNI and CIA Headquarters compounds near its northern end. Normally, the existence of but a single interchange between CIA Headquarters and the first bridge into Washington is a great asset. When, however, an accident blocks the road, it becomes a trap that, this day, had ensnared Admiral Bergen and Hannah Crossman heading downtown in his official sedan.

"Shall I turn on the lights and siren and go down the shoulder, sir?" the security agent in the front passenger seat asked through the intercom.

"No, don't do that," Bergen replied, looking at Hannah who shook her head. "Neither of us has anything pressing to get to this morning. We'll just wait for a while with our fellow citizens," he laughed.

The Admiral was en route to his hideaway in the executive office building next to the White House to review reports for a later meeting on China in the Situation Room. Hannah was to meet, at Bergen's direction, with Paul Rayner, a senior producer for the long-running television show *American Focus,* who had been trying unsuccessfully for more than a year to secure the Admiral's appearance. To his great surprise, the Admiral had been told that the President wanted him to do it, and Hannah had been detailed to negotiate the conditions of the interview and the topics to be covered.

True to the ways of Washington, news of the Admiral's appointment to be National Security Advisor had been leaked in advance of formal announcement. First, a barebones rumor without attribution had surfaced, followed several days later by a more specific story credited to " a usually reliable source not, however, authorized to speak on the subject." The principal purpose of leaking is to test the waters, prior to a formal announcement, against the possibility of an unanticipated negative reaction or revelation. Was there an important Congressman who should have been "consulted" in advance? Does the nominee have a secret mistress undiscovered by preliminary vetting? Leaked information can be denied or a justification altered to accommodate a newly apparent reality. Push come to shove, the subject of the leak can be left dangling in the breeze. In Bergen's case, reaction focused not on his qualifications for the position but on why the President was making the move.

"I've decided to retire from the Navy when I switch jobs, Hannah," Bergen told her. "Military rank is not necessary in the new position, and I'm taking up a four star slot that the Navy can use to make a number of promotions. It will also make Charlotte feel a bit better about me taking another post. She's been trying forever to get me to retire and take her somewhere where we can enjoy a quiet life. Every time that threatens to become a reality, another assignment comes up, and we're off again. If I leave the Navy, she'll have only the next election to fret over."

"Forgive me, sir, but I get the impression you're not very happy about any of this."

"How could I be? I've been in the Navy for as long as I can remember, and I like being an Admiral; I like everything about it. People will call me Admiral for the rest of my life, but when they put that r-e-t after my name it means I'm past it, and I'm not ready to be past it. The good thing about the National Security Advisor job is that it will keep me busy, so that I won't have time to think about that big Navy Exchange in the sky."

"Seems to me your new position could be a lot more difficult than being DNI. There's no structure to it and no real organization to assist you day-to-day."

"Since I will be working directly for the President, theoretically the entire Executive Branch is supposed to support me. But we both know that it's not the same as having your own organization behind you. I will be depending on you, Jim, and Sam for a lot of help and advice."

"I know that Director Detwiler is wondering how you two will get on when he becomes DNI, notwithstanding that you work well together and are good friends."

"An experienced bureaucrat will wonder that instinctively," Bergen laughed. "What have you decided to do? As you know, I'd like very much for you to come with me. The food in the White House mess is pretty good, and I'll get you a reserved parking spot behind the Executive Office Building. If you're really lucky, I will also work you to death."

"I think that I will stay at CIA for the time being, while I resolve an even bigger issue, which is deciding what I want to do with the rest of my life. I've done very well careerwise, and I'm sure a slot at the White House or in the Director's suite at CIA would carry me further, but it would be more of the same thing: working fourteen or fifteen hours a day and disappearing all of a sudden for days or weeks at a time, without being able to explain what the hell it's all about to someone who matters. I suppose it's possible to be in the Clandestine Service and still have a real life, but I'd hate to find myself in the mountains of Afghanistan or in a harem in Yemen worrying about whether my kids were eating their Cheerios."

Admiral Bergen smiled ruefully, as the traffic began to move.

"Tough problems like that are beyond my pay grade, Hannah. You'll have to ask Charlotte whether or not she would have gotten involved with a serving officer, if she knew then what she knows now. I can assure you that the odds would have been against me.

Hannah met with Paul Rayner in the bar of the National Press Club in downtown Washington, within walking distance of the White House. She had never met him before, but he remembered her fleeting appearances on the evening news, when she was seen in the background accompanying the Admiral to Congressional hearings.

"That was a while ago. I'm surprised you remember."

"Television news is my business, Ms. Crossman. Besides, it's not often you see an exceptionally pretty face walking the halls of Congress."

"That's a pretty sexist remark, Mr. Rayner. I would remind you that you're here to lure the Admiral into your studio, not me," Hannah responded in mock anger.

"Rats! I was told you are a team." They laughed.

After ordering, they got down to business. Unlike the majority of current events shows, *American Focus* did not feature a panel format and was not produced live. Thus, each of the two or three segments shown weekly covered its subject in greater depth and with higher production values, such as illustrative film clips. Most important was that taped sequences, such as interviews, could be edited or reshot, if either the producer or guest is dissatisfied. The latter would not be permitted to steer the editing to his or her advantage, but could be confident there would be no "gotcha" moments.

"The Admiral will not agree to scheduling his appearance on your program until the White House formally announces his appointment as National Security Advisor."

Hannah did not say it, but the reason was that, at that point in time, Philip Bergen had no idea why President Kitteridge wanted him to move to the White House and what he was supposed to do when he got there.

"Where would Admiral Bergen like to do the taping," Rayner asked. "The easiest location would be our studio here in town, but we could do it at his home, office, or any combination of places. His will be the longest segment in that program, and we will continue taping until he runs out of interesting things he's willing to say, after which we'll edit it down to fit available air time. You can expect it to air from two weeks to a month after production, unless we find a reason to rush it to your TV screen."

"What might that be?"

"These are dangerous times, Ms. Crossman, and the Admiral has been involved in all kinds of behind-the-scenes operations and negotiations. It would be interesting, for example, for our viewers and the American people to know whether he plans to continue running covert operations from the White House." Hannah swallowed hard.

"Should you ask questions like that, your interview will be very short, Mr. Rayner. I've prepared for you a list of subjects and questions that the Admiral is prepared to address. I would advise that you not push your luck."

Rayner smiled winningly. "Would I be in danger of being relocated suddenly to Guantanamo?"

Hannah returned the grin. "We reserve those places for our enemies. The ones we maintain for journalists are not quite as nice."

"I will keep that in mind," he responded with an exaggerated shudder. "Are condemned journalists entitled to a last meal...like dinner this evening?"

"Only if you accept as fact that taking me to dinner will bring you no advantage."

"I would not dare to think so. I'm sure that, in addition to being gorgeous, you are accomplished at martial arts and silent killing."

"As a matter of fact, I am. But, the Agency won't let me kill anybody here in Washington, so I'm restricted to permanent maiming. I would warn you, Mr Rayner, that you will need to be a very amusing dinner partner."

They laughed, but it turned out that Paul *was* a very amusing dinner partner, and business was barely mentioned during the entire evening. He told her of his adventures as the principal "get guy" for *American Focus* and she told him almost nothing about hers as a CIA officer. Rayner found this difficult, not because he was being unsuccessful in learning Hannah's secrets, but because he was afraid it would appear that he was attempting to pry despite her warning, although he was simply trying to find a subject for small talk that would extend beyond two sentences.

"Suppose I was your husband, also worked at the Agency, and held the same security clearance. Would we be able to discuss our jobs and work problems at the dinner table?"

"To a greater extent than with an outsider, because we would share certain background information. Not everything about the Agency is a deep, dark secret."

"Give me an example of something that's not," he challenged.

"Well," she whispered, "the daily specials at the cafeteria."

He recognized that she was joking, but had no idea where the truth lay. The aura of mystery that surrounded Hannah Crossman contributed to her allure. But, she didn't need it, and Paul found himself beginning to believe she was beyond his reach. As they prepared to leave the restaurant, he asked whether he might see her again, and was surprised that his inquiry seemed unexpected.

"I would like that," she replied, "but I need to warn you that I can't always keep dates, and do not explain why. Any relationship we have is likely to be difficult because there will always be in it at least three of us: you, me, and the Admiral or James Detwiler or Sam Glover or all of the above." She awaited his response, concealing her unanticipated anxiety.

"What did you say the specials were at the CIA cafeteria today?"

CHAPTER THREE

"I am very sorry, Admiral Bergen, that I have apparently mishandled the matter of your prospective move to the White House to be my National Security Advisor. In the mysterious ways of Washington, word of it leaked to the media before I even had the opportunity to formally ask you whether you would take the job. Fortunately, your devotion to duty has both saved me from great embarrassment and given me my first choice for the position. Please be seated, so that I can tell you belatedly what I have in mind."

President Kitteridge, his voice showing concern, had said all of this while coming out from behind his desk as Philip Bergen entered the Oval Office. He noticed the Admiral's brief look of surprise to find the office otherwise empty, since his usual practice was to address Intelligence matters with other Cabinet members present, insofar as they rarely involved only one Department or agency.

"I want to discuss this very complicated business first with you alone, if only to give you a deserved opportunity to opt out. I don't expect you to necessarily agree with my views and concerns, and require that you tell me, when you don't. One of the principal reasons I've chosen you for this largely thankless job is that you are your own man, and will not tell me what you think I want to hear just because I'm President of the United States."

Bergen made no reply, and Kitteridge signaled him to one of the sofas in the center of the room.

"It's difficult to determine where to begin. I'm sure you've noted that relations among the people and nations of the world are becoming more rigid. People and parties in power or seeking to gain it are increasingly unwilling to consider the interests and rights of their rivals, even where their supremacy is not being threatened. Some will argue that it has ever been thus, and I must admit that the past two years as President have brought me a lot closer to political realities than I was before. But, I'm no longer able to ignore the feeling that international relations are fast becoming a zero sum game in which you can either win or lose and there is nothing in between that permits useful accommodation or compromise. Unfortunately, I'm seeing the same distressing tendency in our domestic politics.

"Let's begin with Islamic extremism and our battle against international terrorism. Are we winning or losing? To answer that, we must first decide what 'win' means. How would we like this business to end---in addition, of course, to ASAP? An intelligence report you gave me last week quoted Mir Batani Khan, the new Taliban chief in Afghanistan, as saying that country will begin reverting to the Islamists the day after we leave. Do you agree with that assessment?"

"The same opinion has been voiced by others for quite some time," the Admiral replied. "If nothing else, we have prevented the extremists from taking over, not just in Afghanistan, but in Pakistan as well."

"But, are Batani and the others right when the say that it will all go back to the way it was, after we leave?"

"Is this about finding ways to rationalize taking our marbles and going home, Mr. President?" the Admiral asked, almost sharply.

Kitteridge was surprised.

"No, Admiral! It's about determining what winning really means in terms of true American interests, then figuring out how we get there without sacrificing more lives than absolutely necessary and bankrupting ourselves in the process. We have persisted in confusing the things we need to do to protect the safety and interests of our people with those that burnish our self-image as the world's guardian of democracy. Do we really need to save the Western world from Muslim fundamentalism country-by-country? More importantly, can it realistically be done? If it can't or doesn't need to be done, we should determine the alternative strategies open to us. If we can't see an achievable end to the course we are following, why should we continue to pour manpower and resources down a rat hole. There's got to be a better approach than just bumbling along until someone has the guts to cut our losses and come home, as we did in Vietnam."

Bergen did not respond, hoping he was not the one expected to resolve the President's dilemma, at least not then and there. But, he was not to escape.

"The reason I'm asking you to come to the White House, Admiral, is that I want to expand political and operational contacts with our apparent enemies and competitors, much of which will have to be done covertly. One of the truest clichés of all is that war makes strange bedfellows, and it is, perhaps, more true now than it has ever been. I've been greatly impressed by benefits realized from our arrangements with Abdul Rashid and Mahmud al-Fasal, as well as others you have brokered. What I have in mind, however, is a lot broader in scope and likely to involve the interests and equities of departments and agencies across the Government. The last thing I want to do is foment a bureaucratic civil war, so I plan to have coordination centered here in the White House. I particularly want you to take charge of this because of the considerable experience you've had in the military and the Intelligence Community doing what I believe you people call herding cats. You can have a small staff, but I don't want the Washington Post to discover an office building with a thousand government employees and contractors tucked away somewhere in the hills of northern Virginia."

"Can I bring in people like Jim Detwiler and Sam Glover at CIA?"

"You can co-opt anyone you consider necessary; it's your call. But, if our plans get blown, I will say that I've never heard of you."

"How about that TV program you want me to appear on: *American Focus*? My assistant is making the arrangements."

The President smiled. "The media and our political opponents will be wondering what's going on: why I'm moving you to a new position and whether you're going to be doing things that Tom Brooks didn't do. Your appearance on TV will provide us an opportunity to preempt with our version of what's going to happen. The show is taped in advance, so some smart-ass journalist won't be able to do a number on you. I know you'll be fine, but I want to make a tactical change here. Instead of appearing on the program after you've become Security Advisor, I would like you to do it as soon as possible. That way, if any of the trial balloons you float get badly shot up, we can more easily confess that you were never more than a decoy."

"I appreciate the vote of confidence, Mr. President," Bergen responded dryly, making Kitteridge laugh as he rose to escort the Admiral to the door.

"It will take a while to make the transfers official, with Detwiler's and Glover's appointments requiring the Senate's confirmation. I plan to retire from active naval service before moving to the White House. But, I will start working immediately on the kind of initiatives we talked about. Do you have a preferred starting place?"

Kitteridge pondered for a moment. "Considering our active concern with Pakistan and Afghanistan, we could see whether something could be worked up with Russia and China, either collectively or bilaterally. We have significant issues with both of them, but we all have problems with Muslim extremism, and there may be some mutually beneficial steps we can take together."

James Detwiler and Sam Glover were astounded by the Admiral's account of his meeting with the President.

"This is our reward for having an Intelligence wonk as President," the prospective CIA Director observed with wry amusement. "We complain for years that the White House doesn't understand what we do or appreciate its significance, and now they are going to make us put our sources where our mouths are."

"Why is Kitteridge doing this, seemingly all of a sudden?" Glover wondered.

"Two words," Bergen replied immediately: "Alfred Oberling."

Oberling, Vice President in the previous administration and Kitteridge's opponent in the last election, had left Washington after being soundly defeated and finding little traction for his policy proposals in the capital's post-election environment. Bolstered by the conservative trend evident in the Congressional voting, he had reclaimed his position as senior member of the Kitteridge Administration's opposition, former President Tucker having declared his intention never to come back to politics or to Washington. Oberling had immediately zeroed in once again on the President's international affairs strategy, in particular the global war on terrorism. The White House was not surprised by the criticism or proposed alternatives---only by the rate at which they appeared to be gaining adherents.

Global Security Applications LLC occupied four rooms in a small office building in McLean, Virginia about ten minutes from CIA and DNI Headquarters. Its staff comprised proprietor Reggie Huggins, his secretary and general factotum, and two all-purpose operatives. All were CIA veterans, retirees from the Agency's Directorate of Operations, which is what its Clandestine Service was called back in the day. Reggie Huggins was a legendary operations officer whose adventures had been chronicled (in fact and fiction) so often that many could not believe he actually existed. His critics, who were legion, maintained that Reggie's stellar achievement was to succeed in being a covert operator and shameless self-promoter simultaneously. He had established Global Security Applications in the freewheeling years immediately after 9/11 when imperatives of the Global War on Terrorism overwhelmed consideration of the costs, effectiveness, and legality of initiatives taken to strike back at the enemy while protecting the American people and their homeland. Great opportunities were created for people like Huggins who knew how to operate in the seams and shadows of government, not only in the United States, but abroad as well. They ushered in an exciting new era of long trips in private jets that always seemed to begin and end in the middle of the night, meetings in obscure places with people seen on national television the night before, and the occasional woman willing to overlook evidence that the secret agent groping her was somewhat long of tooth. Reggie realized early on that he had not enjoyed himself this much since the Cold War ended.

Huggins' outsized reputation, however, was largely well-deserved, his performance overseas a legend within the Agency. His specialty, the bread and butter of the Directorate of Operations, was recruiting and running agents and informants among the indigenous population of the countries to which he was assigned. He was somehow able to come up with reliable sources of critical intelligence and do it often enough that his superiors at Langley headquarters could not attribute his successes solely to luck or happenstance. Reggie's reputation as a cowboy actually developed, rather, during those interim periods when he was assigned at Headquarters to supervisory positions of increasing responsibility, in keeping with promotions earned overseas. He had little patience for rules and restrictions far more relevant in Washington than on the cutting edge of agent recruiting and intelligence collection abroad. As a result, he pushed deployed covert operations officers under his supervision to do things that eventually brought the Agency and its Director unneeded grief at the White House and on Capitol Hill.

Huggins was too good to discard, but too ungovernable to be permitted a senior management position, which presented CIA's top brass with a vexing problem that the Soviet Union helped solve by invading Afghanistan. When the indigenous tribal and religious factions there began to cooperate in resisting the foreigners, Reggie was sent to organize the American assistance that enabled them to eventually triumph. His reputation was greatly enhanced by photos that circulated---initially only at the Agency, but eventually via the Washington Post to the world---showing him in combat gear with a Kalashnikov hanging from his shoulder, leading a group of mujahedin somewhere in the mountains of Afghanistan. However, when the Soviet adventure ended and Huggins came home to even greater renown, there was equally greater management resolve to prevent him causing trouble. He endured restraint for two more years before retiring, to rise again after 9/11.

Global Security Applications' big chance came during the Tucker Administration when Huggins was introduced to Roger Norton, the President's *eminence gris,* who was dedicated to protecting Tucker's rear and making him look good to the electorate. Norton was seeking dramatic achievements in the war on terrorism to underscore Tucker's oft-proclaimed dedication to protecting the American people. But he despaired of them being realized by Government agencies, which he considered too cautious and bureaucratic. Like Huggins, Norton was a believer in the magic of the clever and nimble lone wolf. The two hit it off immediately, Norton arranging for Global Security to get a small (in Government terms) contract from Homeland Security to survey prospective counterterrorist initiatives in Pakistan and Afghanistan. The funding provided, three hundred fifty thousand dollars, was sufficient to fuel a corporate expansion, with Huggins searching out and hiring several fellow retirees who had served with him in Afghanistan and were eager to relive the excitement of those days. He also undertook a personal trip to Pakistan and Afghanistan, using his new government contractor credentials, seeking in both countries people with whom he had worked against the Soviets. Returning to Washington, Huggins left behind him a small, but well-placed network of contacts eager to work for the Yankee dollar.

His efforts, however, had come to the attention of Admiral Bergen, then Director of the CIA. Unable to terminate Huggins' efforts because of White House shielding, Bergen had Sam Glover remind him (they were former colleagues) that Tucker and Norton would not be around to cover his ass indefinitely.

The warning proved prophetic when Tucker declined to run for reelection and Vice President Oberling was defeated by Mason Kitteridge. Global Security Applications LLC lost its contract and Government financing, and was forced to scrape along on a meager ration of Alfred Oberling's unspent campaign funds. Its Washington-based staff elected to stay with the firm, although largely unpaid, principally because its members had nothing more compelling to do, and could get along on their CIA retirement annuities. This permitted use of most of the available funding to maintain Huggins' overseas agent network.

After the midterm election, in which the Congressional candidates he had stumped for mostly won, Alfred Oberling moved back to Washington from his base in Missouri convinced that he could beat Kitteridge in the general election two years hence. Roger Norton came with him, and one of the first things they did was to call in Reggie Huggins.

"Are you and your company prepared to dedicate yourselves to our cause, Mr. Huggins?" Oberling asked. "It will be a tough battle and the Administration could decide to come after you."

"We are ready, sir. But the intelligence business is very expensive, especially paying for the services of our people overseas. Are you prepared to provide the funds we require? Given our goals, not having money is the same (or maybe worse) than not having guns and ammunition."

"I understand, Mr. Huggins. We are, of course, not in a position to award you Government contracts, but we have a number of private donors who are willing and able to contribute substantially to our cause. We will need to arrange it so that there is not a traceable link between them and your activities. These people are true patriots, and will not benefit personally from your operations, but they need to be protected from our opponents who would seek to discredit them through slander and libel. If you are prepared to assure their security, I am able to give you an initial sum right now."

Huggins smiled his famous "trust me" smile, but knew that total anonymity for the secret donors could be unconditionally guaranteed only if others who knew of it were dead. This was not a service that Global Security provided, at least not within the United States.

"I will be the only one in my organization to know the details, and I can assure you that no one will hear them from me, Mr. Oberling. What specifically do you wish Global Security Applications to do for you?"

"We are not prepared to provide detailed tasking at this time," the former Vice President replied. "That will evolve with world developments and actions taken or not taken by the Kitteridge Administration. But, you need to know our general objective and strategy."

He nodded to Roger Norton, who took up the narrative.

"We are greatly concerned that the essence of America, the principles for which we stand (if you will), are being increasingly discarded and diluted by the policies and actions our Government is pursuing in dealing with the challenges we face around the world, in particular Islamic extremism. This is not something for which the current

Administration is wholly to blame: it began even before 9/11, but the degradation has accelerated greatly under Mason Kitteridge. Our primary objective in the next election will be to regain control of our national destiny and to restore the true standing of America in the world. This information is for your ears only at this point, but Alfred Oberling intends to run again for the Presidency, presumably against Kitteridge, with this goal as the spear point of his platform."

Surprise, surprise, Huggins told himself, as he contrived to appear cheered by the news. Truth be told, Huggins agreed in many respects with Oberling's objectives. But many years of lurking on the fringes of mobs in foreign countries had taught him that demand for democracy did not automatically justify the actions taken in its pursuit, and that people who acted as though it did were often large-scale pains in the ass. Now, he smiled and protested mildly.

"You understand, of course, that my people and I are not diplomats, Mr. Norton."

Oberling laughed and Norton was quick to reassure: "If diplomats were who we wanted, Mr. Huggins, we would have gone to the State Department alumni association."

CHAPTER FOUR

A platform and rows of folding chairs were set out on the small parade ground of the Washington Navy Yard, which had been the U.S. Navy's first shore installation. Almost every chair was filled, late on a sunny Spring morning, by men in military uniform and women in their Sunday best, seats on the platform occupied, save for a vacant one in the middle of the front row, by flag and general officers and heads of government departments and agencies. They were there to witness the official retirement of Admiral Philip Bergen, United States Navy, Director of National Intelligence; Director, Central Intelligence Agency; Deputy Chief of Naval Operations for Submarine Warfare; Commander, Submarines Pacific; Commander, Submarine Squadron SEVEN; Commanding Officer, USS Cuttlefish; Naval Academy Midshipman, and many stops in between. Hannah Crossman, seated on the stage, noted the presence of the Secretaries of State, Defense, and Homeland Security, as well as FBI Director Donald McGinnis and, of course, the CIA's James Detwiler and Sam Glover sitting near the directors of the other major Intelligence Community components.

The Admiral considered himself a sailor and submariner foremost, and had asked that his retirement ceremony take place at the Navy Yard rather than the South

Lawn of the White House as the President's scheduler had proposed. Looking around, Hannah noted the sudden appearance of men in dark suits on the periphery of the quadrangle and on the roofs of the surrounding buildings. The Chief of Naval Operations stood up and quickly went to the microphone.

"Attention on deck!" Everyone leaped to their feet, those in uniform reaching to their hat brims in salute.

"Ladies and Gentlemen, the President of the United States."

Some of those watching had not believed President Kitteridge would come, particularly after Bergen had refused a White House ceremony. Insiders pondered more the significance of his showing up, agreeing that it was definitely a particular mark of respect and gratitude for the Admiral's service, but wondering what---if anything---it signified regarding Bergen's new position as National Security Advisor. Kitteridge went out of his way to make it clear that Bergen was special, without actually saying it. At the end of a relatively brief ceremony, he pinned the Medal of Freedom on the Admiral's chest and departed, the others repairing to a noisy reception indoors.

"Congratulations, Charlotte! You've gotten him away from the bureaucracy at last." The Admiral's wife could not tell whether her friends were being facetious, ironical, or just plain misinformed. They knew that she had been trying for years to get Bergen to retire and now had apparently succeeded. However, given that her true objective was to get away from Washington and sixteen hour workdays, Charlotte Bergen had a strong suspicion that she had not succeeded. It bothered her more that her husband, who knew a lot more about it than she did, was not noticeably enthused about his future. Well, she told herself as she sipped champagne, at least we own our home, and will not have to move out of Navy quarters.

James Detwiler and Sam Glover were standing nearby discussing their own concerns with Bergen's future endeavors. Given what he had told them of the President's plans for him, it was obvious that the Admiral, in his new capacity, would be active in operational areas within their purview as DNI and D/CIA. They had no fear that he would seek to score points at their expense, but everyone dealing with intelligence matters bearing a high level of ambiguity or uncertainty does not always read them the same way. Neither Detwiler nor Glover wished to run afoul of the President, but certainly not of Bergen.

"Did you notice that the Russian, Estefimov, is here," Detwiler remarked, indicating with his glass a beefy, balding man with a florid complexion standing by himself. "I know that courtesy invitations to events like these are sent to selected embassies, but they rarely respond by sending someone. I wonder why he came, considering that his engagements with Bergen have not been happy ones."

Arkady Estefimov was the senior intelligence and security officer in Russia's Washington embassy and a General in the SVU, successor to the Soviet KGB.

"Maybe he needed to see for himself that Bergen is really going," Sam joked. Just then, the Russian placed his champagne glass on a table and turned toward the door, detouring to approach Detwiler and Glover.

"Good afternoon, gentlemen," he smiled. "A very nice ceremony. The Admiral is to be congratulated."

"I'm sure he will be pleased to know that you came today, General Estefimov," James Detwiler responded.

"Please tell Admiral Bergen that we wish him success in his new position at the White House and look forward to working with him." The Americans were too surprised to reply, as the General walked off. Later, when they gave the Russian's message to the Admiral, they were even more surprised when he smiled and allowed as how he planned to contact Estefimov shortly.

Having reported to Abdul Rashid, Mahmud al-Fasal fled Paris for the sanctuary and comfort of his home on the Mediterranean, relishing the thought of a week's respite before hosting a meeting of his employer's agents and collaborators. The large white house stood on a high promontory jutting into the sea between Nice and Monaco, and was accessible only by a narrow, private road extending from the coast highway. At the edge of its grounds, a massive wrought iron gate blocked the road, requiring all vehicles approaching the house to stop for inspection by members of al-Fasal's security staff comprised of five aging mujahedin of varying nationalities who could no longer endure the hardships of the jihad's front lines. Despite severe limps and the odd artificial limb, they were highly effective protectors of their master's privacy and that of his frequent guests. Al-Fasal himself rarely used the entrance, preferring to base his plane at the airport at Cap Ferrat and take a helicopter to the pad installed behind the house. When arriving back home, he always had the pilot circle the house several times so that he could appreciate the beauty of his most prized and valuable possession, and rationalize once again the seemingly endless days and weeks he spent wandering the globe in sometimes contradictory pursuit of additional wealth and the strategic objectives of the Islamic jihad.

The security and privacy afforded by al-Fasal's estate were rivaled by its amenities, the terraced pool area being one of the favored covert meeting places of senior intelligence officials from around the world. Attendees would fly incognito to one or another of the many airports on the Riviera, to be picked up by al-Fasal's helicopter, which bore the markings of a Greek shipping line in which he had an interest. The French Government was, of course, aware of activities at al-Fasal's villa, but contented itself with simply recording their participants' comings and goings. A great advantage of playing on all sides of a hostile competition, as Abdul Rashid and al-Fasal did, is that participants can't immediately determine which side was being favored at any specific time.

Another not inconsiderable amenity offered by Chez Al-Fasal was escape from the daily strictures of fundamentalist Islam to which most visitors at least nominally subscribed. Alcohol in all forms was readily available and consumed in copious quantities, and the Asian barbecue served outdoors one evening included the most delicious Chinese-style spare ribs. But most noticeable at the business discussions held daily at poolside (participants exchanging their accustomed robes and suits for bathing attire) was the presence of a very attractive woman wearing an ancient YWCA tank suit. This was Hannah Crossman, representing the American Director of National Intelligence. Admiral Bergen had adopted the expedient of sending Hannah, who had no official authority, to such meetings as an observer, which relieved Paris of potential protocol issues and was also a precaution against knowledge of the meeting and its attendees leaking to the American media.

Mahmud al-Fasal looked around the umbrella-shaded table at expectant faces, some now familiar. General Orkamzi of the Pakistan ISI was there, looking particularly tired, and General Atakan of the Turkish General Staff. Colonel Said Jafari, representing the Iranian Revolutionary Guard, was flanked by two newcomers to the recurring conclaves representing the Islamic Front of Somalia and the Egyptian Muslim Brotherhood. Only the Somali seemed surprised at Hannah's presence.

"Last month," al-Fasal began, "General Orkamzi and I held a meeting with Mir Batani Khan the new, self-proclaimed leader of the Taliban in Afghanistan. Its purpose was to hear from him what his strategy against the American invaders would be, going forward. Our expectation was that he would tell of his preparations for increased struggle and his need for greater funding and increased supplies of munitions. We were shocked, however, when he proposed a 'turn the other cheek' strategy designed to convince the Americans that they have won, and are free to go home. Batani believes they will gladly take up the invitation." He looked to General Orkamzi for supplementary comment.

"We were indeed greatly surprised," Orkamzi agreed, "but no more so than my general staff colleagues, who were forced to consider whether or not we really wish the Americans to go home and what will happen, if and when they do."

The others nodded in agreement and sympathy, indicating that the same thoughts had afflicted their governments. They looked to Hannah, who smiled and confessed that such matters were far above her pay grade.

"Americans seem to consider themselves the guardians of democracy everywhere in the world, even in countries where it is none of their business," Colonel Jafari volunteered. The others again nodded, but more guardedly.

"I know Mir Batani Khan from his time in Cairo," the Egyptian informed them. "He was an active member of the Brotherhood before leaving the country to return to Afghanistan. Batani is a very bright and engaging man, with great leadership qualities. He is also ruthless, which creates a very potent and dangerous combination. When he smiles and agrees with you, often putting his arm around your shoulder, one should take no assurance that all will be well."

General Atakan grunted. "We have heard in Ankara that he has, thus far, engineered the assassination of two of his closest rivals, with the help of the ISI and CIA drones." Hannah's and Orkamzi's studiously blank looks were intended to imply that this was news to them. Mahmud al-Fasal quickly sought to move the discussion beyond this awkward moment.

"Abdul Rashid is concerned that, if fully implemented, Batani's strategy could have unforeseen implications and side effects that might create difficulties. It is not that he is against Batani's approach, but that he wishes to avoid having its impact catch us leaning the wrong way, as the Americans would say." Hannah dutifully made a note on the pad before her, signaling that Washington would be apprised of their concern.

"To be perfectly frank," al–Fasal continued," we consider it certain that a resolution of the major issues currently embroiling Afghanistan and Pakistan will not end the conflict between the United States and Islamic fundamentalism. Already we see the focus of confrontation, and many of the fighters involved, shifting to Yemen and Somalia, an area far more dangerous to Western interests than Central Asia because of its proximity to principal petroleum producing countries, to trade routes between Asia,

Africa, and Europe, and unstable countries in Africa (Sudan comes to mind) that could be ripe for radicalization.

"Admiral Bergen and his successor, Detwiler, are highly intelligent and experienced men, and President Kitteridge is a successful international businessman. Abdul Rashid is concerned, however, that they do not yet recognize the day-to-day conflict in Afghanistan, so richly covered by the world's media, to be a diversion from the broader threat of an eventual global confrontation between Islam and the West. As all of you know, the primary task levied on Abdul Rashid by those who provide the financial resources required by the jihad is that he underwrite the efforts of Muslim people everywhere to control their lives and futures in accordance with God's rules and demands. He is being severely tried, however, by evidence that some at the forefront of our campaign would, in achieving this goal, create upheaval in the world that could destroy centuries of civilized development. We must prevent that happening, and all of you must be aware that, ultimately, we cannot rely on the Americans or other outsiders, but only on people like us, from within the movement."

Hannah briefed al-Fasal's admonition and other details of the meeting to a rapt audience in the Director's suite at CIA Headquarters. The Senate had not yet acted on the Detwiler and Glover nominations, so they and Philip Bergen were, in effect, occupying both their new and old positions. Fortunately, they had pretty much been doing that all along.

"I guess the main message that Abdul Rashid and al-Fasal want to convey is that developments in the progress of the jihad are reaching a point at which future change could be unforeseeable and become uncontrollable, and he's not talking just about Afghanistan," James Detwiler concluded.

"I tend to agree with both your interpretation, Jim, and Abdul Rashid's assessment," Bergen responded. "It's going to be critically important that we help the President lean in the right direction."

"I assume we can count on your help in keeping us from going too far astray, Phil?" Sam Glover asked, already knowing the answer.

"As I understand it, that's going to be the main part of my new job."

Hannah added: "I did tell al-Fasal and Orkamzi privately, as you requested, that the three of you intended to meet with them as soon as the Admiral was established in the White House and the Senate has acted on your nominations."

"How did you enjoy the venue, Hannah?" Glover asked.

"Al-Fasal's home is one of my favorite places in the whole world, particularly the pool on the terrace overlooking the Mediterranean. As usual, everyone was very nice to me, but I found it somewhat awkward determining the boundary of propriety governing how I dressed when in the company of Muslim men ostensibly dedicated to the propagation of fundamentalist Islam. When you told me I was going to the meeting, I rushed out to buy a new bathing suit, but could find nothing I thought would meet the demands of modesty. So, I ended up taking an old YWCA tank suit that I've had for almost fifteen years. It turned out to be a bit tight on me. So, I'm not sure that I achieved the level of modesty Agency and Islamic protocol demands, but no one seemed to complain.

Kingsley Yong was exhausted, as he usually was by the middle of the bizarre missions he was often asked to undertake. He had traveled by commercial air from Beijing to Islamabad via Istanbul, and had then been taken by Chinese embassy car to the northern Pakistani city of Peshawar, checking into the local Holiday Inn where he was now trying vainly to catch up on missed sleep while waiting to be contacted for the final leg of his journey. He wasn't sure when that would take place or the prospective means of conveyance, but was confident that, at the end, he would be meeting with Mir Bitani Khan, leader of the Afghan Taliban. Yong was a business development agent of the Peoples' Republic of China, although he was a U.S. citizen by birth and carried an American passport in addition to one issued in Beijing. His parents had emigrated to California as a consequence of World War II, and he had been born and raised in Los Angeles, ultimately achieving an honors degree in international relations and diplomacy at UCLA. After ten years of being shifted from one minor post to another in the U.S. Foreign Service, Yong revisited a contact made while he was attached to the Consulate in Canton, and was hired into the service of the Chinese government, which coveted his ability to speak both native English and Cantonese, as well as his diplomatic experience and university training. His starting pay was five times what he was getting from the U.S. Government.

A business development agent is not necessarily a spy, and Kingsley Yong's basic mission was not to obtain information or items with which their owners did not wish to part. Rather, people like him served as facilitators or conduits whereby agreements that could not be overtly made on a government-to-government basis (or between governments and private entities, such as multinational corporations) could be negotiated and implemented covertly with no opposition, at least for a while. As the impact of economic globalization spread inevitably into the political and military spheres, the role of the business agent became ever more important, and they began to appear in the shadows of world capitals, representing not only governments but also large international banks, commodity trading blocs, and even a nascent trade association purporting to represent Somali pirates.

Kingsley Yong was well known to U.S. and foreign intelligence and security agencies, his name and passport numbers on the watch list of almost every international airport in the world. His file had even been personally reviewed by James Detwiler when the latter was an Assistant Director of the FBI a number of years earlier. Other than to check a bit more closely to verify that it was actually him, however, no one impeded Yong's travels, nor was he closely tailed by the security forces of the countries he visited. The reason for this was highly indicative: the Chinese were everywhere and into everything, trying to grab as much of the available pie as they could, particularly with respect to raw materials. Kingsley Yong was a mine canary: where he appeared, a big Chinese investment deal or construction project was likely to follow, none of it demonstrably illegal. It made far more sense to watch him and to determine with whom he was dealing than to interfere with his movements and activities.

Yong's guide and four bodyguards appeared the next morning, and he was taken north into the mountains in an armored SUV escorted by two pickup trucks with heavy machine guns mounted in their beds. After much jouncing and several panic attacks when the escort feared that unseen CIA missile-launching drones were orbiting overhead, they arrived at their destination, which turned out to be a one-room house similar to the one that Hannah had visited two months earlier. This time, however, the room was warm and well lit, and a much fancier repast set out. Five insurgent leaders, in addition to Mir Batani Khan, greeted Yong warmly as he entered the room. There was no sign of General Orkamzi or other Pakistani representation.

"Permit me to apologize for the ill-treatment you received from the Pakistani roads," Batani said immediately. "When we meet in the future, I promise you it will be in Kabul, and you will arrive in comfort by plane and helicopter. At the moment, I am not entirely welcome in Afghanistan, and would not wish to risk your safety." They spoke in English.

"I have experienced worse," Yong replied graciously, "and the prospect of meeting with you has made the hardship worthwhile." Batani smiled to acknowledge the compliment, while making a mental note to keep a sharp eye on Mr. Yong.

After the formal reception and refreshments, Batani's associates departed, leaving him alone with Yong to address the business matter that occasioned the meeting. His visitor came immediately to the point.

"Several years ago, a team of U.S. Pentagon officials and geologists conducted a survey of the mineral resources of Afghanistan. Their findings revealed the presence of nearly a trillion dollars in untapped deposits of a broad spectrum of metal ores, all critical to modern industry. Given the country's geographic location and difficult terrain, exploiting these finds will be difficult and expensive. But, the most critical barrier is the lack of security in the country due to the ongoing conflict between the Afghan Government, supported by the Americans and NATO, and the Taliban, Northern Alliance, and other insurgent movements supported by the Pakistani ISI and a man in Paris named Abdul Rashid."

"You may not yet be aware of it," Yong continued, "but the government in Kabul has awarded a concession to a Chinese consortium for development of a very large copper deposit in Logar Province, south of Kabul. In addition to development of the mine itself, the consortium will be required to build a railroad running to Afghanistan's northern and southern borders by which to ship the mined ore out of the country."

Bitani did, in fact, know of the mineral survey, that awareness being the underlying rationale for the revised Taliban strategy with which he had earlier surprised Orkamzi and al-Fasal. But, he had not known the Chinese had already begun to develop a major mining concession. Other initiatives would not be far behind.

"How have the Americans reacted to this?"

"Although the idea of helping the Chinese is not popular, the Americans are supporting the project because it will eventually mean thousands of jobs for Afghan citizens. The terms of the concession limit foreigners to management and engineering positions, and that only for an initial five years."

"So, the American military will provide security for the Chinese mine and railroad construction?"

"Yes, until the Afghan army and police forces are able to take over the responsibility."

"Which may be never."

"Yes, which may be never," Yong acknowledged. "That is why I've been sent to see you. We cannot rely on the American support indefinitely, particularly when the unusual circumstances become widely known in the United States. I don't imagine public and Congressional critics will approve the idea of American lives and treasure being spent to protect a Chinese enterprise, however beneficial it might be to the Afghan people."

Bitani's response was immediate. "I agree with you. What do your employers have in mind?"

"The Chinese government would be extremely grateful if you could successfully undertake, as leader of the Taliban, to provide our mining and railroad construction sites protection from attack by indigenous forces of whatever political or religious persuasion."

"How grateful would that be?"

"We would make an immediate good faith payment of three million American dollars against an annual payment of fifteen million dollars. However, two million would be deducted from the total for each serious incidence of failure to provide the agreed protection. What do you think?"

"I think it will do for a start, but I may need more money later. Contrary to popular belief, the Taliban is not the only movement in Afghanistan opposing the government in Kabul and the Americans. The leaders of some are my enemies, and all are my competitors. Much of your money will go to buy their cooperation."

"So, I may tell Beijing that you will subscribe to our proposal?"

"Yes, you may. I will tell you where to deposit the funds. But, I must insist that complete secrecy be observed. My ability to assist you would be severely compromised, if it became known that I was serving multiple masters. At the extreme, I would be required to spend all of my time safeguarding myself from assassination.

CHAPTER FIVE

During his tenure as Director of National Intelligence and CIA Director before that, Philip Bergen had visited the White House on more days than not, and was readily recognized by the President's staff and everyone else who worked there. But he quickly found that visiting and working there were substantially different. In anticipation of his odyssey eventually ending, the now retired Admiral had taken over the West Wing office already vacated by his predecessor, Tom Brooks. It was a nice-sized corner suite on the same floor as the Oval Office, which conveyed a certain superiority to those who had their offices on other floors and were, thus, further from the President.

The most distinctive difference between White House visitors and resident staff was that Mason Kitteridge assumed the latter were available at all times, and would unexpectedly call for discussion or an answer to a question for which the targeted staffer was not always prepared. On occasion, he would come charging out of the Oval Office waving a document and cross into the warren of senior staff offices to search someone out, in the process scattering the small retinue of people whose mission it was to never let the President out of their sight. At those times, it was actually better to have an office on one of the less prestigious floors, since Kitteridge had never located the private stairway connecting to them.

"I will be happy when this transition business is done and you are settled in here at the White House, Admiral," the President told his prospective National Security Advisor one morning. Bergen had tried to react enthusiastically, but was deterred by the knowledge that Kitteridge demanded detail and frequent updates on every pregnant situation, of which there were usually many. The responsibility for providing it would soon be Detwiler's, but Bergen was aware that he would not escape, since the President would know the nearby location of his new office.

Two weeks before the scheduled hearings on the Detwiler and Glover nominations, the President called together his senior intelligence leadership and the Secretaries of State, Defense, and Homeland Security, as well as the Attorney General. Donald McGinnis, Director of the FBI, was also invited to the Principals only session in the Oval Office.

"You are all aware," Kitteridge began, "of my nomination of Admiral Bergen to the position of National Security Advisor. I want to tell you now what I have in mind, other than to put a good man into an important job.

"You will have noticed that all of our government's departments and agencies involved in foreign affairs---political, military, and legal---are represented here, as are additionally DHS and the FBI. In this age of international terrorism, we cannot consider law enforcement solely a domestic responsibility. I recognize that economic matters also constitute a major part, probably the largest single part, of our international concerns and activity, but I didn't want this group to get too large, so I will deal with Commerce, Energy and others separately.

"What I'm going to be talking about here is referred to in the media and elsewhere as globalization, the growing and inevitable interdependence of the world's countries that stems from a number of causes, including an increasing inability to satisfy their populations with domestic resources and effort alone. You are all familiar with examples of industrial globalization that are adversely affecting our country's balance of trade and employment, and the expanding race to secure control of natural resources, such as petroleum and mined minerals. Not surprisingly, this competition and its impact extend to the political and military fields and will do so to an increasingly greater extent as international competition becomes stiffer. Let me give you a critical real world example of what I'm talking about.

"Several years ago, DoD sponsored a geological survey of Afghanistan that found at least a trillion dollars of exploitable minerals, including an enormous copper deposit that has been leased to the Chinese by the Kabul government. I'm sure you've guessed, if you didn't already know, that security for the Chinese operation is being provided by the United States military until the Afghan Army is able to take over, a prospect certainly not imminent. I've yet to hear a complaint from my friend Alfred Oberling about this, but I'm certain it will eventually come."

The President paused to allow his revelation to sink in before continuing.

"Most, if not all of you, expect that I was outraged by this news, but I was not, Mr. Oberling notwithstanding. While I have no great desire to further Chinese interests, the copper and railroad projects will create thousands of jobs for Afghan citizens, which is absolutely essential to our longer range objectives. This is but one example of the truth in the old cliché, newly updated, that globalization makes strange bedfellows---which is my reason for bring-ing you here today."

Kitteridge again paused, this time for effect.

"The pressure of total globalization is creating situa-tions and circumstances that have made the relationships among countries, particularly large ones like ours, even more complex. It seems to me, however, that there may still be significant opportunity for cooperation with our international competitors in the war on terrorism and Is-lamic extremism, which we all oppose, albeit for different reasons. Director Detwiler tells me, for instance, that there is an American with the improbable name of Kingsley Yong wandering around the world promoting business deals on behalf of the Chinese government. Perhaps, we can find some ambitious Chinese who would be willing to make deals for us."

The others in the room looked at Admiral Bergen and James Detwiler for a clue to whether the President was joking, and concluded he was not. The Intelligence people had obviously already been exposed to this lament, but they did not appear smug in their knowledge. This was go-ing to be a world-class can of worms. Kitteridge laughed.

"The looks on your faces alone is sufficient justifica-tion for my holding this meeting rather than sending you all a memo. This will, indeed, be a highly complex and sen-sitive undertaking, one that could easily get out of hand, if we're not very careful. I certainly don't intend and will not condone anything like the Iran-Contra business that got President Reagan in trouble. That is why I decided to bring Admiral Bergen to the White House. Although it will not be openly acknowledged, his principal task as National Security Advisor will be to coordinate our efforts in pursuit of the opportunities I've outlined, as well as to anticipate and forestall adverse consequences."

Everyone stirred uneasily, and Admiral Bergen felt his stomach begin to churn, a sensation he hadn't experienced so acutely since the first time he assumed the con of a warship underway, as a very junior naval officer.

"Can you give us some examples of things getting out of hand, sir?" Secretary of Defense White pleaded.

"First," Kitteridge responded, "I don't want any covert operations run out of the White House. When I call Admiral Bergen 'the coordinator', I mean just that. All of your organizations, alone or in combination, may become involved in our initiatives or in the response to one by another country. The Admiral's responsibility will be to insure that we are all working together in these endeavors, that you receive the support you need, and that I am kept informed in a manner that will allow time for effective action on my part. I do not wish to find myself standing in front of a TV camera telling the American people that I was unaware of what was going on, whether that was true or not.

"Second, things will have gotten out of hand should your departments and agencies come to engage in the sort of rivalry and xenophobia that characterizes our government at times. With Admiral Bergen's help, I will assure that you and your organizations receive all the credit and blame you deserve.

"Finally, I cannot overstress the critical importance of security. The very existence of this program and its senior membership must be accorded the highest level of secrecy we can manage. All of you have been around Washington long enough to grasp what would happen, should the media get even an inkling of it. We could be tied up for the rest of our terms answering endless questions and reacting to worst case scenarios conjured up by cable news pundits. Worst of all, however, whatever benefits and advantages the program offer us would likely be lost."

The taping of Admiral Bergen's appearance on *American Focus* occurred three days after the Oval Office meeting that still filled his mind. The time proximity was coincidental, and he had no viable excuse on which to base a postponement. Hannah recognized that her boss was seriously bothered, but had no idea of the cause except for a guess that it had to do with the President's meeting. It had been decided that the taping would occur at the network's studio in downtown Washington on a set that had Bergen and the interviewer seated in armchairs before a backdrop featuring a map of the world. The latter was Olivia McQueen, doyenne of the program's on-air staff of six, who had the reputation of being a persistent questioner, quick to detect and pursue perceived leads to interesting stories. Although the Admiral could stop the proceedings and refuse to answer particular questions, since the program was not broadcast live, it would not look good and tend to make the remainder of the taping adversarial.

"Admiral Bergen," McQueen began, "you've just retired from the Navy after a long and distinguished career as both a submariner and intelligence officer, in the latter capacity serving both as Director of CIA and Director of National Intelligence. You certainly are deserving of the nation's gratitude for your service to it. But, there are persistent rumors that your career has not yet run its course, that you will soon be named to the White House position of

National Security Advisor by President Kitteridge. Is this rumor true?"

Bergen smiled disingenuously. "Well, I've heard that rumor also, Olivia, and they say that, if you hear a rumor often enough, it must be true. At the moment, however, I can't confirm or deny this one."

"Assuming, for the sake of discussion, that this one is true, Admiral, why would the President want to, at this point in time, move you from a position in which, by all reports, you have been performing very well?"

"I appreciate the compliment, Olivia. But, it's not like my departure would leave a big void. Jim Detwiler is a very talented and experienced man, as is Sam Glover, who would replace him at CIA."

"So, the rumor of your transfer is apparently true enough that the other occupants of the musical chairs have been identified?"

Bergen smiled benignly, having been caught out. "We always take precautions against contingencies, Olivia."

"Given your extensive experience, Admiral, there would seem to be little question but that you could provide useful advice to the President in the White House. But, you are an intelligence officer, and the National Security Advisor position has a traditionally broader charter. Intelligence, I'm sure you'll agree, is but one input, although certainly a very important one, to the policy and decision making process. That again prompts the questions: why you, why now?"

Bergen again smiled. "As you know, Olivia, the National Security Advisor is a member of the President's personal staff, and we've traditionally allowed a President to choose its members by whatever criteria he prefers. I have not attempted to read President Kitteridge's mind, but perhaps he perceives that the changing nature of international interaction has made good intelligence more valuable and worthy of greater attention."

Bergen could figuratively see McQueen's ears prick up.

"What changing nature, Admiral?"

"When you read the current press and watch television news today, Olivia, one word that continually pops out at you is globalization, usually described as the increasing inability of nations to most effectively conduct their economic affairs independently of one another. Most commonly, we hear how millions of American jobs have disappeared overseas and how our trade deficit is helping to bankrupt us. But globalization is occurring in the other major areas of international relations, political and military, and all of them are intertwined. Figuring out who is doing what to whom, or planning to do so is a basic mission of the Intelligence services, and it is becoming even more important and more difficult. And remember, Olivia, that lurking in the tangled web of international political and commercial activities are the terrorists whose only objective is destruction."

"How would the President, with your help, look to deal with this challenge?

"Please remember, Olivia, that I've not yet gotten into the job. But, I think you'll agree that it's nice to have a President who is preparing to take on tomorrow's problems and threats."

"Your boss handled himself very well this afternoon," Paul Rayner told Hannah at dinner after the taping session. "Dropping that bit about political globalization was like throwing a chunk of raw meat into the lion's cage. Olivia has a magnificent instinct for a potentially big story. That's what makes her so great."

"The Admiral's not exactly a novice at this kind of stuff, although he doesn't particularly care for it," she replied. "Fortunately, the Kitteridge Administration has not needed the kind of defending that its predecessor required. So, Bergen has been avoiding public appearances."

"So, how come he's starting to do it now? I suppose this White House appointment is a sure thing, although they're being pretty coy about it?"

Hannah dutifully did not respond, but in truth she didn't know the answers to Rayner's probing questions. Obviously, things were going on about which she was not being told. Whether this was due to their extreme sensitivity or because she would not commit to moving with Bergen to the White House, or perhaps both, she couldn't tell. But the realization that, for the first time in almost four years, she was not aware of what was occupying the Admiral's mind and attention bothered Hannah tremendously.

"Are you planning to go with Bergen to the White House?" Rayner asked, seemingly reading her mind.

"I haven't decided yet, but probably not," Hannah replied, recognizing that her response confirmed Bergen's new assignment, which was going to be formally announced in the next several days. "I expect to continue working with and for Admiral Bergen, but I'm inclined to remain where I am. I work very well with Jim Detwiler and Sam Glover."

"So, the new executive daisy chain has already been decided?"

"Give us some credit, Paul!" Hannah reacted explosively. "You investigative journalism types seem to always start with the assumption that our government is being run by a bunch of boobs."

Rayner started to respond, but then thought better of it.

"It is obviously not wise for me to address that one. But I'm encouraged to know that our personal relationship is progressing: we are having our first fight."

Hannah hesitated, then laughed. "You are damned lucky that regulations prevent me using the tools of my trade here at home. Otherwise, our relationship might reach a quick end right now."

"But we are progressing, aren't we?" he persisted.

"I'll agree to probation," Hannah replied, smiling. She realized that it was not Paul's behavior that had angered her but the annoying thought that she was being left out of the action and, more to the point, that she would prefer to have it both ways. However, when Bergen's appointment and the promotions for Detwiler and Glover were announced several days later, Hannah officially opted to remain where she was, gratified that Bergen appeared

disappointed by her choice, while her new boss was enthusiastic. At lunch with Naomi Benson, Sam Glover's intended, she was assured that the new Director of CIA was also
highly gratified. Apparently, they had already discussed
with Bergen how Hannah could work for all three of them
simultaneously without destroying their friendly relationship and her health.

CHAPTER SIX

Reggie Huggins was in Paris attempting to locate Abdul Rashid, of whose existence he had learned through the old spooks network. Many of his former Intelligence Community colleagues had, like him, gone into consulting firms after retirement in order to make continued use of their talents, experience, and security clearances, generally at salaries much higher than what the Government had been paying them. The firms for which they now worked invariably leased them back to the Government, not infrequently to the very agencies from which they had come. Thus, Reggie had a number of current contacts, one of whom told him of Abdul Rashid, but had no further information, other than that he was to be found in Paris. Huggins knew he had little prospect of locating his quarry, but had come because Oberling and Norton were enthusiastic about locating a man they understood to be a senior member of the Islamic jihad. They readily agreed to pay the expenses of Huggins and his agents, and he was eager to demonstrate to his new employers how valuable and professional Global Security Applications LLC's services could be in extending their reach outside the United States. Reggie's fallback was that he had also learned of Mahmud al-Fasal and the name of the Paris hotel in which he lived.

The latter was extremely puzzled when handed Huggins' business card by his chief of security, along with a report obtained from a contact in the Surete that a man of the same name had been assigned to CIA's Paris Station in the nineteen-seventies. Al-Fasal, of course, had never heard of Huggins or his company, and wondered what his American friends were up to. He thought to call Washington, but Bergen was gone to the White House and he knew Glover only slightly, Detwiler not at all. So, he decided to grant Huggins an audience and gave instructions for him to be placed under surveillance for the remainder of his time in Paris.

"Who are you representing, Mr. Huggins? I'm told you have or had a connection to the CIA."

"I'm no longer with the CIA, sir," Reggie replied, taken aback that al-Fasal was aware of his Agency history. "I represent prominent, politically influential parties in the United States vitally interested in the conduct of our relations with the Muslim world and, in particular, with the war on terrorism. I've been sent to Paris in the hope of locating Mr. Abdul Rashid for the purposes of opening a channel of continuing communications. We understand that you are his close associate, and know where he can be contacted."

Al-Fasal knew better than to ask Huggins who his sponsors were, at least at this early stage of their relationship. The possibilities were not, however, unlimited, and al-Fasal amused himself seeing whether he could guess correctly.

"Abdul Rashid rarely entertains visitors, and I cannot promise you access to him. I would also strongly recommend you not try to locate him on your own. As you can imagine, his security is very closely guarded, and it is possible that an effort on your part to penetrate it could place your safety at risk."

"Thank you for the insight, sir," Huggins replied. "Would it be possible to use you as an intermediary in matters of mutual interest, at least until a higher level of mutual trust is established?" Al-Fasal nodded, and his visitor pondered how to begin.

"My clients are politically influential and highly patriotic. They are extremely concerned that America has gotten so badly bogged down in its so-called global war on terrorism that little progress is being made while costs are soaring. A major change in strategy and rules of engagement is required, and they are preparing to fight for such change at the highest levels of the U.S. Government."

"Why do you come to Abdul Rashid with this?"

"Because our sides have an important goal in common, although for different reasons. We both want to get the United States out of Afghanistan as soon as possible, and to prevent the future intervention of American military forces in the Muslim world. Is that not what you also wish to accomplish, Mr. al-Fasal?"

His response to Huggins' question was studiedly noncommittal, but al-Fasal obviously could not ignore it.

"Assuming that is the case, how would your sponsors propose going about accomplishing that end?"

Huggins pounced. "That is precisely what my clients wish to discuss with Abdul Rashid. I am not privy to the specifics of their proposal, but they insist that its implementation is highly feasible, given the cooperation of both sides."

Al-Fasal, now both intrigued and stuck, stood up and extended his hand.

"I will consult with Abdul Rashid and get back to you. Please tell my assistant outside where you are staying in Paris and how to contact you in the United States."

Abdul Rashid agreed the approach was strange, but did not believe it reflected a new American gambit prompted by the changing of the guard in Washington. At his direction, al-Fasal called Sam Glover on the special secure telephone that had been provided him several years earlier for use in making direct contact expeditiously. The phone rang in the CIA Operations Center, which had standing orders to patch the call through to now Director Glover at any hour of the day or night.

"Mr. Glover, first let me congratulate you on your promotion!"

"Thank you very much, sir. What can I do for you?

"Abdul Rashid asked me to let you know that we've been contacted by a Mr. Reggie Huggins, an American acting on behalf of others of your countrymen, thus far unidentified."

For a long moment, al-Fasal feared the connection had been lost, then Glover responded in a somber voice: "We know Mr. Huggins. What do they want?"

"Apparently to initiate a dialog or negotiation on subjects of mutual interest," his caller replied. Glover did not ask what those subjects were, knowing that al-Fasal would not reveal them nor accept his protestations about Reggie Huggins.

"Thank you both very much for calling to tell us, Mr. al-Fasal"

"Not at all, Mr. Glover. We are always happy to keep you abreast of what is happening in Washington. Abdul Rashid asked me to convey to Director Detwiler and yourself an invitation to meet at the earliest opportunity. Paris is especially lovely in the Fall.

After two days in his new office, Philip Bergen decided that life in the White House did not measure up to his earlier sojourns in the top floor suites of DNI and CIA Headquarters. For newcomers leaving a dusty office on a college campus or even a more palatial one in a Lower Manhattan skyscraper, the transition was undoubtedly magical. But it was not the same as being lord of an enormous enterprise of many thousand employees extending to every corner of the world, the full extent and capabilities of which even he was unaware. What was bothering Bergen most, however, was that he had received just one phone call in the entire two days, and that had been from his wife, Charlotte, to say how impressed she had been to get a call from a pleasant but authoritative female voice saying: "This is the White House operator. Admiral Philip Bergen would like to speak with you." He had discussed with Charlotte whether to drop the "Admiral" now he was retired, and they had decided to experiment with omitting it. But the first time the operator left it off, the person being called answered: "Who?" and it was back in. He had, after all, earned the title.

On the third day, he received a call from General Arkady Estefimov of the Russian Embassy, whom Bergen thanked for coming to his retirement ceremony. Both the Russian's appearance and the Admiral's acknowledgment thereof led to a rendezvous by the carousel on the National Mall, a spot favored by Bergen.

"If what you said on television about President Kitteridge's newly expanded view of globalization is true," Estefimov began, " you and I need to discuss several possibilities that could be mutually beneficial. I know the United States does not wish to become involved in Russia's problems with her Muslim extremists, for which I can't blame you, but you may not be able much longer to both have your cake and eat it. I'm instructed to determine whether our two countries can at least discuss the possibility of cooperative measures."

Bergen led the way to the cafeteria of the nearby National Air and Space Museum where they purchased sandwiches and coffee, then found a table at which they would not be overheard. The huge room was filled as usual with tourists, most of whom appeared to be teenagers on school-sponsored trips. However, the overall noise level was moderate, the visitors absorbed in eating their lunches so that they could get quickly back to the wonders they had come to see. No one noticed the two middle-aged men sitting at a table against a wall.

"My government has recently completed a reappraisal of our situation with respect to Islamic extremism, both at home and abroad," Estefimov continued. "As I'm sure you've guessed, it was prompted by the wave of terrorist attacks in Moscow and elsewhere in the country that we have not succeeded in choking off. Although the survey's general conclusion was, in my private opinion, overly pessimistic, one of its specific determinations was that greater and more applied cooperation among countries opposed to these bastards is urgently required. It also concluded that joint action must be more of an offensive nature rather than confined to exchanging intelligence and securing our borders. I am instructed, as I've said, to explore with you informally potential areas of such cooperation. Moscow, I'm told, will also approach other potentially significant players, such as China and India."

"We shall be happy to hear Russia's thoughts and proposals, General Estefimov, purely unofficially of course," Bergen responded. "One of the principal duties President Kitteridge has assigned to me in my new position is to engage in such dialog and to coordinate our participation in any joint initiatives that might come of it."

Estefimov's smile, the only one Bergen had ever seen, expressed both relief and satisfaction as he appeared to notice the crowd around them for the first time. "I told my superiors this would be so."

"But I am curious," Bergen continued, "what you might have in mind when you speak of greater offensive action, beyond doing more to detect and forestall planned terrorist operations?"

"We have come to believe, Admiral, that we must strike directly at the foundation of terrorism, the source of the one component that has proven indispensable to its success: an ample supply of people readily willing to commit suicide to serve the jihad. Invariably, they are the product of intense indoctrination by extremist zealots of great proselytizing talent, religious zeal, and charisma located all over the world. Most are unknown, not having achieved the rock star status, as you call it, of the sectarian leaders who regularly rail against the infidel West. But they are equally effective in their mission, perhaps even more so, working hard to convince the Muslim masses that their future can only be assured through the willing destruction of their own lives and ours."

"What do the Russians think we should do?" President Kitteridge asked, when the Admiral briefed him on his meeting with Estefimov.

"Kill them, sir! The Russians think we should pool our covert action resources and find ways to assassinate the people who stir up the masses and encourage the fanatics."

"Could we do that?"

"It wouldn't be an easy sell, sir. It's not exactly the American way."

Having received from Kingsley Yong the first installment of his promised subsidy, to add to the remainder (almost half) of the cash received earlier from Mahmud al-Fasal, Mir Batani Khan was ready to launch the next phase of his master plan, which required going back to Afghanistan to earn his Chinese stipend. But first he needed to make sure that his fall back refuge in Pakistan was still secure. Hesitating over the amount, Batani finally put thirty thousand dollars of his hoard into a briefcase and went to Islamabad to wait on General Orkamzi. The latter did not immediately recognize his visitor, who had exchanged his robe and headdress for a well tailored English woolen suit, one of five he had made to measure by the Armani shop in Karachi. He had also trimmed his beard in the latest continental fashion.

"So, Batani, you are going back to cause trouble in Kabul?" Orkamzi reacted, taking the briefcase and shoving it into a compartment of his massive desk, after a quick glance inside. "I congratulate you on an arrangement with the Chinese that will pay you handsomely for doing something you were planning to do anyway. We are very happy for you," he added, nodding toward the place he had just secreted the briefcase.

Batani laughed, while wondering how Orkamzi had come to know about his deal with Kingsley Yong. He should have assumed, he chided himself, that the Chinese agent was also dealing with the ISI, which is what he would be doing in Yong's place. But, the General appeared satisfied with consideration received, so Batani decided to move on to the subject he had specifically come to broach.

"I am interested in your opinion, General Orkamzi, as to how the Americans will respond when they discover the truth about my strategy for getting them out of Afghanistan. I do not believe they will react explosively, since my maneuvers will not cause them additional casualties or expense---actually the opposite. Rather, what I would like to know is whether the Americans will pretend that our efforts have actually created the conditions that enable them to withdraw with honor, which they wish most of all to do. Or will they seek to expose our campaign as a deception and simply go on with the seemingly endless battle between what they consider to be good and evil."

Batani was unaware of Hannah Crossman's presence at his briefing of Orkamzi and Mahmud al-Fasal, as a result of which the Taliban leader's plans and strategy were already well known in Washington. The ISI chief considered telling him now, but decided not do so out of consideration for al-Fasal's credibility and reputation----or so he told himself.

"What if the Americans do neither or both?" Orka-mzi asked instead. "There are influential people in the United States, for example, calling for the creation of permanent bases in Afghanistan that would be used to prevent the country from again becoming the launching point for attacks like that on the World Trade Center. What effect would that have on your plans?"

Batani frowned. "I must believe that, as time passes, the pressure on America to get out of Afghanistan will continue to grow, as it did during the war in Vietnam. Washington has already announced a phased force reduction and conditional end of combat activity, as was done in Iraq. I expect to have much greater difficulty controlling the warfare among my own countrymen than getting rid of the Americans. In shouting and waving our arms against crusaders and invaders, we Muslims tend to forget one important thing: the Americans did not come looking for colonial conquests or cheap natural resources. They do not want to stay, and will leave if convinced that we will not threaten their security and interests or those of their allies. At times, I think they will even accept the imposition of Sharia Law in Muslim states, if only we are quiet about it."

"And what of Pakistan, my friend?" Orkamzi asked. "You cannot separate the future of Afghanistan from that of Pakistan or, for that matter, of China, Iran, and other surrounding states. Throughout history, Afghanistan has always been a prize sought after by an invader from the outside, whether Mongol hordes, British lancers or Soviet armored units. Now that the Americans have found mineral riches in your mountains, the invaders will have even greater incentive."

"If they come bearing truckloads of money, as do the Chinese, we will make them welcome," Batani replied. "But our bond with Pakistan is special because you have supported and given us sanctuary for a great many years, and we shall not forget it. However, Pakistan has its own demons to conquer. You must decide whether the country will be ruled from the halls of government or from the mosques. You and I, dear General, have the same friends in people like Abdul Rashid and Mahmud al-Fasal. But, it may turn out that we also have the same enemies."

"Who did this Huggins say sent him to find me?" Abdul Rashid demanded to know.

"He didn't say, Excellency, other than that they are important, well-placed Americans. I called Glover at the CIA and told him about the visit, but not about what Huggins wished to address." Mahmud al-Fasal was becoming annoyed. This was the third time he had answered the same question for his preoccupied employer.

"Tell me again what that was."

"Huggins was vague. Apparently, he has not been told very much either. His mission was confined to contacting you to determine whether you would be interested in considering direct action against persons in Muslim countries working to prevent the achievement of peace between Islam and the West."

"What persons?"

"He didn't tell me that either, but I don't think he knows. I tried to avoid embarrassing him, and he was grateful for my standard vague response to the effect that we are always interested in things that could benefit us."

"So, what will happen next?"

"I believe Huggins and his sponsors will contact us with a more specific proposal, Excellency."

Reggie Huggins' report to Roger Norton on the same meeting was a lot more fulsome regarding potential developments.

"I didn't get to see Abdul Rashid in person because he's apparently a recluse. He has no legs, and doesn't go anywhere or entertain visitors. Al-Fasal is his main man, and my sources tell me he's very capable and highly reliable. If he says that Abdul Rashid has gotten your message and is interested in hearing more, I believe him.

"You didn't tell him who we are, did you?"

Huggins contrived to appear insulted. "I've been doing this kind of stuff a long time, Mr. Norton, and know pretty well what I'm about and who I'm dealing with. My guess is that you'll have a receptive audience when ready to make specific proposals. Just to be sure, however, I took a couple of my people with Agency experience along to Paris and had them reestablish some contacts I used when posted to our station there in the seventies. One of the things they are prepared to do, on yours or Mr.Oberling's orders, is to trail al-Fasal until he leads us to wherever Rashid hides out."

Norton smiled at the prospect of *Oberling For America* having a covert agent network of its own overseas, and congratulated Huggins on a job well done. Global Security Applications LLC had passed its first client test, and was on its way to bigger and richer things. Fortunately, the small office building in which its headquarters were located was largely vacant and it was easy to acquire space for the additional people Reggie began to hire from the rosters of the spook alumni associations to which he belonged. One day, an extraordinarily attractive woman appeared at 0830, and was sitting in Reggie's visitor's chair when he arrived.

"Who's she?" he asked his secretary. "I didn't think we had an invitation out to anyone who looks like that."

"She says her name is Hannah Crossman and that she's been sent to see you by Mr. Glover."

"Good morning, Ms. Crossman. Jewel says that you've been sent by my old friend Sam Glover," he gushed as he closed the door to his inner office. "One pays attention when sent an employment candidate by the Director of CIA himself." He favored her with his most ingratiating smile.

"There's been a mistake, Mr. Huggins," she replied. "I've come at Mr. Glover's direction, but not looking for a job. He sends his regards and wishes you to know that we are aware of your recent contact with a certain party in Paris, and that we find this to be unhelpful to the interests and security of the United States."

Huggins affected great affront. "I've done nothing illegal, and my company is working on behalf of a highly reputable client who enjoys great stature in this country. I don't propose to give up my rights and livelihood to please Sam Glover."

Hannah smiled. "Mr. Glover predicted you would react this way, and asked me to offer you friendly counsel. Tell Reggie, he said (and here I quote), 'that, if he doesn't knock it off, we will arrange to have his balls cut off.'"

CHAPTER SEVEN

The greatest benefit that, in his view, accrued to Philip Bergen from his change of positions was that he no longer had to appear before Congressional committees to sell or defend the Administration's policies and actions. As an advisor, rather than a cabinet officer or agency head, he was not in the Executive Branch's chain of command and, therefore, not officially permitted to run anything or be held responsible for the way it was run. He could be called to testify at hearings, willingly or not, to defend his advice and views, but could not be held responsible for what the President did or did not do with them. In the public's view (and, significantly, that of the media), the National Security Advisor was a phantom: reported as having attended a meeting, prepared a paper or briefed the President, but without substantive detail. This relative anonymity was President Kitteridge's most important objective in causing the Admiral's transfer to take place.

The role of principal intelligence officer in the Administration passed then to James Detwiler, who was perhaps more qualified for the job than Bergen had been originally. While the latter had far greater experience in the Intelligence Community, he lacked Detwiler's extensive background in law enforcement with the FBI. Insofar as the dominant contemporary threat to the United

States was from international terrorism, which demanded a merger of foreign intelligence and domestic law enforcement, the former CIA Director and FBI Assistant Director could be said to have the edge. Like his predecessor, Detwiler made a marvelous witness: well spoken, decisive, and photogenic. His only disadvantage was the lack of the gold braid-encrusted, ribbon-bedecked Navy blue uniform Bergen invariably wore on visits to the Hill, but rarely elsewhere.

Since the shock of the World Trade Center attack on 9/11/01 and the intensive investigation that followed, the performance of U.S. intelligence services has been under almost constant critical scrutiny, particularly as the scope and cost of its efforts expanded enormously under the cover of official secrecy. Historically, the critical question was always the same: why didn't we have early warning of the Japanese attack on Pearl Harbor or of North Korea's invasion of South Korea in 1950 or the terrorist attack on 9/11. Subsequent inquiry revealed, in all cases, that the necessary indicators were in hand, but not recognized or acted upon, and structural and functional changes in the organization and leadership of what came to be called the Intelligence Community followed. The transition from the relatively straightforward Cold War environment to that of the Global War on Terrorism further complicated matters by introducing into the mix a phalanx of law enforcement agencies on the federal, state, and local levels and the often muddled relationship between them and national foreign intelligence agencies. During his tenure as CIA Director and Director of National Intelligence, Philip Bergen had appeared in many venues on Capitol Hill to explain, plead, and cajole before increasingly dubious audiences, as had James Detwiler and Donald McGinnis of the FBI.

Replacement of the evil Soviet empire by the arguably more evil Islamic jihad as the principal threat to U.S.

national security had major consequences for the Intelligence Community that were underappreciated, particularly by the general public. While the capacity of the Soviet Union to threaten was enormous, by the nineteen seventies and eighties the prospect of nuclear war had become increasingly abstract as both sides strove to avoid confrontational situations like the Cuban Missile Crisis. During this period, little was heard of "intelligence failures," although some fault the Intelligence Community for not predicting the evil empire's rather abrupt demise. The principal task of U.S. intelligence, now equipped with a range of marvelous surveillance and collection systems, was to keep an eye on the huge military resources the Soviets would have had to deploy were they intending to start a conflict with the United States and its allies. Other than the ill-fated venture into Afghanistan, no significant Soviet military deployments were actually ever attempted.

The later rise of al-Qaeda filled the void left by the now defunct Communist threat. There had been a number of terrorist incidents around the world, bombings and aircraft hijackings, but they seemed unrelated, and none had occurred in the United States. The Oklahoma City bombing in 1995, clearly an act of domestic terrorism, was considered an isolated event not representative of a broader, ongoing conspiracy. But, the appearance of an evil mastermind coordinating and supporting international terrorist atrocities, his declared enmity toward the United States, capped by the sophisticated planning and execution of the 9/11 attacks, made the subsequent Global War on Terrorism the lineal successor to the Cold War.

For the greatly expanded intelligence services of the United States, the transition was an enormous shock. The critical surveillance targets were now not massive deployments of troops and tanks or fleets of ballistic missile submarines, but individuals or small groups of men emerging from the weave of local society to kill indiscriminately, often at the knowing sacrifice of their own lives. Although it had not happened in America since 9/11, the fear and warnings were there, their focal points much nearer and narrower. It was not the fear of nuclear war and millions of casualties that most unnerved people now, but the possibility of an attack in their city's subway system or crowded marketplace that killed but forty or fifty---one of whom, however, might be them.

"Are the American people's expectations of their intelligence services unreasonable, Director Detwiler, considering the resources we devote to them and the threats the country is facing?"

Once again testifying before Marcus Crabtree's Senate Select Intelligence Committee, the new Director of National Intelligence silently envied Philip Bergen's escape, although he suspected that his new job would not be a picnic. This hearing was prompted by the Intelligence Community's failure to foresee a bloody uprising by Islamist insurgents in the Caucasus that had been brutally suppressed by the Russian Army.

"No, Senator Crabtree, the American people's concerns are understandable and not unreasonable. But our ability to respond in a timely fashion is affected by the number of bases we are trying to cover simultaneously. We have the capacity to collect and process huge quantities of information almost effortlessly, but when doing that reveals the need to follow up by sending out a reconnaissance aircraft, a pair of agents or a patrol car to investigate, our ability to respond shrinks considerably. We cannot be constantly at general quarters covering all of the threat possibilities. It is true that we did not forecast the occurrence of the Caucasus uprising that occasioned this hearing, but we did advise the President and key Cabinet departments that conditions were ripe for a revolt that could occur at any time, and that the Russian Government would put it down without difficulty. The fact that it occurred when it did was of little consequence to us, since it caused us no damage and required no response on our part."

"Nevertheless, Director Detwiler, there have been other incidents in recent months, perhaps not as spectacular as this one, in which suspicious people and activities have not been pursued, even though evidence and your rules of engagement should have required it. I'm speaking, for example, of the foreign nationals with clear terrorist or at least suspicious connections who were allowed to travel to the United States unhindered."

Detwiler smiled. "We are far from perfect, Senator, and I've been among the first to admit it. In the more tactical areas of counterterrorism, those in which your examples fall, we have still not gotten our arms completely around the enormous expansion in the number of organizations and people interacting on a day-to-day basis as a result of the need for the Intelligence and Law Enforcement Communities to share missions. The complexity of our operating relationships, coupled with the often fragmentary and ambiguous nature of the information we receive, makes for a high level of uncertainty as to what, if anything, should be done, when, and by whom. This at times leads to delay or inaction, even when available indicators call for some response. I have testified before about these problems, and will do so again at the Committee's convenience."

The Chairman looked left and right down the row of Committee members.

"Do any of you have additional questions for Director Detwiler?" Senator Margaret Burke, recently named to the Committee, raised her hand.

"We have heard, Director Detwiler, of yours and Admiral Bergen's continuing conversations with Representative Mary Kingsley and her House intelligence committee on the changed nature of war, as it is now being fought. I believe the specific subject was CIA's use of missile-launching drones in Pakistan and elsewhere. I would be interested in hearing your general view directly."

The new DNI suppressed a sigh and an envious thought of Philip Bergen before replying.

"The American people have long held beliefs about the rules of war governing the circumstances and conditions which make it permissible or impermissible to kill people, particularly those not in uniform and part of organized military units. In this age of terrorism and insurgency, however, the distinction between assassination and killing in battle that we have long made has effectively disappeared. When terrorists mount an operation, say in a subway station, that kills a large number of people, they consider it a battle. But, when we seek out and kill an al-Qaeda leader in his city apartment or an insurgent commander in a mountain hideout, some accuse us of violating the code of conduct that makes America special and gives us the right to lead the world. This is not the time or place to go into what, for this country and its leaders, may be an existential moral issue, but I don't see that our enemies are leaving us much choice. The terrorist we kill in his bed will not be sneaking around the world planting bombs. Do we make mistakes and cause collateral casualties? Unfortunately, we do, and will continue to do so. But, I would much rather kill the other guy by mistake than risk being killed by him on purpose."

Although Senator Crabtree's hearing was classified and attendance restricted to those with the necessary clearance and need-to-know, the last part of James Detwiler's testimony leaked to the media almost immediately. Back at his headquarters, he took a call from Admiral Bergen.

"Congratulations, Jim! It didn't take long for you to make them forget me. The requests for interview that I've been getting since I got to the White House, and to which I've not been responding, have ceased as of this afternoon, at least for a while. And, I owe it all to you!"

"Thank you, Phil. It's an honor to serve."

"By the way, Jim, I need to borrow Hannah from you for three or four days."

Mir Batani Khan, now in the northern Afghan city of Konduz, watched his men put a final polish on the eight identical sports utility vehicles parked in the courtyard of the house at the edge of town on the road north to the Tajik border. The vehicles, brand new, had just been delivered via Tajikistan after a two month wait and a large bribe. All were shiny black, unlike virtually all other SUVs and pickup trucks in Afghanistan which seemed to be either white or another very light color. Batani had chosen black to give the intended recipients of his largesse a feeling of uniqueness and superiority as they motored about the countryside managing the personnel and business of their insurgent organizations. He was also pandering to their belief that the dark color offered some concealment at night from the CIA drones that were assumed to be perpetually lurking overhead preparing to launch missiles. The SUV's were luxuriously outfitted with all available options, leather seating, and bulletproof glass. Concealed among the many gadgets and wires beneath the hood of each was also a sophisticated transponder that, upon interrogation by an aircraft, satellite or line-of-sight ground station would uniquely distinguish the vehicle from its mates and facilitate the lock-on of a tracking or homing signal.

Batani's guests, arriving after dark, had been alerted to bring an extra driver. In truth, almost half of them would not have come, had word about the vehicles not gotten around. The district's warlords were fiercely independent, particularly where outsiders were concerned, as the Soviet invaders had learned many years earlier. Nor were they especially poor, although the area showed no signs of significant prosperity. The opium poppies grown on local farms could have made them wealthy, had their business ventures been managed as assiduously as their conflicts, but the traffickers who bought the crops were also outsiders, not to be associated with any more than absolutely necessary. The opium trade was the source of much religious angst, and had been banned by the ruling Taliban in earlier times.

However, the locals regarded Batani with as much curiosity as suspicion. Although not one of them, he was not exactly an outsider, and they shared his professed goal of getting the Americans and their allies out of Afghanistan. While his shorter hair and stylishly trimmed beard symbolized the foreign influences that scared them, the more thoughtful among the leadership in Konduz Province had begun to realize that it was stupid and pointless to go on fighting for nothing. Thus, they found themselves this night gathered to listen to what Batani had to say and, incidentally, to take home a shiny new SUV.

"My brothers," Batani began after refreshments had been served, "I am not here to harangue you about your duties to Islam or to urge you to engage in jihad against the infidels. My guess is that you have had your fill of both. I am here to appeal to your wiser instincts that must tell you it is time to think of your families and others who depend on your leadership and intelligence. In their sometimes laudable efforts to help our country, the Americans have discovered in Afghanistan deposits of minerals and other natural resources that could make us all rich beyond our dreams, provide work and opportunity for our men and dowries for our daughters. Even more glorious is that, to realize such benefits, we will not have to fight endlessly and sacrifice our lives, but rather do the opposite. To develop these riches as rapidly as possible, Afghanistan will need help and money from the outside, and there are many countries and private enterprises eager to invest in us, if they could be guaranteed cooperation and security. None of them will send engineers and expensive equipment to our country only to have the people killed and the machines blown up."

"We do not wish to have our country overrun by foreigners, particularly if they are infidels," a member of the audience countered. "The Americans have tried to help us, but their ways are not ours and they become rapidly frustrated, as do we."

Batani almost let his exasperation get the better of him.

"My brothers, this is the 21st Century and there is nothing you can do about it. Many times over hundreds of years, invaders have come to our country to take our resources and exploit our people. All of you remember the Soviets coming with their tanks and helicopters. Why do the foreigners come, time after time? They come because our country is rich with treasure, which we its people leave untouched so that others cannot resist the temptation to come for it. That treasure is now growing even larger, and still we sit and do nothing except fight amongst ourselves."

"What do you say we must do, Mir Batani Khan?" a number of his listeners responded virtually simultaneously.

"What we must do is very simple, my brothers," Batani replied. "We must make Afghanistan a place where the foreigners will be happy to come to invest their money because our country is safe and its people are cooperative. At the same time, we must cleanse this country of the corruption and incompetence that deprives our people of their rightful heritage and the fruits of their labor and risk. If we undertake to do this, as an added benefit, the Americans will gladly go home. Unlike those who've come in the past, they do not want to be in Afghanistan.

"There is a large copper deposit in Logar Province that has been leased to the Chinese. Their contract requires them to build a railroad to move the mined ore out of the country. The tracks will come through Konduz and extend into Tajikistan where they will connect with the Russian railroad network. If it is completed, the railroad will connect Konduz with Europe and, in the South, with India and China. Do you realize what that would mean for your province and city?"

Batani looked into their eyes and saw little enthusiasm. It would take a lot of effort, more bribes, and perhaps a couple of extraordinary measures, but he felt confident of success.

"At the moment, construction work on the mine and railroad is being protected by the American military from attacks by our brothers. But, when the American public learns that its soldiers are risking their lives to protect a Chinese enterprise, there will be a loud outcry. We shall help the Americans by not attacking the construction sites and preventing our brothers from doing so. Eventually, we shall do the same throughout Afghanistan, and the American government will be happy to conclude that its mission has been accomplished and that it is safe to go home."

Batani and his guests wrangled for the remainder of the night, the latter leaving primarily because dawn was arriving and they did not wish to be caught out on the road where they could be seen. As they drove off in their new vehicles, two men who had been at the meeting but had not participated, remained behind, seemingly without means of transport. Their host had never seen them before, and grew apprehensive when they approached.

"A very difficult meeting was it not, Sheik Batani? But, I think in the end successful for you," the elder of the two offered. The other one nodded in agreement and shook Batani's hand. All of this was very disconcerting. The men were certainly not local and might not even be Afghans, yet no one at the meeting had said or done anything to bring attention to them.

"I'm afraid I do not know you, gentlemen. What is it you wish of me?"

"We've come to tell you that a very important personage wishes to speak with you, and that it would be greatly to your benefit to attend him."

Batani considered reaching for the pistol concealed within his robe, but decided that the man he did not shoot first would kill him. Besides, the men had not threatened him nor were they brandishing weapons. Having sent his considerable bodyguard away in order to avoid appearing to intimidate his guests, the Taliban chieftain had only his driver to assist him.

"Where is this person who wishes to speak with me?"

Batani found it comforting that his new companions appeared to have no transportation of their own, as they embarked in his vehicle. Their destination turned out to be the airstrip at the edge of town that the Americans quartered in the city jokingly called Konduz International Airport. It had a single, unpaved runway built by the Russians in 1982 and no facilities or amenities other than a rusting, sheet metal hangar well-perforated by bullet holes. But the runway was long enough to accommodate small jet aircraft, its hard packed earth surface meticulously maintained by a crew of local farmers well-paid by the narcotics traffickers who used the strip to evacuate the semi-processed produce of the local poppy fields.

Approaching the derelict hangar, the doors of which were closed, Batani was surprised to see American troops in full battle dress posted outside and in the surrounding scrub. There was no light inside as the three men entered the hangar through a side door. By the darts of morning sunlight coming through the many bullet holes in the walls and roof, Batani could see a small passenger aircraft parked in the center of the hangar, a staircase descending from its open cabin door. His escort propelled him toward the door, then dropped back as he climbed to the cabin. In the well-appointed interior he found a middle-aged man and a very attractive young woman.

"Do you know who I am?" the man asked quietly, pointing Batani to a seat across the narrow cabin. The young woman seated herself further aft, at the periphery of Batani's field of vision.

"I didn't at first, since you are not in uniform, Admiral Bergen."

Bergen smiled wryly. "I'm finding that to be true lately also in Washington."

"And, I'm sure that, had I seen this young lady before, I would remember. I am extraordinarily impressed that you have come all this way to see me. It is said that you have a new position, Admiral Bergen, one that places you very close to your President Kitteridge. Congratulations."

"Thank you, sir. But, as I'm sure you know, new positions generally bring additional responsibility and more difficult problems. At the moment, it would appear that you and I share some of the same problems, and Ms Crossman and I have come to see whether we might help one another with their solutions."

"I am mystified, sir, but intrigued as to what these problems might be."

"To put it directly, our sources are telling us that you are having difficulty consolidating your leadership of the Taliban in this country. Many of the important tribal leaders and a number of the smaller dissident groups apparently do not like you, do not agree with your plans and strategy or all of the foregoing. The events of your meeting tonight indicate the situation still requires improvement."

Batani shrugged. "With your knowledge of our circumstances here in Afghanistan, you know how many tribes and factions there are contending with one another, as well as with you Americans and your allies. In addition, the Pakistanis persist in meddling. Obtaining a true consensus is impossible, so one is reduced to constant maneuvering for position and advantage."

Bergen laughed. "I understand your difficulties, particularly since they are, in this instance, the same as ours. The United States does not wish to remain in Afghanistan as a military force any longer than absolutely necessary. However, we also do not wish to see your country taken over by an extremist regime of religious fanatics after we leave. If that can be precluded, we would be happy to declare victory and go home as soon as possible."

"We are in agreement there," Batani acknowledged, sensing the possibility of more money to go with that already received from Mahmud al-Fasal and Kingsley Yong. "Tell me how you believe we might help each other."

Admiral Bergen smiled.

"First, as a token of our good will, let me inform you that Ms. Crossman here was present at the meeting you held with General Orkamzi and Mr. al-Fasal in Pakistan several months ago. We are aware of your new strategy and its objective, but will not hold it against you as long as our relationship is of mutual benefit. We have been told that you have become adept at deploying our homing signal transponders. You should recognize that we also know how to do that."

It occurred immediately to Batani that the Americans also knew that al-Fasal had given him that suitcase of money. Had both Orkamzi and al-Fasal been aware that a CIA agent was in the room? If only one of them knew, it was probably the Pakistani gaming he and al-Fasal---for what reason Batani didn't know. In his perplexity, one thing seemed clear to the Taliban leader: the Americans had their act together and were very serious about whatever it was they were aiming at. Why else would they send Bergen all the way to Afghanistan to impress him? Batani put aside for the moment his thought about asking for more money.

"We have observed" Bergen continued, "that the course of events in the Muslim world is greatly influenced by the loudly expressed opinions of individuals, particularly those who claim authority and justification in the name of God, and use the mosque as their channel for exhorting the faithful even to deeds the Koran strongly condemns. As you well know, Mr. Batani Khan, the war in which all of us are engaged does not involve large armies or navies, but rather individuals who, alone or in small groups, commit acts that prevent the establishment of peace and prosperity in countries like Afghanistan. Too often, such people respond to what they believe are God's commands, as conveyed to them by their extremist imams and religious scholars. If something can be done to reduce or prevent such occurrences, both Taliban and American interests would be advanced significantly."

"You wish my brothers and I to work with you on this?" a mildly surprised Batani responded.

"You would not find us ungrateful or unhelpful," Bergen replied. "The funds you received from Mahmud al-Fasal and the enterprising Mr. Yong will not last forever." As they stood up, he handed Batani a wrapped box.

"What is this?"

"It is a special satellite telephone that will connect you with us securely from any place and at any time. Please do not try to use it for personal calls, unless you know someone in the CIA Operations Center. You will also find in the box a token of our appreciation for the time you've taken out of your busy schedule to come meet with us today."

The Admiral and Hannah watched as Batani was escorted from the hangar into the sunshine outside. They saw the light through the cabin windows suddenly brighten as the hangar doors were opened, and heard the plane's jet engines whine into operation as it prepared to begin the long flight home.

"I must have rung your apartment a dozen times without a response. If you're not going to be home, Hannah, the least you could do is tell your answering machine. Then I called the number you gave me when we were negotiating Admiral Bergen's appearance on the show, but the people there acted as though I was committing a crime by even suggesting that you exist, much less be reachable at that number. So I pined away, worrying whether you were in danger in some far-off place where the people seem to do nothing but shout and wave their arms."

When he released a well-constructed sob, Hannah laughed.

"I wish you wouldn't whine so much, Paul. I warned you that I would be disappearing suddenly, sometimes for long periods of time. I would take you along, but you don't have the need-to-know where spooks go when they disappear. You should be content to stay at home to welcome me with a stiff drink and a pizza when I return."

"Thinking of the risks you were facing wherever it was you were made me shudder," he replied, his voice quavering convincingly.

"I didn't even get off the plane."

"Yeah, right!"

Hannah liked the attitude toward her job that Paul had adopted, knowing in particular that, despite the humor and playacting, he really did worry about her. Not being able to discuss her work and day-to-day experiences, he insisted, was a great boon because it left much more time for him to tell her about all the great things he was doing. Paul Rayner, in his early forties, was an accomplished international journalist of significant renown, having reported from virtually all of the major areas of conflict in Asia and Africa, often at the risk of his life. He had been riding in an Army truck outside of Baghdad during the American invasion when it hit an improvised explosive device buried in the roadway. The resulting injury and emergency evacuation, covered in detail on national television, had made Rayner a celebrity but put him out of action for more than a year. The network for which he worked astutely offered him the position of executive producer on the staff of *American Focus*, its long-running news magazine. His principal duties were to participate in the selection of the subjects and people the program would cover, then to use his reputation and celebrity to secure the latter's appearance, as he had done with Philip Bergen. But the provisions of his contract also enabled him to select occasional topics and subjects that he would cover himself, something he had not yet done, but told Hannah he was working up to, now that knowing her had renewed his interest in life and career.

Hannah, in turn, had begun to worry about the possibility, however remote, of Paul choosing to investigate a situation in which she was operationally involved, and even dreamt one night that she saw him (through the slit in her veil) consorting with another woman in a Casablanca nightclub where she was lurking undercover. A more realistic concern was the possibility that the Admiral, Jim Detwiler or Sam Glover would see a prospective conflict of interest in their relationship, and force her to choose between her life and the CIA.

CHAPTER EIGHT

Another thing that bothered Philip Bergen about having his office in the White House was that the President knew it. It turned out that the excellent corner room reserved for the National Security Advisor in the warren of senior staff offices was located in the far corner, away from the door to the central anteroom that led to the Oval Office. To the Admiral's dismay, President Kitteridge had taken to walking unexpectedly into the staff offices, waving a document and looking for his Intelligence advisor and tutor. In navigating the maze of aisles and reception areas to reach Bergen's corner, he came across many very surprised and shocked people (a junior staffer discovered asleep at his desk quickly disappeared). After a week of this, Dee Stone (Kitteridge's Chief-of-Staff) had a loud buzzer installed in the staff spaces that could be activated by the receptionist-security officer always present at the entrance to the Oval Office.

When the President stalked out of his office looking preoccupied and determined, the receptionist was directed to sound the alert. There were, of course, false alarms, but the result was a lot better than being suddenly confronted by the President of the United States while your mouth was full of pizza.

"Do you believe the trouble we're taking with Batani will pay off?" Kitteridge asked, after the Admiral briefed him on the results of his and Hannah's flying visit to Afghanistan. James Detwiler and Sam Glover were also present, Bergen being particularly concerned that no gap of trust and confidence be created between himself and his successor as DNI and the new Director of CIA. Although the President might choose to ignore it, the Admiral was no longer his principal Intelligence officer, nor had he any operational authority in the Intelligence Community.

"That's hard to predict, Mr. President. Batani's a shrewd and tough guy, but he's facing opposition just as shrewd and tough, which is, of course, where we might come in."

"In what way?"

"If we are ever to finish up in Afghanistan and Pakistan with useful and lasting accomplishments, the people in those countries whom we support must win. I don't think we can ignore the likelihood that winning may mean eliminating key individuals who stand in our way. Some of them are insurgents with military leadership qualities and experience. But others are radical Islamist zealots whose constant railing against us and our allies is the principal underpinning of our opposition."

"I don't mean to be disingenuous, Admiral, but what does 'eliminate' mean here?" the President asked.

"Whatever might prove necessary, sir. I don't believe we should shrink from killing those who, directly or indirectly, contribute to killing Americans. The extremist cleric who convinces some poor boob to blow himself up in a crowded subway car is just as guilty as the actual perpetrator, actually much more so because his malign influence is significantly broader."

"The men to whom Admiral Bergen is referring illustrates how the threat has expanded with the growth of the Internet," James Detwiler added. If the influence of these poisonous preachers was confined to the people listening to them preach in a mosque somewhere, we would be talking about an audience in the hundreds, perhaps. But, when they videotape their sermons and make them available to millions worldwide on websites, there is no telling where their message will take root. Some of these people are very compelling speakers."

The President moved to conclude the meeting.

"I wanted to make sure we all understood what we're about here. There are leaders in other countries who have the same specific objectives we do, although for different and often diametrically opposed reasons. The program that Admiral Bergen will coordinate should be dedicated to benefiting from such unusual confluences of interests, reflecting the old saying that the enemy of mine enemy is my friend. However, we must be very careful that in winning our war we don't piss off every Muslim in the world."

James Detwiler and Hannah Crossman met with General Estefimov, at the latter's election, in the cafeteria of the National Air and Space Museum. At an earlier meeting there with Admiral Bergen, the senior Russian security and intelligence officer had become enamored of the cheeseburger he had purchased, and seized the opportunity to try one again.

"General Estefimov," Detwiler began, "seven months ago you came to us with a proposal for Russian use of our unmanned aircraft in a campaign against Muslim extremists in your Caucasus region."

"Yes, and Admiral Bergen told your Congressional overseers about it, causing it to be immediately leaked to the press. It was a great embarrassment to my country, and to me personally."

"...for which I now express regret," Detwiler responded. "But how would your superiors react to word that conditions had changed, and we would now be willing to consider adopting your proposal and more?"

"The Chechens and Ingush have not gone away, so presumably Moscow would still be interested, at least enough to listen to your proposal."

"We are about to bring on line a new series of pilotless aircraft, with capabilities far superior to those currently deployed," the DNI revealed. "Details are classified, but I'm sure your intelligence services will soon ferret them out. Arrival of the aircraft will increase our operational capability well beyond immediate need, which would permit us to devote resources to your assistance. We are actually prepared to go beyond your original request, and to sell Russia a number of aircraft with necessary ancillary equipment, as well as to provide training and support to bring your people to full operational readiness as soon as possible. As you know, the aircraft models currently in use are far from obsolete."

Estefimov was astounded, but immediately began thinking how he could claim credit for this remarkable turn of events.

"Aside from money, what will your government require of mine in return?" he asked.

"We would like to have a base facility in Russia from which to originate operations of our own over countries in the Near East and Southwest Asia other than the former Soviet republics. With the new aircraft, we shall be able to greatly expand the range and scope of our activity."

The General's eyes took on a speculative gleam, as he contemplated the potential implications of what he had just been told. "I'm not authorized to decide this matter," he responded, "but it seems to me that what you wish can be arranged. What else?"

The new Director of National Intelligence hesitated, wondering how best to present his next requirement, before deciding there was no good way.

"We would like Moscow's understanding when we blame Russia for drone attacks that, in reality, we will have conducted. You will, of course, deny responsibility and blame the United States, but the resulting uncertainty would be useful in obfuscating public scrutiny of the charges."

Estefimov stared at Detwiler for what seemed like forever, then burst out laughing. "America has certainly changed! My guess is that, within limits, we would agree to that, providing you would permit us a reciprocal privilege, which is likely to be equally believable to the New York Times."

Hannah, who had not been briefed on Detwiler's proposal, was shocked, particularly when the new DNI concluded the meeting by telling Estefimov that she would be the U.S. point-of-contact for the Russians in the matter.

Kingsley Yong, riding his American passport, arrived tired in San Francisco on a non-stop flight from Beijing. After spending the past month visiting obscure places and people around the world on behalf of his employers, he was planning to spend a long weekend visiting his parents in that city's suburbs. As he cleared Customs, declaring the gifts purchased in China, he was stopped by a beefy, middle-aged man in a suit he had obviously not worn for a while.

"Mr. Yong, I am Reginald Huggins of Global Security Applications. I would like to speak with you for a moment." He handed Yong a business card.

"I'm sorry Mr. Huggins, but I don't have time. My brother is waiting for me in the Baggage Claim right now."

"I understand, sir. Let me just tell you that I represent a number of influential people in Washington who are interested in speaking with you on a matter that you are likely to find interesting and profitable. I will be in San Francisco until next Tuesday. My cell phone number is on the card." Huggins nodded and quickly walked away.

Kingsley Yong, tired and in a hurry, would have ignored the interruption and thrown the business card away, except that he wondered how Huggins had known he would be on that particular flight from China and, more importantly, how Huggins had gotten beyond the security barriers into the Customs hall. While waiting for his bags to arrive on the carousel, Yong dialed the local Chinese consulate to ask about Huggins and his company, a query that was relayed to the Washington embassy as a matter of priority. By Monday morning, he had his answer: Huggins was a retired, long-time CIA officer, and his firm was staffed largely by former Agency employees. Whether it was currently an Agency proprietary was unknown, but cautious treatment was directed. Yong was told to contact Huggins to find out what he wanted.

They met on Monday morning at a restaurant near Huggins' hotel. Yong immediately demanded an explanation.

"How come you people know so much about me? Why is the CIA so interested in what I do? I'm a business representative, not a spy!" Actually, contact by the CIA was not exactly the great surprise Yong implied. He had been visited by an Agency representative shortly after going to work for the Chinese and asked whether he would be sympathetic to his homeland's intelligence requirements. Yong had declined, not knowing then what his obligations to either his employer or the CIA would be. He had not, however, reported the CIA contact to the Chinese Government. As far as he knew, he had since done nothing illegal in performing his duties.

Huggins held up his hands defensively.

"First, Mr. Yong, let me set the record straight. I'm not here representing the CIA, nor am I planning to ask you spy or do things against either China or the United States. On the contrary, the people I represent are seeking to enlist your aid in a program intended to help both countries."

That silenced Kingsley Yong, who now felt obliged to listen.

"As a matter of security, I cannot tell you at the moment who my clients are, but you would learn fairly quickly, should you agree to work with us. Suffice it to say, they are prominent and influential American citizens very much concerned about the growth of the extremist threat in the Muslim world and the failure of our current government administration to deal with it effectively. They perceive that China, although at odds with the United States over a broad range of issues, shares its concern with regard to Muslim extremism, albeit perhaps for different specific reasons. Defensively, for example, Beijing is extremely sensitive to separatist activities along its northern and western border by Muslim Uighurs. Offensively, China has undertaken a very large and expensive copper mining development in southern Afghanistan that it would, I'm sure, like to protect from Taliban attack."

The latter example, of course, pricked Kingsley Yong's interest, and he decided to pursue the conversation further than originally intended. He had assumed, going in, that Huggins and his people were a lunatic fringe group to be ignored. He had not yet changed his mind, but decided that his Chinese employers deserved a more fulsome after action report.

"Do you foresee this convergence of interest developing into joint undertakings? If so, how?" he asked Huggins.

"That's not yet been determined. My immediate assignment is to determine whether or not you are interested in serving as my clients' intermediary with your employers in China."

Yong's mind was immediately filled with thoughts about the prospects opened by Huggins' proposition, but also of the potential dangers, including that of unknowingly straying over the line into illegal activity: espionage on behalf of a foreign power. That scared him, and he replied to Huggins without enthusiasm: " I will pass what you've told me on to my employers."

On Monday, Kingsley Yong flew to Washington, thinking about his meeting with Huggins throughout the long flight. The following morning, he rooted out the business card left with him by the man who had approached him years earlier on behalf of the CIA. Not surprisingly, his call was transferred from office to office and person to person, with the last one telling Yong that he would be called back. After 5 PM, the telephone rang and a female voice inquired whether he was indeed Kingsley Yong.

"Fortunately, Mr. Yong, you have a very distinctive name that our computers recognized. My name is Hannah Crossman. What can I do for you?"

"We've had our first contact from Batani!" Sam Glover reported to the Admiral and James Detwiler. "He called the Ops Center on the special phone we gave him, and the call was patched through to me. Batani wants us to do a Predator strike on a building in Konduz City that he says is being used as a storage facility by the biggest narcotics trafficker in Afghanistan. The man uses his enormous revenue to pay bribes to Batani's competitors and to equip his own self-protection force. At the moment, he is near the end of a poppy harvest and processing cycle and the target building is full of semi-processed opium base that is about to be shipped north into Tajikistan. A drone strike now would deprive the trafficker of a large amount of money and keep a lot of heroin off the world market."

"How many people in the building?" Bergen asked.

"Usually very few, I was told, but it may be possible to time the strike for when the big boss himself is in the building."

"What do you all think?" Detwiler asked.

"Sounds like maybe win-win," Bergen replied. "But, it's yours and Sam's call. I'm just an advisor these days."

Batani confirmed that he had a supply of transponders on hand, and was instructed to place one on the roof of the target building where it could be interrogated by the launch aircraft and used to home its missiles. He was also asked to supply the times at which the narcotics kingpin was to be found in the building. Within a week, this had been done and mission planning completed. Drone strikes were not usually conducted in the Konduz area, but it was well within the operational radius of the aircraft based in Pakistan and their control facilities. The optimum strike time, as supplied by Batani, turned out to be after dark, so an Air Force low altitude photoreconnaissance mission was scheduled for the next morning to assess damage caused by the strike. The target building was a single-story warehouse of considerable dimensions, so two aircraft were assigned, each to launch two Hellfire missiles.

Admiral Bergen briefed President Kitteridge and secured his permission for the proposed strike, which went off without apparent hitch, video cameras aboard the attacking drones showing huge balls of flame billowing from the target. It was still burning the next morning, when photographs showed almost the entire building collapsed. The first hint that something had gone wrong was that Batani proved unreachable, and was actually not heard from for more than two weeks following the attack. Thus, it was primarily from the screams of anguish and recrimination immediately surfacing in the world media that it was learned the warehouse that night had been the site of a celebratory dinner and entertainment hosted by the drug lord. Attendance was mandatory, if one wished to live without threat of assassination, and everyone who was anyone in the Konduz district was there. More than 150 people had been killed, including the Uzbek musicians and dancers brought in for the occasion.

CHAPTER NINE

Fallout from the Konduz raid reached James Detwiler and Sam Glover in the form of official expressions of Congressional dismay, in particular from Mary Kingsley, chair of the House Permanent Select Committee on Intelligence. She had been Admiral Bergen's nemesis on the use of drones, and the latest incident had reinforced her view that this was not a form of warfare in which Americans should engage. There had, indeed, been large quantities of drug ingredients destroyed in the attack, which significantly ameliorated public criticism. However, the trafficking kingpin had not even been in the country and the dead comprised virtually all of the leading governmental and religious figures of the Konduz District, including, as it turned out, the leaders of three insurgent factions contesting the dominance of Mir Batani Khan.

"Another one like that and we'll never get anything through Congress" Admiral Bergen observed somberly. "But the problem is that we need Batani, duplicitous bastard though he may be. Someone needs to keep the Taliban in Afghanistan under control, and there's no substitute for Batani in sight.

"Perhaps, we should send Hannah to lean on him," Sam Glover threw in, only half joking.

James Detwiler smiled grimly. "I think there may be a better option. Hannah called last night to tell me that our reluctant friend Kingsley Yong called the Ops Center and was referred to her because the computer linked his name with the Admiral's on the watch list. He told her that Sam's friend Reggie Huggins came to see him with the same kind of pitch he gave to Mahmud al-Fasal. It occurs to me that we might connect with the Chinese through Yong and get them to square Batani away. They need him even more than we do to help protect their construction projects in Afghanistan."

"Let me talk with the President to double-check that he'd be okay with that," the Admiral reacted. "And you, Sam, need to have another chat with your boy Huggins. Apparently Hannah wasn't convincing enough."

A week later, Yong called Hannah to convey an invitation for a discreet, informal visit to Beijing by a senior American intelligence official---ASAP. The President quickly decided that Admiral Bergen would go.

"This is the main reason why I asked the Admiral to change jobs," he told Detwiler and Glover. "National Security Advisor is not an intelligence position, so it provides a certain amount of cover for the interaction we need to do with foreign powers like China. We will not publicize Admiral Bergen's trip or anything that might result from it, but some or all of it is likely to leak. No one may believe our explanation, but I would like our activities to be as ambiguous as possible. Please thank Mr. Yong for his assistance, and tell him to keep his mouth shut."

Arrangements having been made, Admiral Bergen departed for Beijing in an Air Force extended-range passenger jet, larger and more comfortable than the Agency's aircraft. Hannah Crossman went with him as DNI Detwiler's liaison to provide continuity on follow-on Intelligence Community actions and responsibilities that might be agreed upon by the Admiral and his hosts during their meetings. "Also," Bergen noted with a smile, "she usually gets more attention and better service than I do."

The Admiral had last been in China on Navy assignment during the post-Vietnam years when that country was opening to the West. Despite all of the photographs he had seen and TV coverage of the Beijing Olympics, Bergen was amazed by the size and modernity of the city, as their plane circled overhead prior to landing. They were met at the airport by the CIA Station Chief driving his personal car, their visit being treated as private to avoid reflection in even the mundane protocol records of the American Embassy. The Ambassador, who was apprised of the visit, would meet with the Admiral privately before his departure for home.

Their host turned out to be Jian Gai-min, a very senior governmental and Communist Party official, who greeted his visitors cordially.

"Welcome to China. We are very pleased that you have come. Your reputation has preceded you, Admiral Bergen, and I am looking forward to our discussions."

The Admiral was both flattered and surprised that he and Hannah were being greeted by so lofty an official. Their surprise was even greater when one of his aides beckoned to Hannah and their embassy-provided interpreter and led them out of the room. Bergen was prepared to protest, but couldn't quickly think of grounds on which to do so.

"Do not be concerned about your colleague, Admiral Bergen. I wish to discuss with you matters of extraordinary importance and sensitivity, and prefer to have as few people as possible present. As you can see, my English is sufficient to enable us to dispense with an interpreter. You should be aware that our ambassador in Washington has talked with your President Kitteridge and was told that you enjoy his fullest confidence."

Bergen was not sure he could accommodate any further surprises.

"Mr. Kingsley Yong has reported to us," Jian began, when they were comfortably seated in his private office, "an encounter with a man named Huggins, who wished him to approach us on behalf of unidentified, prominent Americans apparently seeking to sponsor covert operations against troublesome Islamic extremists. You should be aware that Mr. Yong is employed by the Chinese government as a business development representative, not an intelligence agent (Bergen was not always sure of the difference), and we advised him to notify your CIA of this occurrence, which I assume he did. That matter is now yours to handle as you see fit.

"However," he continued, rising from his chair, "the broader matter of possible cooperation between the United States and China in combating the expanding threat of Islamic extremism is of great interest to us. We recognize that there are many specific matters and issues on which our two countries disagree and will actually oppose each other, but surely we recognize that continued spread of extremist ideology in the Muslim world and among its growing minorities in the West will bring great harm to the entire world by disrupting international political, economic, and social progress."

Jian paused to gauge the Admiral's reaction, and Bergen pretended to consider what he had been told before responding: "I have been authorized by President Kitteridge to discuss this possibility."

Referring to a large map of Asia that almost covered one wall of his office, Jian quickly sketched the background, of which he was certain Bergen was already aware.

"With respect to our relations with Muslim countries, China is in the position of being simultaneously on the defensive and offensive. As you can see, we are bordered on the west and south by countries with large Muslim populations that are themselves disrupted by internal dissension caused by religious differences. We see significant danger in the prospect of an Islamist regime taking power in Pakistan and attempting to extend its sway into Afghanistan. There are also Muslim factions within our border, notably the Uighurs, likely to be encouraged by more aggressive support and encouragement from a radicalized Pakistan, as are those in Kashmir and elsewhere in India.

And, to the south, are the large Muslim populations of Southeast Asia. While they are not a current difficulty for us, we fear the effects of a campaign by radicals to enlist all of the world's Muslims in a crusade against the infidel who, of course, is you and me."

Jian paused and smiled.

"My colleagues accuse me of being overly Americanized and, indeed, I spent a great many years living in the United States. But, what they are really talking about is that I don't share with them the ingrained Chinese fear of national disintegration. When you Americans have serious problems ---racial conflict, economic dislocation, political polarization, whatever---no one is seriously concerned that the country might fall apart, not since your Civil War anyway. China, an ancient civilization extending centuries beyond yours, has been constantly beset by the failure of dynasties, empires, and modern governments to maintain the country's cohesion in the face of internal and external enemies. The dominant lesson we Communists brought with us when we gained power in 1949 was that the central government must be extremely strong and never seriously challenged. The sheer size of the country and its enormous, highly diverse population are sources of both great strength and great difficulty. They have enabled us to make remarkable strides toward modernization in the past thirty-five years, but also constitute a tinder box waiting for a match. You have seen in the Middle East and North Africa what happens when the masses decide they've stood as much as they are willing to bear from their rulers. Were something like that to occur in China, it would be orders of magnitude larger and could eventually engulf the entire country.

"I don't believe Chinese are more prone to mass protest and riot than other peoples, but once they begin, the size and scope of such disruptions expand virally, particularly with the availability of modern communications like the Internet and mobile telephones. The world criticizes us for brutally suppressing small demonstrations in minor provincial cities, and we---to be perfectly honest---have been guilty of overreacting. We are trying harder now to fit the extent of our reaction to the actual threat, but are having difficulty managing the security forces in the outlying provinces, which is where many of the problems arise. Although the complaints that motivate the protests are generally local, their trigger is often a protest occurring elsewhere in China or in a foreign country, often over some different alleged injustice. This is one of the main reasons we are so sensitive to foreign social and political influences, given that it is impossible these days to keep out information from abroad. It is also the reason why we are interested in cooperating with you to combat the influence of those individuals who preach revolution and destruction in the name of God, wherever they might be."

"You spoke also of China being on the offensive" Bergen reminded.

"The offense and defense are obviously interrelated," Jian responded.

"We have succeeded in maintaining peace and order in China largely because of the great improvements achieved in the economic well-being and prospects of our people. But, we are riding a tiger, and cannot stop or get off lest we be eaten. Not only are there millions of people who have not yet benefited significantly from our prosperity, but those who have demand not only that it be maintained, but that it continue to grow. Thus, we must continue to feed the tiger more and more.

"Unfortunately," Jian sighed, "China lacks natural resources commensurate to her population and ambition. We must continue to secure external sources of practically everything in ever-larger quantities, and do it in competition with the rest of the world. It turns out, as you know, that the most promising sources of what we need are often to be found in underdeveloped, politically volatile countries where such competition is exacerbated by corruption and inefficiency. China has had to commit to far larger projects and greater investment than other countries and companies would find prudent in order to satisfy greedy national leaders and trump the competition. Because of both our need and the risks being taken, we will go to great lengths to secure what we require and to safeguard it. In doing so, we sometimes act contrary to what the United States perceives as its national interests and moral scruples. But, there are indeed situations in which our countries' interests and objectives coincide, and I would propose to you and your President that we cooperate on those to the extent we can."

"Can you give me an example?" Admiral Bergen asked, guessing with near certainty what Jian's response would be.

"My government has acquired a large copper mining concession in Afghanistan, south of Kabul. In addition to paying a huge amount of money, we are obligated to build a railroad from the Uzbek border on the north to the Pakistani border on the south to facilitate removal of the mined ore for processing and export. Naturally, the security of these projects is of vital concern to us, and we will go to great lengths to assure it. Although our reasons may be different, I believe we have a commonality of interest in pacifying Afghanistan by defeating extremist elements that disrupt economic progress and support international terrorist activity. Will the United States support such initiatives?"

Bergen responded immediately. "President Kitteridge has authorized me to negotiate arrangements of this kind. We have in fact been thinking along the same lines you have." Jian smiled.

Hannah and her escorts reappeared and, while Jian Gai-min hosted everyone at lunch, had a private moment in which to fill the Admiral in on the briefings she had received.

"They were very forthright, assuming (I think) that we already know about most of their projects in Afghanistan. In addition to the Aynak copper mine, there is a huge iron ore deposit in the Hindu Kush, among other concessions, that Beijing is trying to capture. It was obvious they believe or have been told that we will work with them on operational matters, at least in Afghanistan and Pakistan, because they provided me with information that I'm sure we would consider classified."

After lunch, Jian and Bergen---with Hannah present this time---reconvened to talk about Mir Batani Khan.

"His tactics have been brilliant," the Admiral acknowledged, "which means he cannot be trusted one iota. He's come a long way in consolidating his power among the insurgent tribes and factions by killing off his rivals, frequently by getting us to do it for him. I can't call him unscrupulous or dishonest because we've not yet tested him on fulfilling commitments. But, we clearly need to be on guard against double dealing."

"We've given him several million dollars in return for protection of our copper and railroad projects and the people working on them," Jian revealed.

"We also rewarded him for exactly the same thing," Hannah added, "and I know that he's also collected from others. Some of the money, I'm sure, is going to necessary bribes and operating expenses, but a lot is being reserved to fuel his broader ambitions. Our Mr. Batani is a very shrewd and capable man."

"However, we are agreed, are we not, that for the foreseeable future he is indispensable?" Jian asked. Bergen nodded and added: "Which means that, in addition to accommodating him, we also need to protect him, a task likely to prove a lot more difficult than just feeding him money."

Mahmud al-Fasal, on another round of visits to Abdul Rashid's franchisees, was in Islamabad commiserating with General Pervez Orkamzi.

"I can't tell whether our situation has gotten better or worse," the ISI chief told his visitor, who nodded consolingly. "The Taliban and other dissident groups continue to mount attacks here in Pakistan aimed primarily at the government and the army, but killing a lot of innocent people in the streets and marketplaces. This campaign, which is not centrally organized or directed, was begun as an effort to force us to stop supporting CIA drone operations, which have succeeded in killing many of their leaders and scaring hell out of the rest. But, even more extreme elements have taken to attacking Christians and other Muslim sects, and now plain criminals have joined in. The government is weak and disunited, and the army is caught between defending itself here at home and pursuing our interests abroad. And everyone blames the intelligence services for not being able to read peoples' minds in time to prevent the attacks."

Orkamzi fell silent, seemingly overwhelmed by the weight of his troubles. Al-Fasal noticed for the first time that the General was fingering worry beads. He could not tell how much of Orkamzi's apparent distress reflected the seriousness of his situation, as opposed to a plea for more of Abdul Rashid's cash.

"Take heart, my friend. Although you may be having difficulties here in Pakistan, our affairs in Afghanistan appear to be progressing nicely. How have you been getting on with Batani since our meeting?"

"He has been making progress in reducing the rivalries among tribal and provincial leaders," Orkamzi reported, "mostly by having them killed off. The Americans have been very helpful in this regard, although not necessarily aware of it at the time. Fortuitously, this gives their President cover against political opponents' criticism that he is condoning assassinations, which the American moral code does not permit.

"On the negative side," Orkamzi continued, "Batani has received a large amount of money from a Chinese agent named Kingsley Yong and is, therefore, far less dependent upon our support and that of Abdul Rashid. We are told he received an additional sum from the Americans during a covert visit by Admiral Bergen to Konduz, and may also be receiving a stipend from the government in Kabul.

"As you know, most of this money is ostensibly being paid to Batani for the protection of the Chinese copper mining and railroad building projects, which he appears to be doing successfully . To be perfectly frank, I have a significant personal reason to protect and encourage him: several of my direct army and government superiors have financial interests in the success of the Chinese ventures, and would be greatly vexed by a perceived failure on my part to support them."

Al-Fasal nodded sympathetically. "My dear General Orkamzi, I fully understand. However, I can't help wondering, if everyone we know is concerned that the Chinese projects succeed, why we have to pay such enormous sums to have them protected."

"I've heard from the Agency again," Reggie Huggins told Roger Norton, "this time from Sam Glover himself. He and I go back together to the old Directorate of Operations days."

"What did he say?"

"He said that, if he catches me breaking the law, Guantanamo will be too good for me. I much prefer the good looking chick he sent the first time."

"What do you plan on doing?" Norton asked. "You're not going to be much good to Alfred Oberling, if Glover has got you scared shitless."

"Don't worry about me and my people. We learned in the same school Sam did, and know how to get the job done, particularly outside the United States. I came here today to report that I've reestablished most of my old network in Europe, and am ready to accept Mr. Oberling's assignments."

Norton duly reported Huggins' readiness to the former Vice President. "What is it you want him to do first?"

"The truth is, Roger, that I don't know yet. We need to do something dramatic to draw attention to the fact that the extremists continue to get stronger in the Muslim world and more successful in inciting the masses against both us and their own moderates. If something isn't done about it, we will end up with the kind of us against them face off we had with the Communists, except that it won't be a cold war this time. The saving grace with the Communists was that they were not ready to die for their cause, but the Islamists are, and not solely as a last resort. The scariest thing about countries like Iran getting nuclear weapons is that the fanatics who run them could come to believe that destroying themselves and a good chunk of the world would be a great achievement.

"So, Oberling concluded, "we must take action against those who would lead their followers over the cliff and, realistically speaking, the only reliable way to do that is to kill them. I don't know whether our President has realized this as yet or what, if anything, he'll do when he does. But, I don't want to bail him out, so that he can take credit for saving the Western world. That's why I'm not yet sure what I want Huggins and his people to do. Whatever it is, however, it must be timed to occur after *Oberling for America* has become publicly active and well known, so that the voters know clearly who's going to bat for them."

"In the meantime," Norton complained, "Huggins and company are costing us a fortune, and the Party controller's office has begun to ask questions. What shall I tell them?"

"Tell them to fuck off!" the candidate heatedly replied. "I'm having a hard enough time saving the world from murderous religious fanatics without also having to save it from accountants and bookkeepers."

CHAPTER TEN

Representative Mary Kingsley, Chair of the House Permanent Select Committee on Intelligence, was irate and focused again on what had become her number one bete noir: CIA's Predator drone program.

"I can't believe you are planning to provide aircraft and missiles to the Russians," she scolded James Detwiler. "It wasn't even a year ago that Admiral Bergen rejected a request from Moscow that was limited to providing operational assistance against their radical insurgents, not the technology itself. What has happened in the interim that I don't know about?"

Suppressing unkind thoughts of Bergen and the President, the DNI attempted to provide a convincing explanation:

"Two major aspects of this situation have changed, ma'am. First, we have brought more advanced airframes and sensors into use at an accelerated pace, encouraged by the great success the program is achieving. We also have a more capable successor to the Hellfire missile. The hardware we're proposing to sell to the Russians is far from our current best, and will not include the most capable electronics. Secondly, and more important, we are likely to have increasing need for Russian assistance and cooperation in Central Asia and the Middle East as extremist activity spreads and we withdraw our forces from the area. Coming generations of drone technology will permit us to target any spot on the continent without actually having base facilities or people within thousands of miles. But, we are not there yet, and there will always be a need for intelligence to help locate targets for the aircraft sensors to acquire. Russian territory extends across the entire top of Asia, and Moscow still has significant influence in the tier of former Soviet republics that border on countries in which we're interested."

Kingsley frowned. "Shouldn't we be afraid that the Russians could use the drone technology against us or our NATO allies?"

Detwiler smiled sheepishly. "Our success in employing drone aircraft has obscured their critical limitation: they are relatively slow and not all that maneuverable. We have been able to use them effectively largely because they have been operating over countries that lack a modern air defense system: radar and ground-to-air missiles. This is not true of either the United States or Russia, which could easily shoot the aircraft down, once they became aware of them."

"I expect the Taliban and other insurgent will learn of this, if they don't already know it."

"We've discovered anti-aircraft guns in weapons caches captured in the mountains of Pakistan and Afghanistan, and we know the insurgents have shoulder-fired missiles that can be very effective against helicopters and low flying aircraft," Detwiler acknowledged. "But radars, AA guns, and their ammunition supplies, being very heavy and bulky, limit cross-country maneuverability, which the insurgent bands must have. Without radar, insurgents on the ground cannot locate the drone aircraft, and first learn of their presence when a missile explodes among them."

"Do the Russians know of these limitations?" Kingsley asked.

"I expect they do. But the Chechens and Ingush are in much the same situation as the Taliban, with respect to air defense," Detwiler replied.

General Arkady Estefimov, for one, was not concerned about the combat limitations of the unmanned aircraft systems. As hoped, he had been given credit for changing the Americans' mind about the Russian request for drone assistance and for obtaining much more from Washington than had been originally considered possible. The ministry in Moscow had appointed Estefimov Project Manager, and given him considerable staff to facilitate and coordinate the transfer of American drone technology and the establishment of a covert American operating base in Russia. Having first visited Moscow to receive both praise and directions, Estefimov spent the next two months at an obscure former Soviet military airfield in southern Russia monitoring the arrival of massive, unmarked air transports carrying equipment and personnel via a circuitous route through Alaska and Siberia. Inasmuch as the drone support facilities were designed to be modular and readily transportable, they became operational quickly and training of Russian operating crews had begun almost immediately. The General had arrived earlier that day to be present at the launch of the first operational mission against Chechen insurgents.

At their new base nearby, the Americans had been flying their aircraft for more than a month, although Estefimov didn't know whether the flights were operational or practice missions. It had been agreed that Russia would not ask what her guests were doing as long as the aircraft flew over Russian territory only in a narrow corridor between their airfield and the border. Thus far, the relationship between Russians and Americans had been businesslike and cordial.

"Does CIA ever let its spooks go on vacation?" Paul Rayner asked, Hannah looking at him sharply to see whether or not he was serious.

"Of course. We're treated just like any other government employee. Why do you ask?"

"If I'm ever going to be able to decide how much I really care for you, I'm going to need more than a day here and there. Every time I get myself excited about our relationship, you disappear someplace or other like you did last week. If the bosses will permit it, I suggest we go away together for a week or so to some place that's not close to CIA Headquarters or the White House."

"Like what?"

"How about Paris? I haven't been there in years, and I hear it's still romantic."

Hannah found it disappointingly easy to get James Detwiler, Sam Glover, and Admiral Bergen to deprive themselves of her assistance for a week (they felt guilty of overworking her), and she and Paul were soon off for the French capital. They stayed at a small, Left Bank hotel recommended by the Embassy. Both of them had been to Paris often enough to not be interested in the usual tourist attractions, and they spent the days mostly walking, hand-in-hand, through the city, with frequent stops at sidewalk cafes. They went to dinner each evening at a different restaurant chosen from a list provided by the CIA Station Chief. Hannah avoided contact with officialdom of any kind and, to Paul's great satisfaction, turned off her ubiquitous secure mobile phone, except to check for messages once a day (fortunately, there were none, due to a conspiracy in Washington to help her have a good time).

On their third evening in Paris, Paul and Hannah went to a restaurant that specialized in North African cuisine. In honor of the occasion, she had spared nothing and looked especially gorgeous. The large room in which they were greeted by an admiring maitre d' looked to her for all the world like Rick's in Casablanca and, as they were led to their table, Hannah could see heads turn. Paul ordered champagne cocktails as he looked around, equally carried away: "Wow! What a place!"

When their waiter returned, however, it was not with two cocktails, but with a silver ice bucket containing a bottle of vintage champagne. Behind him was another man with a tray holding a crystal bowl of beluga caviar and accompaniments.

"There must be some mistake," Paul reacted. "We didn't order this."

Hannah reached for the business card perched on the edge of the tray. It read: Mahmud al-Fasal – International Management. She looked around the room, finally spotting him standing near the entrance. He smiled at her, touched a forefinger to his nose grifter-style, and disappeared through the door.

"Who was that?" Paul asked.

"Just a business acquaintance."

"You have some acquaintances," he marveled, taking a bite from a caviar-laden round of toast.

As the evening progressed, Hannah became increasingly relaxed, realizing ultimately that she was the victim of subconscious apprehension over the possibility of business intermixing with pleasure while she and Paul were in Europe. Now that it had actually occurred, the apprehension was gone.

"Shall we dance?" Paul proposed. "Maybe they'll play *As Time Goes By.*"

They were moving slowly around the crowded floor, when Hannah suddenly came to a dead stop, staring over Paul's shoulder. He turned to find a handsome man in evening dress----Egyptian or Iranian, perhaps---staring back at her.

"It is you, Miss Crossman, is it not?" the man asked in astonishment. "This is the third time we have met under unexpected circumstances. I believe we have the right to call it fate."

Hannah was speechless, as Paul watched agape.

"Paul," she finally explained, "this is Mr. Mir Batani Khan, another business acquaintance."

"Paul was very impressed," she told Sam Glover in an early morning phone call. "But, how in hell did Batani get to Paris without our knowing about it, and what's he doing here?

"Since you also saw al-Fasal at the restaurant, my guess is that the two were together. We know that al-Fasal just made a swing through Pakistan, so the odds are that Batani came to see Abdul Rashid."

"Are you planning to ask al-Fasal?"

"I wouldn't expect a straight answer, if I did. But, it is very interesting that he was apparently not concerned that you would spot Batani, and may even have staged it. That would mean that al-Fasal and Abdul Rashid are aware of the meeting you and the Admiral had with Batani in Konduz."

"What the hell, Sam?"

"At this point, Hannah, I just don't know. Have fun!"

Upon investigation, it turned out that Batani had an Egyptian passport, having lived in Cairo for some ten years. He had simply trimmed his beard, changed clothes, and gone to Kabul International Airport for a flight to Paris. Glover told Bergen and Detwiler of the events in Paris after the President's intelligence briefing later that morning.

"We need to restrict Hannah's vacations to Atlantic City from now on," the Admiral laughed.

It was late Spring in Afghanistan, but the early mornings were still cold and chill winds blew down from the surrounding mountains. A fire was burning briskly in an old oil drum, the men trying to get as close to it as possible. Their leader, a lieutenant of Mir Batani Khan, searched the fading darkness for signs of movement in the railroad workers camp. Other than smoke coming from the tin chimney of the kitchen tent, there was nothing. But, the more than two hundred men would soon be roused to continue pushing the new track southward toward the Pakistan border. Thus far, progress had been peaceful, but the railhead was now extending beyond more easily defended flat lands into mountain passes where attackers had the advantage of concealment and surprise. Batani's agents in rival bands had already sounded warnings of coming efforts to disrupt construction.

Except for, perhaps, twenty Chinese engineers, construction supervisors, and equipment specialists, the construction crew comprised Afghans recruited locally, as required by the concession agreement with the Kabul government. None had worked on a railroad before, few having even driven a car or truck. But, railroad track laying could still utilize largely unskilled labor, just as it did in the nineteenth century when large numbers of Chinese immigrants came to work on railroads in the American West. The major difference between then and now was the advent of specialized, heavy construction equipment that reduced the amount of manual labor required and speeded progress.

The Chinese construction company had brought in earthmovers, cranes, track layers and the like, as well as the specialists to operate and maintain them. That equipment and those key people were the primary targets of the insurgent groups dedicated to preventing the railroad and the copper mine it would serve being built. Their leaders quickly realized that destruction of a massive earthmover had much greater impact than killing a gang of men with shovels. It also permitted them to order the deaths of fewer of their fellow Afghans, many of whom were sympathetic to the Taliban cause, but simply needed the work. At the new mine, which would be a deep open pit affair, the importance of the massive front end loaders that scooped the ore out of the sides of the pit and the enormous trucks that carried it to the surface and loaded it on to the rail cars was critical. Far more money and effort had been put into protecting the equipment than the workers, who were quickly and easily replaceable.

The first explosion occurred a hundred yards away near a wall of sandbags built to shield parked vehicles. It was followed quickly by two more, the second of which landed among the trucks beyond the barrier. The men gathered around the fire scattered, searching in vain for the source of the shells that continued to explode in a line advancing toward a fuel dump on the far side of the storage lot. These were not grenades, Batani's officer realized, but mortar rounds being launched from positions in the hills outside the construction camp's perimeter. There was nothing his men could do, except wait for the American army.

Within minutes, the sound of helicopter rotors could be heard overhead, followed by the explosions and flares of rocket launches, as the Americans found targets in the hills with their night vision devices. The incoming mortar fire had by now ceased; with daylight, however, would come the threat of direct assaults by bands of men who looked eerily like those Batani had deployed to oppose them. Their primary targets were again the specialized vehicles, which would be attacked with rocket-propelled grenades as though they were tanks or armored personnel carriers. At railroad worksites that lacked natural defenses and protective barriers, attacks had started coming almost every day. Progress in advancing the track was slow, too slow to meet the date whereby the Chinese were committed to ship the first load of ore from the new mine. Everyone knew that, when the rail line was completed, the insurgents would switch to the time-honored tactic of blowing up the track in front of approaching trains, which would then be plundered.

Kingsley Yong was directed to warn Batani that China expected far more return on the protection money he had been given. Beyond the obligations that came with the funds he had taken from Yong, the Americans, and Abdul Rashid, Batani's basic credibility as a leader and trustworthy co-conspirator was being challenged. His entire strategy and personal safety depended upon making himself indispensable to most, if not all, of the significant players in the struggle for Afghanistan's future. Batani knew that many of those attacking the railroad and mine construction were being paid and protected by General Orkamzi's ISI, under orders from his superiors. Pakistan was supportive of the railroad project and the development of Afghanistan's resources, but wanted a controlling influence in their management and a share of the resulting revenue dedicated to the good and welfare of the Pakistani military and its leaders. Orkamzi was delaying progress until the Kabul government and the Chinese agreed to Pakistan's terms. His intelligence support to the CIA drone strike program carefully omitted locating and targeting data on the insurgent bands that were attacking the construction sites. At the time he left for Paris, Batani had not yet discovered a remedy for this grave threat to his future, and carried his frustration with him.

Mir Batani Khan had been invited to Paris by Abdul Rashid, who had come to believe he could profitably work with the Taliban leader. He liked Batani's strategy for getting the Americans out of Afghanistan, and was duly impressed by the man himself when they finally met. Perhaps it was the education and the years in Cairo, but Batani did not appear the cunning, backwoods religious fanatic prepared to see a lot of people killed to preserve his fiefdom. At the same time, his attractive qualities made him a potentially dangerous competitor dedicated to his own goals rather than Abdul Rashid's or those of the international jihad. The reclusive mastermind was struck by the similarity of his prospective relationship with Batani to that he and al-Fasal maintained with the Americans. He knew the Taliban leader had also met with Bergen, presumably for reasons similar to his connections with al-Fasal. As he reached for his worry beads, Abdul Rashid looked forward to the arrival of Batani and al-Fasal later in the morning. It would at least make the day a bit less lonely.

"Some delay is not unexpected, given the conditions under which the work is being done," Batani later admitted grudgingly. "But, the attacks have set the Chinese back months, and the disruptions are growing. The bastards are very clever: they aim their rockets and grenades at the earth movers and transporters that are hard to repair and even harder to replace." He wanted badly to stand up and pace the room, but would then tower over Abdul Rashid, seated on his cushions unable to rise.

"What about your own fighters?" al-Fasal asked.

" They are badly outnumbered, and the Americans will provide only air support because they fear their troops taking too many casualties. Apparently, the idea of sacrificing soldiers' lives to protect a Chinese construction site does not resonate well with the American public and, without Orkamzi's intelligence, the CIA can't effectively target covert missile strikes."

"It would seem that, if the Pakistanis won't help, the Americans would be your only hope," Abdul Rashid observed.

"I agree, but I can't simply call Washington," Batani lamented. I don't know Detwiler and Glover, who are now in charge."

"Bergen's former assistant, Hannah Crossman, happens to be in Paris on vacation, as you know" al-Fasal reminded them. "She now works for Detwiler. We could talk with her; there is nothing to lose."

"How will we find out where she and her friend are staying?

Mahmud al-Fasal laughed. "That's easily done. Visiting CIA people always stay in the same hotels when they come to Paris. It's a relic of the Cold War when the Ministry and Surete security people used to maintain special hotels for visiting spies, of which there were a great many. The hotels were considered neutral territory and, in return for behaving themselves while in town, the visitors were provided first class accommodations and assurances that the only hidden microphones were French. The buildings have long been returned to their commercial owners, but old customs do die hard, and they are excellent hotels. I will find out for you where Miss Crossman is staying, but I will also call Mr. Glover in Washington and tell him that you propose to contact her. Relationships are becoming so complicated these days that we may have to establish a chain of these special hotels all over the world.

CHAPTER ELEVEN

"I don't know what Batani wants," Sam Glover told Hannah, "and al-Fasal may not know either. At least he didn't tell me. He called me, so that when Batani contacted you, we wouldn't think that he and Abdul Rashid were involved in something sneaky. In short, he was covering his ass."

"How do you want me to handle this?"

"Find out what Batani is looking for, and let us know. From what our sources tell us, he's in pretty deep trouble because his Taliban organization in Afghanistan, such as it is, is not gaining the upper hand. His enemies have gone on the warpath against everything that was not there in the fifteenth century, which includes Batani himself and all foreigners, especially the Chinese."

"Can we help him, Sam?"

"I don't know. We can always give him more money, but my guess is that wouldn't help. If money was what Batani needed, he would have gotten it from Abdul Rashid. I suspect that what he needs is firepower, but don't promise him anything. The Admiral and Detwiler want to find out how far our friends in Paris will go to support Batani, because that will signify their broader strategy and objectives."

"How is Batani supposed to contact me?"

"That's been taken care of," Glover replied. "It's been arranged for Batani to meet you at al-Fasal's hotel apartment at noon today your time. Call me immediately after the meeting."

Hannah's biggest problem was Paul Rayner, who was understandably irate, particularly since she couldn't tell him why she needed to leave him.

"We leave Washington to get away by ourselves, and here they spirit you away after three days. It's not fair, Hannah!"

"I'm sorry, Paul, but it will be only for a few hours. It was your idea we come to Paris," she teased.

"With that damned satellite cell phone," he scoffed, "they would have had no trouble intruding on us in Tierra del Fuego!"

Batani was already there when Hannah arrived at al-Fasal's apartment, which she had visited with Admiral Bergen on previous occasions.. It was enormous and entirely self-contained, staffed by al-Fasal rather than the hotel. Its operating costs must be astronomical, Hannah always speculated, but no more so than those of the villa on the Riviera that al-Fasal considered his primary residence. They were testimony to the financial success their owner was experiencing in his many international business ventures, as well as the considerable reward he was likely receiving from a grateful Abdul Rashid.

Al-Fasal's chef had prepared a light luncheon for them, which was served at a small table in a bay window that overlooked the Place de la Concorde and the Arc de Triomphe. Hannah found the entire business exceedingly bizarre, starting with her sudden assignment to meet with a sworn enemy of the United States in a plush, highly civilized environment which she could never hope to duplicate in her real life and, finally, sitting across the table from a man who looked more like the young Omar Sharif than a wild-eyed Muslim fanatic. Despite her Agency training and professional focus, Hannah wondered momentarily whether her makeup was smeared or she had a hair bump. Batani had seen her at her absolute best at the restaurant the night before, and Hannah knew that she had to create a much more subdued appearance appropriate to the CIA business to which she had been assigned, something she had not anticipated when packing for Paris.

"So, we meet for the fourth time, Miss Crossman. There is obviously something significant in this that is not yet apparent. May I call you Hannah?"

Having no alternative, Hannah nodded, Batani smiling at her obvious discomfort.

"I will tell you the name my very close friends call me, but you must agree not to laugh." He waited until she nodded.

"At school in Cairo, they began to call me Mike---we all had American names for one another---and it stuck. I've not heard it used for many years. My friends from those days are either dead or far away, but you may use it, if you wish."

On an official mission, Hannah decided she could not deal with Batani on a first name basis, which would further confuse an already confusing situation.

"Well, Mr. Batani---Mike---you asked to be put in touch with us, and here we are. I was fortunate enough to be in Paris when Mr. al-Fasal called, and am pleased to meet with you."

Batani detected the difficulty with which Hannah said the last, and began to laugh. "I understand you are here on vacation with your lover, and apologize abjectly for disturbing your peace. I must admit, however, to being unexpectedly bothered by the knowledge that you are already romantically engaged. But, to business!"

He hurried on in order to give Hannah the opportunity to say nothing.

"As you know, I have undertaken to provide protection to the Chinese copper and railroad development projects in Afghanistan. The truth is that I am having great difficulty fulfilling my commitment because of determined opposition by several of my rivals. I, of course, knew from the outset that I would be opposed by those leaders who simply don't want me to succeed. But I did not anticipate opposition from the Pakistanis, who are working to delay the projects until Kabul and the Chinese give them what you would call a piece of the action. Orkamzi is providing my enemies materiel and intelligence with which to attack me, while withholding from the CIA intelligence needed to target its drones against the attackers."

"Under the circumstances, what do you believe we could do to help you?" Hannah asked.

"Eight months ago, you were present when I received a great deal of money from Mahmud al-Fasal. I used some of that to purchase fancy, well-equipped vehicles that I gave as gifts to my Taliban rivals in the hope of improving our relationship. Four of the five leaders whose fighters are now making trouble for me were recipients of those gifts."

"Not all bets are winners," Hannah commiserated.

"That is very true," Batani agreed, "which is why I concealed in each of the vehicles a transponder that can be remotely activated. It is a Chinese copy of one of your models called, I believe, the HT-25." He had pulled from his pocket a small notebook from which he was reading.

"My request is simple," he continued. "I will provide you with the signal signatures of these transponders, and ask you Americans to use them to engage my enemies and kill them."

"How do you know we are able to do that?" Hannah asked.

"Mahmud al-Fasal told me. Abdul Rashid believes that you can help, if you wish to do so."

Hannah confirmed the last with al-Fasal before reporting to Sam Glover, who did not seem surprised.

"We can, in fact, help Batani," he confirmed, "but it would be very tricky. The problem is that Orkamzi believes that he has limited our drone capabilities by withholding targeting intelligence and mounting close surveillance of the airfields in Pakistan at which we base the aircraft. If, despite this, we should strike the factions attacking the copper mine and railroad, Orkamzi could start to believe that we've begun to freeze him out and get pissed off. We're not prepared to have him do that, since we continue to need his help, particularly within Pakistan."

"So, what do we do, Sam?" Hannah asked impatiently, anxious to get back to the hotel and Paul.

"I don't know yet. Jim Detwiler and I are about to go visit with the Admiral over at the White House. I'll call you later." Given the time difference, this was not a happy prospect for Hannah, who knew the call would come in the middle of the night, which it did.

"We talked with Bergen, Hannah, and he talked with the President, and we need you to go to Pakistan tomorrow morning. The Ops Center has gotten you a reservation on the Air France flight to Islamabad that leaves Paris at 0930."

"Marvelous, Sam! Just what I need. What am I going to do in Pakistan?"

"You'll be met at the airport in Islamabad and taken care of. Remember the meeting you and Detwiler had with General Estefimov at the Air and Space Museum several months ago? Well, it's about that. You'll find out more later."

"Sam, we're talking on a secure, encrypted circuit. Why are you being so damned obscure? What the hell is going on?"

"I'm sorry, Hannah, but I can't be more explicit at the moment.

"What am I supposed to tell Paul?"

"We're very sorry to have to do this to you, but this situation is totally unexpected and you happen to be the only one in position, at the moment, to help. As for Rayner, if you wish, we can take his mind off you by having him renditioned to Tahiti or maybe Guantanamo."

"Don't be a wiseass, Sam. You're ruining my life."

Hannah had been told that someone would meet her plane in Islamabad, and that someone turned out to be Bob Berke, field name Jed, whom Hannah had known well at CIA Headquarters and during his earlier tour as the Agency's Chief of Station in Islamabad. Badly injured in the suicide bombing of a Pakistani police station, Jed had been evacuated back to the States, and had only recently returned to full duty.

Tired and disheveled though she was, Hannah was nevertheless happy to see him, particularly since he had arranged for a room at a local hotel in which she could bathe and get some sleep. Upon awakening the next morning, she did not immediately recall where she was, and looking out the window didn't help. Not for the first time in recent months, Hannah wondered why she was no longer able to convince herself that her life was a great adventure.

Jed drove her to the CIA Station's offices at the Embassy later that morning.

"I thought you were planning to retire, Jed?"

"I thought about it momentarily, and it scared me to death, Hannah. Then, after I recovered from the bombing, I got tired of being the Headquarters invalid. So, I talked them into sending me back out here. It wasn't difficult: I'm well qualified for the job and nobody else wanted it. So, here I am. "

"I haven't the foggiest idea what's going on, Jed. Everyone is being so obscure."

"I had a call from Sam Glover," he responded, "asking me to fill you in on this current business with Batani, and what Headquarters wants you to do in connection with it. You'll recall that the arrangement we now have with Moscow permits us to operate our Predators from a 'secret' base on Russian territory against targets located any place but in Russia and the former Soviet republics. The base is considered 'secret' not because no one knows about it, but because we and the Russians will 'officially' deny it exists, permitting each country to reject responsibility for attacks mounted from the base, we blaming them on the Russians, while Moscow attributes attacks by its new drones to us. A good example of how that works is the way the Pakistani government and military scream every time we kill a bunch of Taliban with a drone attack in the mountains, when it is well known that the ISI has provided the intelligence needed to target the aircraft, including identification of the key people being hit."

"So, where do I come in?"

"We're going to use the transponder frequencies and codes that Batani gave you to take out the Taliban faction leaders giving him a hard time. We'll hit them in their vehicles, if necessary, but it's preferable to wait until the vehicle is parked outside a house with a bunch of others, indicating that a meeting is going on. Then, you shoot the missiles through the roof of the house. That approach has given us our greatest success.

"But, the aircraft we've been using for missions in Pakistan and Afghanistan are being closely monitored and inhibited by the Paks. When we attack anyway, using the aircraft now operational in Russia guided by Batani's transponders, Orkamzi will be mightily pissed. More significantly, he is likely to be in big trouble with his superiors, who don't like things happening that they don't know about and don't control. Despite his working against us in this particular business, we need Orkamzi to be kept on because he works with us in others areas. The previous tenure of ISI chiefs has not been notably long, and we have no idea who we would get as Orkamzi's replacement. This is where you come in, Hannah."

"What?"

"It's true. Sam talked it over with Detwiler, then both of them discussed it with Bergen, and he (I'm told) talked it over with the President. You are to be a covert, very unofficial emissary of the Director of National Intelligence to the government and military leadership of Pakistan. Should you find it unavoidably necessary to the accomplishment of your mission, you may also judiciously drop President Kitteridge's name."

"And my mission will be what?

"To convey to the Pakistani leadership that our attacks, which will have occurred just before you surface here in Islamabad, were not directed against Pakistani interests and security, but are part of a new, broader strategy of cooperation that will better protect Pakistan. You will apologize for them not getting warning of the attack, and explain that the demands of attacking all targets almost simultaneously left no time for advance warning."

"Why should they believe anything I tell them?"

"They won't. But they will be impressed by the fact that we consider them important enough that we would go to the trouble of trying to soothe their hurt feelings. The clincher, of course, will be you. Everyone of consequence out here knows you or, at least, knows who you are. They've seen you with Admiral Bergen at important meetings, and know that you often attend the conferences at Mahmud al-Fasal's home. In this instance, you are the perfect representative: no high level position and, therefore, no authority, but well connected to people on top. The fact that Washington would go to the trouble of having you bring the Paks an explanation more than compensates for its lameness."

"I'm impressed with my own importance," Hannah laughed sarcastically. "When's all of this going to happen?"

"Undoubtedly, Orkamzi already knows that you've entered the country, and is wondering what the hell's going on. If all continues to go according to plan, the attacks will be made tonight or tomorrow morning. Our birds have been up for two days looking to pinpoint the targets in the vicinity of the mine and railroad operations. We can't delay much longer. Orkamzi is sure to come looking for you tomorrow."

The ISI director had, indeed, been notified of Hannah's arrival in-country, and become duly alarmed. Had she come on business of which he was not aware? Were Abdul Rashid and Mahmud al-Fasal involved? Did it, perhaps, have to do with the Americans' dealings with Batani? Maybe, it was all of the above! Orkamzi established continuous surveillance of the CIA Station Chief and the hotel in which Hannah was staying, and also issued a general alert to his deployed agents to report even the smallest thing that appeared out of the ordinary. His office was soon swamped with phone calls and messages, since no one wanted to be accused of missing something significant.

The attacks were actually carried out in mid-afternoon while their targets were in the field or at meetings with their subordinates. Good luck permitted all of them to be carried out within the same hour, largely preserving tactical surprise. Two of the three Batani enemies targeted were caught at apparent command posts in the mountains surrounding the copper mine site, while the third was found fleeing in his new SUV, having been alerted to the attacks by the sounds of missile warhead explosions in the distance. Batani Khan immediately announced a great victory in Afghanistan's struggle against foreign domination.

General Orkamzi spent the better part of the following day standing uneasily at attention in the private offices of his military and governmental superiors being thoroughly chewed out. None of them cared about the Taliban leaders who had been killed or that much about the impact of their deaths on the campaign to delay the construction projects. All, however, wanted to know why Pakistan hadn't been consulted in advance and whether this signaled a change in American policy and attitude. Orkamzi assured them he was on the case and had, in fact, summoned to Islamabad a personal representative of Admiral Bergen and Director of National Intelligence Detwiler to explain what was going on. Returning to his own office, the General was relieved to find a message from Hannah proposing they meet.

"Orkamzi is certainly going to ask what we're up to. What do I tell him?" Hannah asked Jed.

"First of all, you can acknowledge that we were responsible for yesterday's attacks on behalf of Batani. Orkamzi has no doubt already assumed that. What he's really interested in is where the attacking planes came from. You can tell him that we have a new base in Russia from which we can reach all of Central Asia. That will give the Pakistanis something to think about, because it means that we are no longer dependent upon them for ground support and intelligence needed to operate our drones. Remember that Orkamzi doesn't know about Batani's transponders, which means he doesn't know how we got the intelligence needed to target the insurgents harassing the mine and railroad. If we have done this right, he will fear that we don't need the Pakistanis any more, and will be grateful when you reassure him that we do (which, of course, is true).

"Thank you, Jed! You've made me feel a lot better," Hannah complained, her exasperation palpable. "It looks like everyone else is winging it, so why shouldn't I?"

Orkamzi's staff car came for her promptly at noon; she was surprised to find the General already in it.

"It is such a fine day, Miss Crossman, that I decided to show you Islamabad's famous Rose and Jasmine Garden. We can talk while we are strolling about looking at the flowers. I believe there is a show there now."

It was indeed a warm, sunny day, and walking in the park was very pleasant, even for the squad of paramilitary police whose truck had followed the General's car. When Orkamzi and Hannah got out, the policemen established a moving perimeter around them at a discreet distance. Strangely enough, it did not seem to distract the many strollers crowding the Garden.

"It is a sign of the times," the General lamented, "that I cannot go outside even in Rawalpindi or Islamabad without fear of attack by extremists. This is partly a result of the success you are having with your drones attacking their leaders in the mountains. They have no way of fighting the aircraft and missiles, so they come to attack our cities with cars filled with explosives and suicide bombers, blaming us for helping you or for, at least, not stopping your attacks. We are paying a great price for that assistance."

While enjoying the sun, Hannah recognized that meeting outdoors enabled Orkamzi to escape the microphones and recording devices that likely populated his offices and conference rooms. He was understandably nervous about the message he would be able to take back to his senior colleagues in the headquarters compound. Hannah attempted to reassure him.

"My understanding is that most of the people killed in our attacks are your enemies as well as ours, although perhaps for different reasons."

"What you say is largely true," Orkamzi admitted. "But, we have difficulty getting foreigners, including many of you Americans, to understand how badly fragmented our country and society are. Such unity as exists is far more a reflection of tactical convenience than loyalty or patriotism. What you call the Taliban is really a collection of contending factions fighting with both the government and one another, depending on the issue. There are only two causes that will unite the country, at least temporarily: the first is opposition to foreign invaders, the second is the protection and propagation of Islam. The two, of course, combine in the more extreme factions, which do not hesitate to make war simultaneously on foreigners and fellow Pakistanis alike.

"The overriding mission of our government, in particular the Army, is to prevent these centrifugal forces from causing Pakistan's disintegration, leaving us vulnerable to outside enemies and competitors, whether it be India, China, Iran, or even a successful Afghanistan. That is why the help given to us by the United States, particularly to our armed forces, has been indispensable and we, of course, would like it to continue. To be perfectly candid, Miss Crossman, we have facilitated CIA's drone program as much or more for that reason than for its direct benefit to our domestic objectives."

"You have done that sometimes, General Orkamzi, and sometimes not," Hannah reacted forthrightly. "When your domestic interests outweigh your need to help us, you have not hesitated to find reasons not to assist us, and even to obstruct. This current controversy with Batani about protection of the Chinese projects in Afghanistan is a good example. We understand why you do these things. But, you must understand, however, that we have had to create the capabilities that you are unwilling or unable to provide. As the attacks carried out in Afghanistan the other night illustrate, our drone operations are no longer dependent on your facilitation."

"I understand that your new base for the drones is in Russia. I assume you intend to share your capabilities with the Russians?"

Hannah did not answer the question, telling Orkamzi that his assumption was correct. She felt certain that she had already exceeded her instructions, as far as representing her government's position and interests were concerned. But, she had left Washington to vacation in Paris, not to play ambassador in Islamabad. If Sam Glover and the other bosses didn't like the way she conducted the interview with Orkamzi, they should have left her with Paul Rayner, whom she did know how to handle.

"You can be assured, General Orkamzi, that we value Pakistan's assistance as much as ever, and do not intend to withdraw our support. At the same time, however, we cannot be put in the position of having to subordinate our requirements to your internal political and financial priorities. The conflicts you've described will go on forever, if there is no real will to resolve them. As the recent uprisings throughout the Muslim world have shown, the fundamental problems are underdevelopment, corruption and economic inequality, for which a tougher, more dogmatic Islam is surely not a cure. You will not find America's patience endless, should action on this realization not be forthcoming."

As they returned to the General's sedan, Hannah told herself that, if she was not canned, they should seriously consider making her Secretary of State. Facing his superiors and peers at the end of the day, Orkamzi put the most favorable spin on what Hannah had told him, warning them also, however, that establishment of the capability to operate drones from Russia could be considered strong evidence that the United States was taking contingent measures against the prospect of Pakistan's disintegration or loss to extremism.

"It could have been worse," the Army Chief-of=Staff admitted. "We might have to give up the income from the mine and railroad projects, but American aid will still be there, at least for a while. Did you enjoy negotiating with the American emissary, Orkamzi?"

"She is much better looking than Bergen, but told me the same things."

The Chief-of-Staff laughed, along with the others in the room."Washington's decision to send her to talk with us reminded me of an American musical film I saw many years ago," he told them. "In it, there was a song about a spoonful of sugar making the medicine go down."

CHAPTER TWELVE

Reggie Huggins had been in the CIA Headquarters complex hundreds of times, but not since he retired. A visitor now, he checked in at the main gatehouse on the edge of the wooded compound, showing a unformed officer his retired employee ID card. He was given a sort of welcome home smile, a visitor's badge, and directions to the shuttle that would take him to the main entrance of the Headquarters building, a massive affair surrounded on three sides by parking lots. At the security check point in the lobby, Reggie passed through a metal detector and waited in an adjacent lounge until someone from the Director's suite came down to escort him to the private elevator and up to the seventh floor. Arriving there, he was shown directly into Sam Glover's office, his escort wordlessly retreating and shutting the door behind her.

"What the fuck are you up to, Reggie?" Glover stood looking out through the floor-to-ceiling windows that made up the large room's front wall. He did not give Huggins the opportunity to say hello.

"I thought that Hannah Crossman made my message clear: you are screwing around in very sensitive business, and your Government does not appreciate it."

"Sorry, Sam. I'm just trying to make a few bucks. The client came to me. I didn't go looking for him."

"Who is it?"

"Sorry again, Sam, I can't tell you. But, it's someone important, who may have a lot of clout someday."

"I already know who it is, Reggie. What have they got you doing?

"You know I can't tell you that, Sam. Suffice it to say it's the kind of stuff I did for the Agency, but only the legal part."

Pointing to a chair, Glover barked at Huggins: "Sit down, Reggie, and listen carefully. The guys you're working for, Oberling and Norton, are looking for dirt to use against President Kitteridge in next year's election, and expect you to help them find some. Now, there's nothing illegal about that; it's the good old American way. But, we've learned that you've been making trips overseas on their behalf and reestablishing contact with people you worked with while on assignment for the Agency. That can get a bit dicey, Reggie, and I called you in to assure you that, should you make a pain in the ass of yourself, we will find something illegal in what you're doing and fix it so that you spend most of your remaining years in your lawyer's office. Am I making myself clear?"

"I hear you, Sam. But, what am I supposed to do: I've taken a lot of money from them, and much of it has gone to pay debts and overdue expenses."

"I don't want to hear about it, Reggie! Just stay out of our way! This business is complicated enough without everyone playing both ends against the middle. If you guys keep it up, sooner or later someone is going to start shooting, and people we know will be in deep shit, if not dead."

Glover's warning did not impress Oberling and Norton, who assured Huggins that the CIA Director was the one who needed to be careful. After the next election, he would be gone. Reggie was not all that confident in the predicted outcome, deciding that a bit of butt protection of his own was in order.

The formal establishment of *Oberling For America,* an exploratory committee authorized by current election law, permitted Roger Norton to begin actually collecting the funds informally promised by the organizations and individuals anxious to see Alfred Oberling in the White House and, more urgently, Mason Kitteridge out. It also facilitated trial campaigning by the candidate and major supporters that served to identify and field test prospective platform planks, in addition to generating additional contributions. President Kitteridge had not yet announced for reelection, giving Oberling more media access time than he would later get. Now that the spotlight had been turned on, Roger Norton marshaled the field commanders whose efforts were to be focused on international relations.

"Our principal theme in foreign affairs," he told them, "will be the failure of the Kitteridge Administration to move the war on terror and Islamic extremism more rapidly to a successful conclusion that will eliminate the threat to our American homeland and allow us to bring our troops home. The theme that Alfred Oberling ran on the last time, Keeping America Safe, is still valid and will also be used. But we cannot, unfortunately, cite instances where Kitteridge has failed to protect the homeland, which makes the point less compelling. The American people don't want to get involved in godforsaken places like Somalia and Yemen. We need to determine what they will support in the way of strategies and actions, and base our campaign on them."

The small group of advisors to which Norton was speaking nodded approvingly, but noticeably without enthusiasm. Finally, the senior minority member of the Senate intelligence committee spoke up:

"That's all well and good, Roger, but what new strategies and actions do you have in mind? Some of us believe that it's not a question of making a final push to victory in Afghanistan, but rather of figuring out how to cut our losses and get out, as we did in Vietnam. We are in the process of withdrawing from Iraq and giving up whatever capability we had to influence events there. What do we do if, as some of us believe will happen, the government we left in place disintegrates into civil war and everything we sacrificed our people and money for starts to go down the drain. That could very well begin to happen in the middle of our campaign.

"Then, there's Afghanistan. Many of the people I talk with don't think it's worth fighting for, and that we can't win in any event. We went in there, in the first place, only because we needed some place to hit back after 9/11. What is our election platform going to say about that, Roger, or about what we should do in the other places that could fall to Islamist extremists?"

Roger Norton stared silently at them for what seemed an eternity before replying lamely: "That would depend a lot on what Kitteridge is doing about those problem areas."

"Surely, Roger, you're not saying that our campaign strategy is simply to advocate the opposite of what the Administration is doing or proposing?"

"Certainly not! But, at this early date, Vice President Oberling doesn't yet possess all of the data he needs to make informed decisions in these areas, and we will not be able to count on the Administration to help us. *Oberling For America* has engaged a consulting firm of former CIA operatives to advise us in these matters. Their people have already been conducting interviews overseas on our behalf."

"What are they learning, Roger?"

"I'm sorry, Senator, I can't tell you that at this point."

"You're as bad as the damned CIA, Roger!"

Admiral Bergen had just finished briefing President Kitteridge on the results of the drone strike operations against Batani's enemies. He, Detwiler, and Glover had been called to the Oval Office, which meant that the Chief Executive had more on his mind than just the briefing. This was confirmed when they found that the Secretaries of State, Defense, and Homeland Security had also been summoned, as well as the Attorney General and the Director of the FBI.

"Did launching the operation from the new base in Russia create any problems?" Kitteridge asked.

"None at all, sir. Once the aircraft were in the air, they were controlled as always by pilots here in the U.S. to whom their point of departure made no difference. We, of course, had to scrupulously obey all the rules the Russians set for us, and the flying time to and from the target area was much longer, but none of that proved a problem. The aircraft had to orbit quite a while looking for their targets, but it ultimately proved to be a piece of cake, given that we had the transponders to home in on. Going home, the birds rode a beacon from the new base."

"Excellent!" Kitteridge responded. "As all of you know, I authorized a deal with Russia to get us a base for drone operations in Central Asia that does not depend on the assistance and good will of Pakistan. I consider it an important hedge against the possibility of that country, and indeed Afghanistan as well, coming under the control of unfriendly governments. Our ability to check out the new facilities through the Batani operation was a fortuitous break. But, acquiring the base reflects a broader rationale that I want to talk with you about this morning.

"Looking at it realistically," the President continued, "our direct involvement in Muslim countries, like Iraq and Afghanistan, is going to come to an end sooner rather than later. The American people will not stand for it much longer and, frankly speaking, we are unlikely to be able to claim 'mission accomplished' when we leave." He saw no disagreement in the faces of his listeners.

"Given that probability, what measures do we take toward protecting America and its people from enemies operating from Islamist countries? This is essentially the same question we faced at the outset of what became the Cold War, with respect to the Communist Bloc, although the circumstances and conditions were obviously different. Without overstressing the analogy, let's consider a possible future in which the Soviet Union is here represented by an Islamist Pakistan and, perhaps, a Taliban-governed Afghanistan. As during the Cold War, albeit for different reasons, we know that achieving our goals by invading those countries or massively bombing them are not viable options. But, their radical governments are making no secret of their enmity toward us and willingness to support, or at least tolerate, terrorist organizations directed against us and our allies. What do we do?"

"But we are not talking massive nuclear threat here," the Secretary of Homeland Security pointed out. "None of these countries is likely to be capable of mounting a significant attack on us."

"That's true," Kitteridge acknowledged, "but nowadays our people are likely to view the greater probability of an attack that kills fifty or a hundred people in the New York City subway system a lot more anxiously than the prospect of a nuclear holocaust. Ultimately, it's not the magnitude of a threat that is most affecting, but rather the strength of fear that it will be realized.

"You are all, of course, wondering whether I've got answers to the questions I've posed. Actually, I believe there are not many available courses of action. The real question, I think, is not what we should do, but when should we do it. I hope that events will enable me to avoid both the questions and the actions indicated by their answers. But, I believe it prudent that we take steps to prepare ourselves against the possibility or probability that a worst case situation will eventuate.

"Obviously, I want us to be able to deal with developing threats and adjust to changing circumstances as rapidly and effectively as possible. To do that, I believe we must be prepared to take what timely preemptive action we can. Secondly, we must act in concert with other nations that are in the same boat we are, regardless of how we stand with them on other issues. All of your organizations are likely to become involved, to one extent or another, as we implement such initiatives. Admiral Bergen is my designated coordinator in these matters. If you have something to report or need something, he's your man."

"Why all the extra security and secrecy, Mr. President?" Secretary of State Grant wondered.

"A number of reasons, Wilma. First, we're doing things to prepare for worst case circumstances that, hopefully, will never materialize. Should the foreign governments and individuals who would be affected get wind of our precautions their reactions might not be helpful. Second, we will probably be seeking cooperative agreements with governments and individuals with whom we might very well be at odds on other issues, including some of great interest to our allies. In short, we may have to play the ends against the middle in some situations. Finally, and unfortunately not least, there is the likelihood that what we're doing, should it leak, would become entangled in election polities. I have little doubt that Mr. Oberling and his merry men would not refrain from exploiting already oomplex situations to gain advantage in the coming campaign."

The President could tell from their body language that he had generated more questions among his listeners than he had answered.

"Let me give you examples of what I'm talking about," he resumed. "As indicated, I am particularly worried about the future stability of Pakistan, specifically the ability of a leadership friendly to us to remain in power and not be replaced by a fundamentalist regime. While we continue to heavily support the Islamabad government with money, arms and covert CIA assistance, I have hedged the possibility of losing our influence and facilities there by entering an agreement with Russia to provide us a basing facility for CIA missile-launching drone aircraft. It recently became operational and known to the Pakistanis when aircraft launched from there conducted operations in Afghanistan that we were not permitted to mount from bases in Pakistan because senior officials there have interests opposed to ours. Needless to say, the Director of the Inter Services Intelligence Directorate was mightily shocked and unhappy, but became usefully aware that we are no longer completely dependent upon his assistance and good will.

"The situation in Afghanistan is somewhat similar. I am hedging the prospect of losing the cooperation and assistance of the government in Kabul, such as it is, because of its ineptitude, corruption, defection from our cause, or some combination of the three. Although it is admittedly risky, we have begun to provide covert support to the recently self-proclaimed head of the Taliban, Mir Batani Khan. While we assume him to be completely untrustworthy, Batani is a nationalist rather than an Islamist fanatic, and appears to influenced more by the law of supply and demand than by the Sharia. It is entirely possible, of course, that we shall have to change our minds sometime in the future, and be forced to rectify our error.

"If all of this sounds very strange to you, let me add a final note. Admiral Bergen has recently returned from China, where he conferred with very senior people about arrangements between our countries similar to those I've just described to you. The Chinese are very much interested.

The meeting ended quietly after a reminder from the President about the need to maintain the security surrounding what they had been told. As they filed out, the attendees stared at Admiral Bergen. He couldn't tell whether they were looks of dismay, pity or outrage.

Back in Washington, Hannah tried repeatedly to contact Paul Rayner, without success. The answering machine at his home number had stopped taking new messages because its memory was full and the persons who answered his office number would say only that he was on assignment, refusing to reveal where that was. When Rayner finally called her a week later, Hannah was both relieved and angry.

"Where have you been, Paul, and why didn't you return my calls?"

"I wanted you to feel what it's like for me when you disappear into your spook world without telling me where you're going and when you'll be back. I had decided, after the business in Paris, that enough was enough. But, here I am back again for more. You do have redeeming qualities, my Love, even if I don't get to appreciate them as often as I'd like."

"Thank you, Paul. I will try to make it up to you: but, I did warn you how it would be. Ironically, if we had gone to Atlantic City or Branson, Missouri to get away from Washington, I would have been safe from my bosses. But, the errand they grabbed me for turned out to be really important, so I can't whine too loudly."

"I can't tell you that I understand," he replied, "because it would imply that you can keep doing it to me. But, I will grant that what you did was important. I know now that the guy we ran into on the dance floor in Paris, the one you introduced as a business associate, is really head of the Taliban in Afghanistan. I know you won't tell me what the hell he was doing in Paris, but I am impressed and now prepared to believe all those warnings of how you might injure me, should I make improper advances."

Hannah laughed with some relief. "I want you to know that I do exercise restraint in such matters."

"Our adventure in Paris had another effect," Paul added. "I came back determined to get off my butt and back into real journalism instead of being just an arranger. One of the reasons you didn't hear from me sooner is that I've been off after a story. It wasn't a particularly spectacular one, but I'm not going to tell you about it anyway, just so you'll appreciate what it feels like to not to have a need-to-know."

Hannah laughed again. "I will use my spook training to worm it out of you. How about dinner tonight?"

"Is it safe?" he asked in a convincingly quavering voice.

CHAPTER THIRTEEN

Mir Batani Khan's stock rose sharply after the CIA drone attacks had rid him of three among his strongest and most dedicated enemies. In Afghanistan, the swiftness and accuracy of the strikes had, at least temporarily, convinced his remaining rivals that Batani had powerful magic working for him, in addition to the Americans. The Pakistani high command and ISI knew the truth of the matter, but recognized that Batani's activities could no longer be controlled to the extent they had been. General Orkamzi also fretted over reports that the Taliban leader was dickering with the Chinese. The immediate challenge for Batani was how to exploit his new-found prominence to further his ultimate goal of gaining complete control of Afghanistan, which meant getting both the Americans and Pakistanis out of direct involvement in his country's affairs while, simultaneously, keeping them aboard as supporters. The master key was money: he needed more, a lot more. With money, Batani could not only offer more and larger bribes, but also take over and operate functions and responsibilities that normally belonged to the government in Kabul. He would manage them better and more reliably, showing the people where their path to true progress lay.

His chosen demonstration program was opium poppy production, in which Afghanistan was the world leader, ultimately responsible for almost 90% of the world's heroin supply. When the Taliban ruled the country, in strict accordance with Koranic law, opium production had been forbidden. Following their invasion in 1979, the Soviets had enforced the ban by burning the poppy fields and other drastic methods of physical eradication. When they left the country, poppy cultivation, which is relatively easy and requires little rain and no fertilizer, rebounded quickly. As with any other lucrative business, an infrastructure for processing and transporting the harvested crops quickly developed, its rewards so great as to provide substantial incomes not only for traffickers, but also for military and civil officials in the jurisdictions affected by the trade in Afghanistan and neighboring states. Batani had no idea of the full amount of money involved; but he knew it was very large, and wanted a major piece of the action for his own cause.

The obvious approach would have been to muscle in, gangster-style, and simply demand a cut of the take. However, Batani realized his action would anger the Americans, who were trying to suppress the drug trade, as well as the Russians, who were suffering a serious heroin addiction problem on a national scale. The latter had not yet given Batani any money, and he speculated that they could be willing to pay to play.

However, Batani knew no one in Russia, especially someone with connections in the intelligence and security agencies. After mulling the problem for a while, he went to his clothing chest and located the satellite telephone given him by Admiral Bergen. Turning it on, he was a bit surprised to find it had held its charge, because five or so seconds after he extended the antenna and pushed the Send button, a female voice responded in English: "Operations Center. How may I help you?"

"This is Mir Batani Khan calling to speak with Miss Hannah Crossman. Do you know who I am?"

"Yes, Mr. Batani Khan, we know who you are. I will try to locate Ms. Crossman for you immediately."

It was just past 0730 in Washington, and Hannah was sitting, in her underwear, on a bench in the locker room of the fitness center in the basement of the CIA Head-quarters Building complex, having just come from a post-workout shower. Fortunately, she had already opened her locker, and did not have to fuss with the combination when she heard her phone ring.

"This is the Special Communications Duty Officer, Ms. Crossman. Mir Batani Khan is calling. I am switching it to your cell phone."

"Hello, sir! This is a very pleasant surprise. What can we do for you?"

"It is a pleasure to speak with you, Ms Crossman. You will forgive me for saying so, but it is much more en-joyable speaking with you than with your Admiral Bergen. I am in need of assistance in making a connection with the appropriate officials in another country."

"What country is that?"

"Russia. I know from your last drone aircraft opera-tion in my country that you have a new cooperative rela-tionship with the Russians, and I was hoping it could be of assistance to me."

"In what way, sir, and on what subject?"

"The subject is drug trafficking, but the specific mat-ter is too complex to be discussed adequately on the telephone. Suffice it to say that I have a proposal I think would interest both you and Moscow, and I would like an early opportunity to discuss it with the appropriate officials."

Throwing on her clothes haphazardly, Hannah rushed from the locker room to Sam Glover's seventh floor office, only to find that the CIA Director was going to the White House directly from home.

"Were you attacked in the elevator, Hannah!" his aide asked facetiously. Given the rush hour traffic headed into the city, Hannah knew it would be impossible to meet with Sam in less than an hour, so she called his cell phone, hoping that he was not already in the Oval Office or some-place else where he could not talk with her.

"Sam! Batani called, and wants us to help him get with the Russians on something to do with the drug traf-ficking business."

"Shit! What did you tell him?"

"What could I tell him? He wouldn't go into the spe-cifics of his scheme, just wants us to set up a meeting. Be-sides, I don't have the authority to even order pizza without one of you grand poobahs having to tell me what toppings to get."

Since James Detwiler also happened to be down-town, they met in early afternoon in the Situation Room, then moved to Admiral Bergen's office when he returned from a meeting in the Pentagon. Bitani was not stupid enough to become a drug trafficker, they agreed, or at least not stupid enough to tell them about it. One could be sure, they also agreed, that whatever he had in mind was calculated principally to advance Taliban interests, as defined by Mir Batani Khan. He didn't appear to believe in partnerships, nor was he obviously dedicated to amassing personal wealth. Most of the money he had gotten from al-Fasal, Yong, and Bergen had already been given away or invested in future benefits, mostly involving killing off his rivals.

"We have no choice but to find out what he's up to," Glover reasoned, "but to do that we need to facilitate the connection with the Russians he's looking for."

"I don't mind us doing that," Detwiler reacted, "but I don't want it to appear to the Russians that we are necessarily part of Batani's scheme, particularly when we don't know what the hell it is."

"Well, we can't have it both ways," the Admiral interjected. "We can't introduce Batani to the Russians on one hand, while telling them on the other that we deny any responsibility for what he proposes. It would look like we were being jerked around."

"Why don't we just play it straight?" Bergen finally proposed. "We'll tell the Russians that we have no idea what Batani has up his sleeve, and will be hearing it for the first time just like them."

"Who do we contact on the Russian side, and at what level?" Glover asked.

"The obvious person is Estefimov, who owes us big time since we made him a hero in Moscow with the drone business."

"Who do we send?"

"I will make the initial contact," the CIA Director decided, "because Estefimov is after all a General. But, I believe Hannah should be our action officer. All of the parties know her, and she's shown that she can handle herself in situations like this. The other thing is that it is important that neither of the other parties gets the idea that the United States intends to play in whatever this game is. Hannah, who has no executive authority, is perfect for the assignment."

Seated quietly against a wall, Hannah said nothing, but had a premonition that Paul Rayner was once again destined to be disappointed. Her concern grew when it turned out that General Estefimov was in Russia tending to his new drone empire. When contacted through the Russian Embassy, he agreed to meet with Batani, sensing another possible career-enhancing coup. He proposed the meeting take place in Dushanbe in Tadjikistan, which borders Afghanistan on the north and is on the route taken by drug shipments to Russia. Batani agreed and Detwiler could, therefore, not decline. Once again, Hannah had a long, boring plane trip during which to wonder why she continued doing what she was doing, particularly on the last leg from Moscow in a rickety Aeroflot Ilyushin.

Dushanbe, the capital of Tadjikistan, at least offered Hannah the support of a U.S. Embassy. She was met at the airport by the CIA Station Chief, whom she had known slightly at Headquarters. He had made a reservation for her at the best hotel, but was directed to tell her that the Embassy could not be associated with her or her mission while she was in town. Asked why, he revealed that continuous controversy over counter drug strategy dominated the Embassy staff, to which were attached representatives of every Washington organization with claim to a role in protecting America from dangerous drugs. Their focal point was, of course, the opium poppy derivatives coming out of Afghanistan, controversy centering on the question of what to do about it. Eradication had once been the primary objective, tactics concentrating on spraying, burning, and otherwise destroying the growing poppies, while compensating the growers to keep them from starving and revolting. Programs were also established to transition poppy farmers to other crops. None of this worked long term, in great measure because the government in Kabul and its allies exercised little control over the growing area and its population. During the years it ruled the country, after expelling the Soviets, the Taliban had effectively put a stop to the raising of opium poppies by declaring it a violation of Islamic law. But, after the American invasion, it reversed that policy as a way of striking back against the West while raising needed cash. Afghani poppy farmers soon regained their market share and U.S. counterdrug agencies shifted the emphasis of their campaigns to prevention and treatment of addiction rather than eradication of the drugs at their source. Standing orders to CIA stations were to stay out of narcotics related debates and operations, dealing with terrorists being trouble enough.

Checking into her hotel, Hannah was handed a note from Mir Batani Khan asking her to meet him later for dinner. She almost didn't recognize him in the hotel lounge, sitting at the bar nursing a glass of fruit juice. He had further trimmed his beard from what she had noticed in Paris and had his hair cut in the latest Western style. The business suit he wore was well-cut Savile Row with a large plastic name tag on the right lapel that associated him with the Central Asia Development Corporation and identified him as Robinson Wahby in English and what Hannah assumed to be Tadjik.

"Good evening, Mr. Wahby. I almost didn't recognize you."

"All well and good, Miss Crossman. If I was easily recognizable, I couldn't travel safely without a large escort and would not be able have a pleasant dinner alone with a beautiful and charming woman. I have an additional name tag inscribed with the name of my wife, Bathsheba Wahby, which will insure that no other man will stare at you during the evening. Or, I can inscribe it with the name of a well-known movie star, which will cause all who see us to envy me. I am prepared to submit to your will, if you promise not to tell my brothers in Afghanistan."

Hannah laughed and agreed to be Mrs. Wahby, perhaps a bit too readily she thought later. The hotel restaurant, a refuge for foreigners in a strange land, was filled with westerners and Asians (many bearing name tags) grateful for not having to wander poorly lit streets in search of an indifferent meal. Batani, however, had reserved a small, private dining room to which he led a very surprised Hannah.

"You've been here before," she recognized.

"The name Wahby is honored throughout the land," he replied

"Is the food good?"

"That much honor no name can command."

But the food *was* good and the service attentive as the Wahbys wined and dined in high style. They were serenaded by piano and violin players who ran softly through a remarkable repertoire ranging from what Hannah assumed to be Tadjik folk songs to Broadway show tunes. She was enjoying herself immensely.

"The Taliban business must be very good for you to be able to afford an evening like this." Batani laughed.

"I am only following the example of my illustrious tutor, Mahmud al-Fasal, who is actually funding this enjoyable interlude, along with his mentor, Abdul Rashid.

Al-Fasal is, by the way, a great admirer of yours and would undoubtedly approve of my expenditure, if he knew of it."

Hannah felt herself blushing and feeling guilty about it for reasons she found too complicated to contemplate at the moment.

"Your mention of my Taliban business interests me," Batani continued, "because, as you know, there is not a single or unified Taliban in either Pakistan or Afghanistan. In terms more familiar to the West, I consider myself the Taliban's business agent, at least that is what I'm trying to become. I have no desire to tell warlords how to live or rule their people, much less to replace them. But they need to know that they cannot continue to ignore the world pressing in on them and that, if they follow my lead, I will show them how to prosper from change while retaining, actually expanding, their rights and privileges."

"Do you really believe you can do all that?"

"I do, at least to the extent that, once these people begin to benefit from my initiatives, they will forget about the ancient enmities and religious constraints. You will hear an example of what I have in mind when we meet with the Russian tomorrow."

Arkady Estefimov arrived the next morning to find that the Russian embassy in Dushanbe had essentially the same instructions as its American counterpart: keep Batani and Crossman at arm's length to avoid being drawn further into the drug war controversy. The three met in the hotel lobby and walked out into the city to get away from the inevitable listening devices. Eventually, they settled around an unoccupied stone chess table in a nearby park; its location away from pedestrian traffic yielding privacy sufficient to their needs. Hannah noticed at least seven men loitering in various locations surrounding their position, one of whom was certainly the driver of the car in which CIA's Chief of Station had transported her from the airport.

"We are apparently being well guarded," she informed the others. Estefimov looked around.

"Four of those men are from my organization," he explained. "It is not safe for Russian security officers in Dushanbe. We recently discovered an information leak at our embassy, and it is possible the drug traffickers know about our meeting."

"Marvelous!" Hannah exclaimed, turning to Batani.

"Two of the other men are mine," he informed them. "Let us sit here and talk, rather than run around the city looking for privacy that probably doesn't exist. We will have the advantage of seeing first anyone who would surprise us, and what I have to propose to your superiors will not, in any event, take that long to relate."

So, they sat around the small table looking over one another's shoulders into the distance before becoming totally absorbed by Batani's proposal.

"Both Russia and the United States," the Taliban leader began, "are vitally interested in suppressing the production of opium poppies in Afghanistan. Russia would like simply to continuously eradicate the crops, as they did after invading the country in 1979. The Americans, however, have now come to the conclusion that eradication does not work in the longer term, and have urged the world focus on prevention and treatment campaigns.

"We do not agree," Estefimov interjected, "but Moscow does not wish to take direct action, which would involve us in America's adventure in Afghanistan. We have had enough of that."

"The truth is," Batani continued, "that neither of your countries is in a position to implement a practical strategy for getting rid of the heroin because neither of you has lasting control of the land and the people involved. The Americans could do it, if they wished to frequently send helicopters over the poppy fields to spray them with herbicides, but that is no longer their strategy, as I've said. My proposal is that I serve as your agent for gathering the poppies produced, which I would turn over to you for destruction."

The simplicity of Batani's proposal left the others speechless, as they rapidly considered its implications.

"How would you propose to accomplish that?" Hannah asked.

"It would be relatively easy," Batani shrugged. "These are my people, and will deal with me before any foreign drug trafficker, particularly when I offer them a fair price and a consistent income. They could continue to grow the poppies, as they wished, but it would be safer and more profitable to sell them to me than to the foreigners. Gradually, I would wean our peasants to other crops by paying them more for those than I do for the poppies. Our farmers and district leaders are not international businessmen or narcotics kingpins. They would be glad of a reasonable and steady income from someone they know in their own country. They would also be assured that the drugs themselves were going to be destroyed, so they will not have violated outstanding fatwas."

"Where will you get the funds?" Estefimov wanted to know.

"From you and the Americans, of course. The traffickers now pay the growers very little for their poppies. I would pay them more, but it would still be far less than you and the rest of the world pay annually to combat heroin and its effects."

"What about the drug traffickers now being supplied? They would surely cause trouble," Hannah noted.

"I would need your help there as well. I know where the people managing the trafficking business are to be found in Afghanistan, just as I'm sure the Russian security services know where they are in Tajikistan and the other border states. I possess a supply of the transponders used in your recent drone operations against the fighters harassing the Chinese construction sites, and would undertake to have them installed in the houses and vehicles of the key drug traffickers in Afghanistan. You would then be able to kill them with your missiles."

Hannah and the Russian general looked at each other. Although Batani's plan was simple and straightforward enough to be promising, neither of them had authorization to pass judgment on it, certainly not to give the Taliban leader assurance of support. Estefimov responded:

"We will take your proposal to our superiors. But, I for one am impressed with it." Hannah nodded agreement.

"If your leadership should agree to execute my plan," Batani added, "I would like the necessary air strikes to be carried out by aircraft now based in Russia, so that my contacts in Pakistan are not implicated."

Their conversation was, at that point, interrupted by a commotion that had broken out at the edge of the park near where several of the minders were posted. One of them came running in their direction as what sounded like shots were heard in the background. Nearing the group at the table, he shouted in Russian to Estefimov who immediately rose and told the others to follow him in the direction away from the noise. Running to the opposite edge of the small park, they reached the curb just as an armored SUV with the CIA driver pulled up. Turning to the others, Hannah asked: "Can I give you a lift, gentlemen?"

CHAPTER FOURTEEN

"Do we know where Hannah is?" Philip Bergen asked of James Detwiler and Sam Glover at the beginning of the early morning conference call they had made standard practice since the Admiral's move to the West Wing. Every morning at 0700, the White House operator rang the three and linked their office or secure cellular phones for a brief session to coordinate their day's schedules and make sure that all were aware of anything new that had occurred during the night.

"She's at home, hopefully asleep," Glover replied. "I had our security people meet her plane at Dulles at 3 AM, expedite her through Customs, and drive her home. She called me from the car, sounding completely out of it. The security guys told me this morning that she looked like crap. Can you die from jet lag?"

"Next time we ask her to do something like this, we need to assign her a plane, whether her grade rates it or not," Detwiler resolved.

"We could promote her," Glover offered. "She mumbled something last night, half asleep, about how Mahmud al-Fasal treats her better than we do."

"But, if we promote her," Bergen noted, "she will then be too senior for us to send on missions where we can later deny she had the authority to commit us to something we don't want to be held to."

"She did tell me," Glover reported, "that Batani has a very interesting proposal. I told her to get some sleep and to meet us at your office, Phil, late this afternoon, if that's okay? By the way, I got an email from our Station Chief in Dushanbe saying that Hannah's meeting with Batani and Estefimov was apparently attacked by parties unknown. They think it was either Muslim extremists or drug traffickers, which doesn't help much."

By six that evening, Hannah was somewhat restored (at least visually), her recovery delayed by failure to find messages from Paul Rayner on her answering machine. As she related the details of Mir Batani Khan's proposed intervention in the Afghani opium poppy trade to her triumvirate of bosses, Hannah wondered whether the absence of attempted contact by Paul meant that he was now comfortable with their strange relationship or that he had given up on it?

"What do you think?" Bergen asked of the others, when Hannah had finished. "Do I take this to the President?"

"Seems to me that the first question we need to answer is whether or not Batani is capable of delivering on his commitment," James Detwiler responded. "He calls himself the head of the Afghani Taliban, and we oblige him, but he is unlike any Taliban we've ever known. He's made himself leader by killing off many of his rivals or, more often, getting us to do it for him. One of the principal unifying elements of the Taliban, we've been led to believe, is religious extremism. Batani has shown little evidence of even being a Muslim, much less an Islamist fanatic."

They all looked to Hannah, who yawned as she nodded in agreement.

"I'm pretty sure Batani is a Muslim, but of the Mahmud al-Fasal variety. When I saw him in Paris and Dushanbe, he looked and dressed like a young Omar Sharif doing business development for a major multinational. Although born and raised in Afghanistan, he's spent little time there as an adult until recently. He's bright, charming and very well-spoken, definitely leadership material."

Hannah felt herself blushing as she spoke, and wondered whether the others had noticed.

"You omitted ruthless and cunning from his list of quals," Sam Glover added. "He's playing a very dangerous game, and may very well end up dead before all this is over."

"Just our kind of guy," Detwiler laughed. "But, assuming the Russians agree, I don't see any reason why we shouldn't give him a shot. The most it could cost us is killing some people we would like to have killed anyway and a bunch of dollars down the drain, something we are more than used to."

"I agree," Bergen nodded. "I particularly like Batani's request that the drones in Russia, both ours and the Russians', be used to strike the traffickers. That will further mask the sponsorship of the strikes, an ability that may be of use to us later on. It would also remind the Pakistanis again that we have alternatives to purchasing their good will."

He looked at the others and saw no disagreement.

"After I run it by the President, Jim, I'll ask you to arrange it with the Russians. If they won't play, we don't."

As Hannah was leaving the White House, her phone rang. It was the Operations Center Watch Officer: "Ms Crossman, we have Mir Batani Khan on the line. He wishes to speak with you."

"I am glad to hear that you've returned home safely, Hannah. I'm just calling to tell you how much I enjoyed our evening together in Dushanbe, and will not take much of your time. It would be interesting to hear the reaction of your superiors to my proposal, but I would not presume on your discretion."

"I also enjoyed our dinner together, Mr. Batani."

"I thought we had agreed that you would call me Mike?"

"I don't recall such an agreement, but the alternatives don't seem promising."

"Both of us should work on a pretext to meet again soon. If you delay too long, I shall create a major problem here in Afghanistan and insist that you are the only one to solve it. That way, facilitating our next meeting would become a vital national interest of the United States."

"I will work on it, Mike," Hannah told him, and blushed again.

Kingsley Yong was in a very good mood. His business development efforts on behalf of the Chinese Government were going well, and he had been given an unexpected bonus on his last visit to Beijing. Even better, he was just coming off a two week vacation during which he did absolutely nothing but hang out, virtually incommunicado, at his parents California home, going to the beach during the day and napping on the living room sofa in the evening. Just not having to go to airports and make interminable trips in planes was itself a major break for him. Perhaps best of all, the Chinese mining and railroad venture in southern Afghanistan had finally begun to progress at a rate that kept his employers in Beijing off his back. At some risk to his safety, Yong had chosen to personally deliver to Mir Batani Khan his next payment of protection money, rather than wire-transfer the funds to Batani's bank as usual. He had been picked up at the international airport in Kabul by three men he later described as thugs in police or army uniforms, and taken blindfolded to a location outside the city, where Batani met him to receive his stipend. Despite the fear and rough handling, Yong felt his trip had been worthwhile, inasmuch as it had emphasized to the Taliban leader Beijing's concern about his performance. It had also gotten him a detailed briefing of Batani's capabilities and activities. It was impossible to verify the accuracy of what he had been told, but Beijing was impressed that Yong had taken the trouble and accepted the risk involved.

What Batani had apparently done was to outsource protection of the mining and construction sites to the very militants who had been attacking them, paying them with the funds Yong had given him and additional sums he must have gathered from other donors. His success in getting the Americans to kill off his rivals had so impressed and scared remaining opponents that they became receptive to his seemingly naïve argument that it would be possible for them to earn enormous returns with little effort or risk by pretending to guard the construction sites from themselves. Once they found that what Batani had told them was largely true, their joy and admiration was increased many fold by the sly knowledge that they were putting a big one over on the infidel foreigners.

Their sentiments were not shared, however, by General Pervez Orkamzi of the Pakistani ISI, who found himself caught in a growing dilemma. He had been one of Batani's original sponsors and had introduced him to Abdul Rashid and the CIA, both now sources of the funds Batani was using to dominate the insurgents of his country and secure his independence from Pakistan and Orkamzi. Of even greater significance, was that the Americans had begun to see in Batani an instrument for pursuing their aims in Afghanistan without first securing the assent and cooperation of the Pakistani government and military high command.

Influence in Afghanistan was critical to Pakistan's future security and prosperity, whether as a democracy or an Islamist dictatorship. Orkamzi and his superiors were realists enough to recognize the essential weakness of their country's long term position: resources insufficient to underwrite the improvement in living standards demanded by a large population that continued to grow rapidly and was already dissatisfied. They also acknowledged, at least in private, that Pakistan's most valuable current asset was her ability to cause trouble regionally and beyond, and to exploit that facility in order to extract international assistance, principally from the United States. But, a serious war with India could not be won, and might result in Pakistan's destruction, a certainty if nuclear weapons came into play. China had been a long-term ally, but mainly because Beijing had seen Pakistan as a counterweight to India and, therefore, to America. But, contention between Pakistan and China over access to and control of resources in Afghanistan could change that to the detriment of Islamabad's interests. Finally, there was the porous border with Iran, already the site of clashes between Shiite and Sunni bands supported by their national governments.

After centuries of abuse by Asian and European invaders, Afghanistan was quite possibly on the verge of a great renaissance initiated, of all things, by a comprehensive resource survey sponsored altruistically by the U.S. Department of Defense. The critical determinant would be the ability of the government in Kabul to effectively manage the coming economic boom and to keep the inevitable greed and corruption from thwarting realization of its promise. Thus far, the auguries had not been encouraging.

Enter Batani. In a relatively short time, he had significantly reduced the dissension and warfare within the country, largely by killing off many of his rivals and bribing others in the name of peace and industrial development. Thinking about it, General Orkamzi could not decide whether the Taliban leader would ultimately be viewed as a national hero or an arch villain, but either way was becoming a major pain in the ass for Pakistan. The ISI chief knew that his own future was tied inversely to Batani's, but did not know at the moment how to proceed. He could have Batani killed, but that would create chaos in Afghanistan and mightily piss off the Americans, probably Abdul Rashid as well. Instead, Orkamzi reviewed his personal escape plan for, perhaps, the three hundredth time. He had money stashed in accounts overseas, false passports and identification papers, and a tacit promise from Mahmud al-Fasal of a comfortable asylum somewhere in Europe or Turkey, should he have to leave Pakistan unwillingly. Finally, he looked in his office desk to check the loaded pistol that was his ultimate precaution.

When *Oberling For America* was announced and proclaimed its mission and the importance of achieving it, Reggie Huggins began to understand what was going to be expected of him and Global Security Applications LLC. He recalled Oberling's activities during the Tucker Administration. But one pays little attention to a Vice President unless he somehow screws up or, heaven forbid, succeeds unexpectedly to the top job. Oberling's name had been far more prominent during his losing run against Mason Kitteridge, but Reggie was busy at the time getting his company started and doing overseas chores for early clients. The election post-mortem by the Vice President's backers had, in fact, concluded that too many voters who might very well have voted for him were not paying attention. Resolved not to let that happen again, OFA hit the ground running with its criticism of President Kitteridge, establishing Oberling's agenda for change within the first week of what was going to be a long campaign.

Sam Glover's warning in mind, Huggins arrived for the first Oberling strategy session, and was told by Roger Norton to sit unobtrusively against a wall and to simply listen to what the candidate and his senior advisors were considering. Norton would meet with Reggie afterward to put what he had heard into perspective, as well as to translate it into tasking for Global Security Applications. Oberling had segmented his campaign brain trust into three parts: Domestic Social and Political, Economics, and Foreign Affairs/Homeland Security, the last transcending the domestic-foreign divide in recognition of the terrorist threat. This was the segment Reggie Huggins was attending.

Alfred Oberling chaired the meeting in person, since it involved the area of Presidential affairs in which he felt Mason Kitteridge most vulnerable. Huggins counted fourteen people present, in addition to the candidate, Norton, and himself. All were middle-aged, prosperous-looking men wearing business suits. When each introduced himself at the outset, Reggie learned that those who were not head of a substantial company---determined by the fact that Reggie Huggins had heard of it---were senior members of one or another of the not-for-profit think tanks that abound in the Washington area. Oberling introduced Reggie as "Mr. Huggins, late of the CIA, who is advising us on strategy and action in the war on terror." When he heard that, Reggie thought again of Sam Glover's threat.

"The Kitteridge Administration," Oberling began, "has failed to answer---or even adequately address---the questions that are foremost among the concerns of the American people: where is the mess in which we're involved in Southwest Asia and the Middle East taking us, and when is it going to end. These, I believe, are the issues our campaign needs to focus on."

"But, Alfred," a member of the group was quick to interject, "our opponents are likely to argue that, as Number Two man in the Tucker Administration, you were as responsible for our being in this mess as anyone."

"You are right!" Oberling responded. "They will charge that, and a lot worse. But, recriminations don't get you very far in an election. The voters want to know how we plan to handle today's and tomorrow's problems, not yesterday's. After we bailed out of Vietnam, I don't recall anyone complaining later that Nixon abandoned the country to the Communists. It is virtually certain that our outlook on the Muslim world is going to change in the not distant future. The questions for us now are: one, what changes in relationships do we anticipate and, two, how do we propose to deal with them. How we present to the voters our analysis and plans for continuing to keep America safe will, as much as anything, determine our prospects of winning the election."

The others at the conference table nodded agreement, but Roger Norton reminded them that agreeing what the issues were was the easy part. They would probably find similar views in the strategy sessions that President Kitteridge had undoubtedly begun to hold. The coming election campaign would hinge, however, on which of the contending parties had the most convincing prescription for moving forward. Alfred Oberling asked the director of one of the nation's most influential think tanks to brief the group.

"There are three major forces currently at work in the Muslim world," he began. "The first is the rebirth and expansion of Islamic fundamentalism. There is already an aggressive, fundamentalist regime in Iran and the potential for more in countries like Pakistan, Yemen, Somalia, and Afghanistan. You all know the threats we already face from extremists hiding in these countries. It could become much worse, if the terrorists can claim the full support and resources of their governments. Beyond that, lies the possibility of extremists succeeding in a country that has a critical role in world affairs, such as a major oil producer. We might have to intervene directly to prevent such a development.

"The second major force is the continuing popular unrest that has swept Muslim countries in North Africa and the Middle East, and may very well spread further. Many observers in the West have labeled this a pro-democracy movement, but it is basically a drive for a more promising economic future. An extraordinary percentage of the population in Muslim countries is very young, under 30, increasingly better educated, and without jobs or the promise of one. They blame the greed, corruption, and ineptitude of their current dictatorial regimes, in power for many years, and have succeeded in toppling a number of them. Problem is that the rebels do not have the wherewithal to implement lasting, more effective governments. In addition, it is not clear that every one of these countries, Pakistan comes to mind, will ever have the resources and infrastructure needed to support their large and growing populations on a level comparable to developed countries in the West and Asia.

"The third major factor is the struggle of existing political and economic establishments in the Muslim world to maintain themselves against the other two major forces. At the center of this struggle are Saudi Arabia and the Gulf states, which have the substantial advantages of oil wealth and relatively small populations. Because of this, however, they are the ultimate targets of Islamic extremist movements, such as al-Qaeda. The Saudi monarchy, probably the most religiously conservative regime in the world, has attempted for years to play on all sides, looking to the U.S. for protection while devoting huge sums of money to fundamentalist causes. Its perceived rationale for doing that has become increasingly less viable.

"In Pakistan, which is poorly endowed with resources, the struggle is between Islamist fundamentalists and the educated, largely secular, middle class and military establishment which are arguably that country's greatest assets. Should Pakistan fall to extremist rule, the impact on world affairs would likely be enormous, even without consideration of that country's nuclear weapons."

There was silence in the room as the speaker waited for his audience's reaction. Finally, the candidate asked the think tank director an obvious question.

"Given the complexity of the situation, and the variety of potential outcomes (none particularly great), what are your thoughts as to positions *Oberling For America* ought to take and actions we should recommend?"

"I'm afraid, sir, that I haven't the foggiest idea at this point," he replied. "I'm sure that President Kitteridge and his advisors are dealing with much the same analysis and view of prospects. My recommendation to you, from a tactical standpoint, would be to say nothing at this time. For the moment, this is the Administration's tar baby: let them deal with it. There will be time for us to pounce when they make mistakes, as I'm sure they will."

CHAPTER FIFTEEN

The small house in Kandahar Province stood at the edge of poppy fields now denuded of the distinctive long-stemmed bulbs. The recent harvest over, growers were preparing to ship their produce northward, their progress closely monitored by agents of the traffickers who would transport the opium base across international boundaries, convert it into heroin, and sell it on the insatiable world market.

Although its few windows and door were open, the house was stifling hot, with almost forty men squeezed into its largest room. Almost all were poppy growers from the surrounding district who had come at the summons of Mir Batani Khan principally because they feared the consequences of not showing up. There was also more than a little curiosity to hear what the increasingly fearsome Taliban leader wanted of them. Batani entered the house without the expected heavily armed guard and climbed onto a stool in a corner of the room.

"My brothers! I will not detain you long, lest we all dissolve into pools of sweat. I wish to congratulate you on another bountiful crop, which your customers in the north are eagerly awaiting. I also wish you to know that I am prepared to buy your produce at prices greater than what the foreigners are now paying you, and without the fees, bribes and other deductions usually taken from your payments. I can also assure you that no drugs produced from your crops will addict the people of Afghanistan or other children of Islam."

When Batani paused, the room erupted as all of the assembled farmers began talking to one another at the same time, turning frequently to stare at the Taliban chieftain, who reached into his robe and withdrew a handful of small gold coins that he dropped on a table in front of him, where they lay glittering in the light of a lantern hanging overhead. Batani repeated this maneuver again and again, until there was a substantial pile of the coins, each about the size of an American dime, lying before him.

The effect of the gold was opposite to that of Batani's purchase offer: the farmers fell quiet as they watched the pile of coins grow, and they strained to hear what he was going to say next.

"Many of you have daughters for whom you would like to have fine dowries that will attract worthy husbands. Some have sons for whom you would wish worthy brides. Others of you have many sons and many daughters, and do not know how you will do right by all of them."

The room was filled with knowing laughter, and Batani chose that moment to pull from another pocket a bracelet and necklace made from the same coins attached to gold chains.

"Picture your daughters and your brides wearing these on their wedding days and you will know what to do. Each of you shall today receive one of these gold coins as a token of my friendship and good will, whether you choose to sell your crops to me or not."

The next morning, Batani assembled a well-guarded fleet of trucks in the center of a nearby village, and waited to see whether his pitch had worked. At first, only a few wagons appeared, but the word quickly spread that the elders approved, and there was soon a long line of vehicles waiting to transfer their cargoes into the trucks. Batani had set up a table, in a location visible to all, where he settled accounts with those who had brought him their poppies, handing out both currency and gold. A celebration ensued among the farmers, but the many fighters brought along by Batani for security stood nervously looking for signs of retribution. Surely, the drug traffickers already knew what was occurring and would be compelled to react rapidly and violently.

But the remainder of the day and night passed uneventfully and, by noon the following day, all the trucks had been filled and the remaining farmers told to return with their merchandise two days hence. The trucks were formed up in a line, with a pickup truck armed with a heavy machine gun or recoilless rifle in between each, and strong forces of armed vehicles in front and rear; their destination a compound in Kandahar City. Batani himself rode in a truck at the center of the convoy, coordinating its movement via walkie-talkie, the immediate task being to cover the forty odd miles before dark.

The assumption that the traffickers would know what was happening was both obvious and correct. Among the locals eager to share in Batani's largesse were those who hedged their bets by tipping off the people with whom they had done business in the past as to what was transpiring. The latter were infuriated, as were those up the chain whom they supplied. A plan was quickly developed to intercept the convoy when it passed through the mountains en route to Kandahar City. Its objective was not simply to regain control of the opium product but, more important, to teach an unforgettable lesson to anyone who would even consider messing with what the traffickers considered theirs. The organization's chief overseer for Afghanistan was directed to go to Kandahar to oversee the intercept operation, and he ordered his subordinates into the mountains to make sure that everything went as planned.

A narrow pass through low foothills was chosen as the site of attack because the roadway could easily be blocked to prevent the convoy from moving while its protectors were being picked off. The attacking fighters, who normally provided security for drug shipments and the warehouse in Kandahar City that served as the traffickers local headquarters, were reminded again and again that the trucks and their cargoes were not to be damaged. The attackers were already on station when advised that the convoy had departed for Kandahar City.

Progress was slow: the trucks heavily laden and the road narrow and unpaved. Batani was certain they would be attacked, the only question being where. He devoted his attention to keeping the convoy from becoming strung out along the road, and was caught off guard when a series of explosions erupted some distance ahead of the lead vehicle causing all to stop. To the drivers' surprise, however, Batani ordered them to keep moving forward, even after another, closer series of explosions. He also ordered the fighters escorting the trucks to push out along the road ahead of the convoy. A few minutes later, the sounds of small arms fire and screams of pain and anger replaced the explosions. Eventually, the convoy inched past what was obviously the site of the explosions and skirmishing. It was littered with bodies, and the sounds of gunfire from the gullies and bush flanking the road told Batani that his men were taking no prisoners. The Russian drones had done their job, and the convoy passed through to its destination undamaged.

A still adrenalized Batani described all of this in minute detail to Hannah, half asleep after being awakened by the Operations Center Duty Officer in the middle of the night. The plan he had outlined to her and Esefimov in Dushanbe was working perfectly. The boss of the traffickers in Afghanistan had been standing in a group outside his warehouse in Kandahar listening to the explosions in the distance when a single missile had done for them. Batani didn't know whether it had come from a Russian drone or an American one. Neither did General Pervez Orkamkzi when he got the report a short time afterward.

"The gold coins are a nice touch, Mike," Hannah told him. "I hope you plan to continue them."

"Oh, yes! I've laid in a large supply. They are Canadian five-dollar Maple Leaf coins I obtained through one of Mahmud al-Fasal's trading companies. He and Abdul Rashid are being very helpful, although I don't believe they knew the purpose for which I wanted the coins."

Hannah relayed Batani's report to Bergen, Detwiler, and Glover during their morning conference call, apologizing for the occasional yawn. "I seem to be operating on Kabul time these days," she explained.

"Batani's done well," Detwiler, the new Director of National Intelligence opined, "but this is just beginning. The traffickers are not going to give up 90% of the world's heroin supply. From now on, Batani will be a target of both the drug lords and the Islamist fanatics. He will need an army to watch his back."

"On the other hand," Admiral Bergen noted, "he's now got twenty or more million dollars worth of opium base to peddle to the Russians or the DEA, and there's a lot more where that came from.

Sam Glover and Naomi Benson were married one Sunday in a small ceremony performed by a Navy chaplain friend of Philip Bergen's. Neither bride nor groom had relatives or childhood friends they wished to invite, other than Naomi's grown daughter, Nancy, so the wedding party except for the wives looked a lot like a gathering in the director's office of an Intelligence Community agency. Charlotte Bergen remarked, only half in jest, that she was surprised Sam hadn't held the wedding in the CIA cafeteria.

Following the formalities, a small reception was held at the Fort McNair Officers Club, after which the newlyweds went home. There were no plans for a honeymoon because the groom, unbeknownst to his bride, was preparing to leave covertly for Europe, with Admiral Bergen and James Detwiler, to meet with Abdul Rashid for an important review of threat perceptions and strategy. Neither he nor Detwiler had as yet met the reclusive jihadi strategist.

Hannah brought Paul Rayner to the wedding, after making him swear that there would be no leak to the media (The Washington Post noted the event three days afterward in a squib in the Style section). Paul considered the invitation a good omen in his relationship with Hannah, and was overjoyed. The new Mrs. Glover took Hannah aside at the reception to register approval of Paul, whom she hadn't previously met.

"You look like hell, Hannah," she added. "You can't make up all at once for lost opportunity. Get some sleep!"

Hannah laughed. "Actually, I think I'm dying of terminal jet lag, and it's the fault of your husband among others. Not only do they send me to far off places to meet very strange people, but those strange people keep calling in the middle of the night, even after I get back. I wish I had the time and energy to make up for lost opportunity."

"The solution," Naomi responded, "is to hook up with a spook, like I did. He'll be so concerned about breaching security that you will spend all of your time in bed, and never leave the house."

CHAPTER SIXTEEN

Abdul Rashid left his Paris home for the first time since occupying it fifteen years earlier. It was testimony to the depth of his depression over the parlous state of his affairs that the departure had actually been his own idea, which had both surprised and shocked Mahmud al-Fasal. In retrospect, al-Fasal had seen some kind of break coming, but would not have guessed that his severely handicapped employer would leave his beloved home and loyal staff. One day, however, Abdul Rashid told al-Fasal that he was no longer able to think straight, that he had found himself discovering as new ideas discarded weeks earlier as unworkable. A complete change was needed. Abdul Rashid was finding himself caught in the realities of developing events in the Muslim world, which seemed to be arguing for a strategy opposite to the one he was being paid to pursue. His efforts to maneuver between the extremes and to hedge his bets had yielded little progress, and his endowment of operating funds had begun to shrink as some of his sponsors reconsidered their investment, while others lost their positions of power and wealth to persistent, chanting mobs.

It was resolved that Abdul Rashid would be moved to Mahmud al-Fasal's home in the South of France, where his mood and health could benefit from the sun and fresh air. With typical efficiency, al-Fasal removed Abdul Rashid from his Paris compound in a specially equipped van to a nearby French military airfield into which he had been permitted to bring his jet transport in return for having advised the security services of his employer's intended relocation. This arrangement provided much greater privacy and security than having to depart from Charles DeGaulle airport. Immediately following the departure of the van from Abdul Rashid's garage, a second truck loaded the furnishings and contents of his private study for express shipment to al-Fasal's villa, although it was unknown how long Abdul Rashid would be staying there. By dawn of the next day, he had been installed in the master suite of al-Fasal's seaside home, to sleep in the darkened bedroom through most of the day.

Admiral Bergen, scheduled to visit Abdul Rashid with James Detwiler and Sam Glover, was pleasantly surprised when told that the meeting had been shifted from Paris to the villa overlooking the Mediterranean. It was decided to add Hannah Crossman to their party, inasmuch as she was already slated to attend a meeting of al-Fasal's intelligence contacts at the villa after her seniors departed for home. The group left Washington on Saturday morning to take advantage of an invitation by al-Fasal to spend Sunday recuperating from their journey on his much-admired pool terrace. Abdul Rashid had not been outside his home in fifteen years, and could not immediately avail himself of the amenities offered by the French Riviera because he was unaccustomed to full daylight, especially sunshine. Even dark glasses did not suffice, and the American visitors were forced to join him, on Sunday afternoon, in al-Fasal's darkened study, which had been refurnished to replicate Abdul Rashid's Paris sanctorum. Since their meeting would consider matters above her pay grade, Hannah put on her YWCA swim suit and went to the pool.

"By tomorrow, hopefully, my eyes will have adjusted, and I will be able to join you outdoors, gentlemen. I greatly appreciate your indulgence and cooperation in coming all this way to chat with me," Abdul Rashid told them, as they awkwardly collapsed onto the cushions set on the floor before his now familiar low table. His major domo, brought from Paris with the furnishings, offered tea and---with Mahmud al-Fasal's customary thoughtfulness---single-malt scotch for the infidels.

"I am very happy to meet you, Monsieurs Detwiler and Glover, and congratulate you on your appointments. Hopefully, our relationship will be as productive and mutually stimulating as the one Admiral Bergen and I have enjoyed these past several years.

"I am particularly pleased that we shall be able to discuss, in person, a critical challenge concerning which, even after long and intense consideration and such consultation as I could safely venture, I cannot decide upon a strategic direction in which I would have confidence. I tell you this only because I am willing to wager much of my sponsors' money that you are facing the same dilemma from your perspective. If we cannot muddle through this together, perhaps we can at least avoid unnecessary casualties."

"What is it that's troubling you, sir?" Bergen responded. "Perhaps we can indeed help one another once again."

Abdul Rashid adjusted his glasses and took a sip of tea before turning to Mahmud al-Fasal: "Do you think God would indulge me this once and permit some of that whiskey?" The others laughed, and the tension was broken.

"I have been watching on television," Abdul Rashid (glass now in hand) began, "the protests occurring all over the Muslim world. What strikes me about the people you see crowding the squares and avenues is that they are mostly children, maybe in their early twenties, and I find it very difficult to believe they are demonstrating for a greater role in their lives for Islam. I see the police and military attacking them to protect those in power and to prevent the upheaval from expanding beyond the ability of the government to control. The demonstrators shout for democracy, but what they want mostly is something different from what they have now: a more promising future. The disorder may eventually run its course, but the people who created and supported it will still be there, and they will not remain quiet. My problem, gentlemen, is determining who represents the true jihad."

"We are having somewhat the same problem, as I'm sure you suspected," Admiral Bergen commented wryly. "Our analysts have also observed the youthful character of the protestors, as well as the rarity of clerical participation and Islamist propaganda. But virtually all of the protests have focused on getting rid of existing regimes and ruling elites. We've seen very little about what and who would replace them, and are very concerned about the creation of power vacuums that would provide opportunities for the extremists to whom you and we are opposed."

Abdul Rashid smiled. "We apparently share that perception as well. You fear a repetition of what happened in Iran when the Shah's ruling apparatus was immediately replaced by Khomeni's, including all-important control of the military and internal security forces. There was virtually no opportunity then to oppose the establishment of a theocratic dictatorship. However, things have changed since 1979, and it is no longer certain that money, power, and military strength will guarantee success in suppressing a revolution, as I am learning. The single most significant reason for that, I believe, is the radical improvement in public communications, specifically the mobile telephone and the Internet. It seems that every young person I see, no matter where in the world, appears to possess the latest model mobile phone, even though he or she is wearing ragged clothing and might appear half-starved. The ability to communicate information and pictures to thousands, even millions, of people almost instantaneously, wherever they might be, is the operational equivalent of a mass demonstration in a central square. A resisting regime may shut down the telephone system and Internet access, but such moves are ultimately self-defeating because they, in effect, disrupt the entire country and spread discontent far beyond the actual protestors. Even I, I'm told, receive more than a hundred email messages each week."

"You look surprised, gentlemen," al-Fasal interjected. "Abdul Rashid does, in fact, have an electronic mail account, although he has never been anywhere near a computer or a mobile phone. One of my assistants monitors the traffic, which often contains useful reports from our agents and collaborators around in the world. You will be interested in knowing, Mr. Glover, that we recently received an inquiry from the gentleman I called you about several months ago---Mr. Huggins I believe. He professed interest in connecting with Abdul Rashid on something called Linked-In."

Admiral Bergen stared at Sam Glover, who smiled sheepishly and shrugged. James Detwiler brought the discussion back to the principal subject.

"What we are most concerned about, of course, is what happens after the mob in the square succeeds in toppling its government in the name of democracy and a better life. Perhaps we are being cynical, but it would appear that the prospect of such improvements in the Muslim countries currently under great stress is at best limited and perhaps unlikely. We are concerned about the creation of power vacuums---even where the military restores or maintains order---that could be filled by extremists in the name of Islam. Pakistan, Yemen, and Somalia are the most worrisome, at the moment. The creation of an extremist-ruled state that could be used as a base for exporting terrorism and upheaval could substantially change the fundamentals of international relations."

Abdul Rashid reached for his worry beads before responding. He had obviously pondered this issue.

"I, of course, am not as concerned as you are about the prospective establishment of fundamentalist Islamic states. It is actually what I have been employed to promote. I believe, however, that fundamentalists should not be extremists and, in that regard, I share your concern. Leaders whose eyes and attention are focused on heaven alarm me, because they are not truly concerned about the welfare of their people and because one never knows what they might do in the name of God. This conflict between my duty and my belief has been causing me much pain."

"What are your thoughts about what we might do together to combat the extremists?" Admiral Bergen asked.

Abdul Rashid rocked forward and back, then took a sip of whisky while framing his answer.

"We Muslims are united only when facing a common outside enemy: the most useful being one who is both a foreigner and an infidel. Otherwise, we will eventually succumb to the age-old sectarian conflicts, of which Sunni versus Shia is only the best known. You Americans help the extremists, obviously unwillingly and unintentionally, by being that outside enemy. What they say about you in the mosques is mostly untrue, but the imams say it very convincingly; it is their trade."

"You are saying, then," Bergen reacted, "that, if we went home, the extremists would leave us alone?"

"Unfortunately, it is not that straightforward," Mahmud al-Fasal volunteered. "Because you are so valuable as a scapegoat, the radical imams will make up calumnies as needed. And then, there is always your support of Israel."

"So, what can usefully be done?" Sam Glover asked.

Abdul Rashid took another sip of whisky and wiped his forehead.

"The extremists' first goal is to gain control of the resources of the Muslim world, principally the oil wealth of Saudi Arabia and the Gulf States. They would use the wealth and power gained to extend their dogma throughout the Muslim world and to influence events in the world as a whole. What you must do, to answer Mr. Glover's question, is to defend those vital areas at all costs. Without them, the extremists cannot win. You, as well, will not be able to win, but you will also not lose."

Abdul Rashid fell silent and became absorbed in his worry beads. Realizing that the meeting was at an end, the others left the darkened room for the bright sunshine of the terrace, and the sight of Hannah in her aged tank suit.

After a fine meal prepared by al-Fasal's chef, brandy, cigars, and a lengthy review of world affairs in the cool sea breeze on the terrace, Admiral Bergen went to bed, only to be awakened in the small hours of the morning by the ringing of his satellite cell phone.

"This is the White House operator. The President's Chief of Staff wishes to speak with you, Admiral Bergen."

"You're up late, Dee!"

"It's not yet nine in the evening here, Admiral. The President wanted me to advise you that Alfred Oberling appeared this evening on the television show *American Focus*, and outlined the strategy he would adopt to deal with Muslim extremism, should he be elected. If all else fails, he said that he would go for an all-out containment strategy that would isolate extremist-ruled countries from the West. He used Pakistan as an example."

"Sounds like our Cold War approach to the Communists all over again."

"The people you're visiting will probably not yet be aware of the program, but the President wanted you to know about it, in the event they did bring it up. As you know, we are not yet prepared to comment on the issue."

But, by breakfast the next morning, Abdul Rashid and Mahmut al-Fasal had seen a transcript of Oberling's interiew prepared by the latter's staff in Paris and emailed to the villa. A courtesy copy was on the breakfast table at the place of each American. Abdul Rashid surprised everyone by coming to the long, ornate table in the sunny dining room, although his dark glasses seemed to do little to relieve his discomfort. He had come specifically to discuss the Oberling interview.

"Is this course of action being seriously considered in America?"

"Many possible courses of action are being considered," Admiral Bergen replied noncommittally. As the President's personal representative, he spoke for the three Americans present.

"What concerns us most," he continued, "are the fanatics traveling around the world plotting to kill large numbers of innocent people and causing permanent disruptions in all aspects of daily life, both domestic and international. At present, these murderers operate at least semi-covertly within the countries in which they are located. We shudder at the prospect of their becoming officially sanctioned and supported by the rise of regimes that reflect their extremist ideologies. Whatever responses are adopted, we are not likely to tolerate such developments."

"I completely understand, Admiral, why the United States would react strongly to such threats. But, do you think that a containment defense would be effective? I am aware that it served reasonably well during the Cold War, but the relationship between the West and the Soviet Union was radically different from that between Muslim extremists and what they consider to be the infidel world."

Bergen smiled wryly. "There is no obviously good strategy. One of the principal reasons containment is being considered is that it is the least drastic or violent of the options perceived to be available to us at this time. I share your concern as to how effective it could be. But, let me ask you, sir, how you view this confrontation, presumably from the opposite perspective?"

Abdul Rashid grimaced involuntarily---he normally did not show emotion.

"I am even more conflicted than you are, gentlemen," he admitted. "I fear, ironically, that success would bring disaster, that the victory of what you call Islamic extremism would irretrievably rend the fabric of civilization that holds the world together. His voice heavy with regret, Abdul Rashid abruptly swiveled his wheelchair around and quickly left the room, followed immediately by Mahmud al-Fasal, who returned shortly thereafter.

"Abdul Rashid apologizes; the sunlight was bothering his eyes,"

James Detwiler intervened to move the table conversation beyond the awkward moment. "While we are here, Mr. al-Fasal, it would be useful to discuss the status and prospects of yours and our relationships with Mir Batani Khan in Afghanistan. Since you so kindly arranged for our Ms. Crossman to attend yours and General Orkamzi's meeting with him in Pakistan, there have been a number of very interesting developments, which we consider quite promising. What is your view?"

He nodded toward Hannah, who had been studiously concentrating on her croissant and coffee throughout the preceding discussion. Mahmud al-Fasal reflexively looked around the room to assure that everyone one present had a need-to-know, a precaution that Sam Glover noticed and appreciated.

"Batani Khan," al-Fasal began, "illustrates the dilemma to which Abdul Rashid and Admiral Bergen were referring. Interestingly enough, however, it is not because he represents the extreme of fundamentalist Islam, but rather because he potentially represents the opposite. Every student of the Islamic jihad has recognized the critical importance of developments in Pakistan to the future of not only the region, but of the entire confrontation between the Muslim and non-Muslim worlds. Of late, however, it has become apparent to Abdul Rashid that the future of Afghanistan may be equally critical, and that perception is changing our engagement strategy.

"Much of the credit for this revised analysis is due to you Americans, specifically to the detailed survey you

sponsored to assess the extent of Afghanistan's natural resources, the immediate effect of which has been to elevate
the economic potential of Afghanistan over that of Pakistan, except that the former's lack of a stable and effective
national infrastructure and, of course, the continuing hostilities are greatly retarding progress. Ironically, Pakistan
has more infrastructure than it needs but relatively few resources, while Afghanistan now appears to be overflowing
with potential riches, but lacks the infrastructure needed
to realize them.

"We now know enough about Batani Khan to assess
his capabilities as being considerable. He is undeniably intelligent; but, more than that, he is resourceful. The tactics
whereby he has succeeded thus far have often been brilliant, and his broader objectives strike us as logical and
realistic. Beyond that, he is ruthless in eliminating his opposition or getting you Americans to do it for him. Batani
has visited us in Paris to consult with Abdul Rashid, who is
inclined to support him."

"Forgive me, sir," Bergen interjected, "but I sense a
note of hesitation in what could otherwise be considered a
ringing endorsement."

"You are very perceptive, Admiral. It is our concern
with Batani's intentions that causes us to hesitate. He is,
after all, not in our employ or yours. He obviously has
lofty goals and great pretensions, but it is not yet clear on
whose behalf he is pursuing them. Batani is a Muslim, but
it seems obvious that he is not seeking to establish an Islamic theocracy in Afghanistan, as the Shias have done in
Iran and some would do in Pakistan. If that is, in fact, the
case, he will continue to face strong opposition among the
Islamist tribes and sectarian factions of his own country,
as well the enmity of the Pakistani Taliban who espouse an
even more extreme theology. He has, thus far, been able to

cope, but his opposition will become more determined, as it becomes more desperate.

"That being said, the true reason for our hesitation is that the success Batani achieves in establishing effective control of Afghanistan must come at the expense of Pakistan, the fortunes of which concern Abdul Rashid greatly. It is has always been tacitly assumed, based on the evidence of history, that Afghanistan could never prosper on its own, but would continue to be victimized by foreign powers. Every invader coming to that country, including most recently the Soviets and now you Americans, has eventually learned that reinventing Afghanistan to their requirements is too hard and not really worth the effort and expense. Given their long common border, across which people and things have flowed virtually unimpeded for many decades, Pakistan has regarded Afghanistan as sort of a retarded brother, in need of guidance and protection, from which it could expect little reward.

"Now, Afghanistan's retardation threatens to be cured, and Batani will be seen as leading it to an independent existence at the expense of Pakistan, something that Islamabad, in particular the Army, will not tolerate. The challenges that ruin Abdul Rashid's rest, gentlemen, are determining which side he wishes to prevail and what he must do to help assure that outcome."

Paul Rayner was happy with himself, enough so that he almost forgot that Hannah had once again disappeared without warning. First, the interview of Alfred Oberling had turned out a winner, which had pleased both his boss and Olivia McQueen. Then, he had prevailed upon the network to advance the airing of the interview from its originally scheduled slot three weeks hence. The recent proclamation of *Oberling For America,* coupled with the absence of a competing sporting event or country music awards show had allowed the airing to achieve almost double *American Focus*'s normal audience. Rayner had been called by the network president in New York and told that, as a reward, he would be authorized to pursue a story of his choice and produce it as an *American Focus* segment on which he could appear as interviewer or delegate to someone like Olivia McQueen, if he chose.

The leadership of *Oberling For America* was also ecstatic, for the feedback from the interview was enormously favorable in terms of both the public's impression of the candidate and the substance of what he had said. Press reaction tended to slight the former (arguing that the public did not yet know Oberling) and fixate on the latter. The general impression expressed was that the American people were totally fed up dealing with the Pakistans and Afghanistans of the world, and would support drastic measures designed to tell them so.

"I believe the poll results and feedback we've been getting are telling us that we don't need to pull our punches about how to deal with countries that shelter and support terrorists," Oberling told his advisors. "Kitteridge is stuck with the Government's track record and we're not. The voters are tired of putting up with the crap we've been taking from the Paks, Afghanis, and Iraqis while our guys are getting killed over there and we piss away billions of dollars."

"What shall we recommend doing? Roger Norton asked. "My sources tell me that Bergen and the CIA guys are over in Europe now communing with that jihadi mastermind Huggins tried to contact a month or two ago. Could be they're working out some sort of deal."

"We should not be making deals with terrorists," Oberling reacted categorically. "I think we should expose what Kitteridge is doing and establish firmly that an Oberling administration would not deal with those bastards."

Reggie Huggins, sitting quietly in the background, was alarmed. The others were surprised when he spoke.

"I think, Mr. Oberling, that we need to be extremely careful in trying to expose covert intelligence activities. Not only can that risk our peoples' lives, but also our national security interests. The fact that we may disagree with what the Administaration is doing, doesn't necessarily make it wrong or ineffective."

Oberling stared at Huggins with obvious disdain, while Norton volunteered, with a chuckle: "Reggie is very sensitive about these things. Glover sent one of his people, a good-looking chick named Hannah Crossman, over to warn him that he risked having his balls cut off, if he made a pain-in-the-ass of himself."

"I would guess that has already happened," the candidate responded contemptuously. Later, Norton talked him out of summarily canning Huggins, pointing out that exposing classified information was against the law, and that it would be dumb to give Kitteridge an excuse to initiate a high profile Justice Department investigation of his election opponent. He prevailed upon Oberling, instead, to assign Huggins and his people to investigate the Administration's activities overseas, particularly in southwest Asia, to see whether politically useful leads could be developed.

Hannah Crossman remained at Mahmud al-Fasal's villa after her seniors left for home, awaiting the arrival of the other participants in the meeting she was to attend. She enjoyed a marvelous day in the sun being pampered by al-Fasal's staff and not having to think about the increasing danger and complexity of the international intrigues in which she was enmeshed. Al-Fasal was busy tending to Abdul Rashid, and had time only to inquire periodically whether she was wanting for anything. General Atakan of the Turkish General Staff arrived the following day, followed several hours later by Colonel Said Jafari of Iran's Revolutionary Guard. Only General Orkamzi, who had the longest distance to come, was not yet present. Al-Fasal was unwilling to begin discussions without him, so Hannah's respite was extended into another sunny day, both Atakan and Jafari proving to be very pleasant company at poolside.

Orkamzi failed to appear on the following day, however, and Mahmud al-Fasal began making inquiries in Islamabad. When none of these yielded useful insight—even sources that he knew should certainly be aware of the General's whereabouts—al-Fasal became concerned that something was amiss. Finally, he called a Taliban contact in Karachi, and asked him to check, a response coming back quickly indicating that Orkamzi had been relieved of his responsibilities and confined to quarters pending charges that he is an agent of a foreign entity, thus far unnamed. Given the circumstances, al-Fasal went ahead and assembled those present in his study to await a visit from Abdul Rashid. But, everyone was too engrossed in speculation about Orkamzi's situation to focus on al-Fasal's agenda. In particular, they wondered for whom the Pakistani general was being accused of covertly working. As all of them knew from personal experience, it could be anybody or everybody. When al-Fasal was called away to the telephone, all pretense of decorum was abandoned, and the room did not become quiet again until their host returned, after a lengthy interval, looking extremely somber.

"A highly reliable source in Pakistan tells me General Orkamzi is dead, apparently killed trying to leave the country. Speculation is that he was unable to secure a plane and attempted to go by road into Waziristan, perhaps hoping to contact Mir Batani Khan for assistance. The official report is that his vehicle was moving at a high rate of speed when it left a mountain road and dropped into a ravine."

"Is that report credible?" General Atakan wondered aloud.

"You are free to believe whatever you choose," al-Fasal responded.

CHAPTER SEVENTEEN

The news of General Pervez Orkamzi's abrupt departure from the world left Mir Batani Khan feeling depressed and disconcerted. It was not that he had liked the late ISI chief, much less trusted him. Rather, it was that he had felt confident he understood Orkamzi's motivations: how much his decisions and actions were influenced by the directives of superiors, how much by patriotism and Islamic theology, and how much by personal greed and self-preservation. Now, he would be forced to deal with an entirely different mix in an officer of whom he probably will have never heard.

Batani realized it was time for a thorough reassessment of where he stood and where he thought he was going. He needed to review a strategy that had developed more or less of its own accord as opportunities had presented themselves and he had moved to seize them, hoping that, cumulatively, they would enable him to achieve his grand vision of an Afghanistan free of foreign intervention and united internally under his leadership. His review reminded him that his most effective weapon was audacity, which would be effective only as long as his many remaining opponents didn't stop fighting one another long enough to join against him.

Batani wanted the Americans to leave his country. He also wanted the Pakistani military and ISI to stop meddling in Afghan affairs. But, he needed the Americans to help keep the Pakistanis at bay and both to fight off his enemies and competitors within Afghanistan. Then, there were the countries--- notably China, but also India and others---that wanted a large piece of the action in exploiting Afghanistan's economic potential. Eventually, Batani knew, there would also be problems with Iran, with which Afghanistan shared a long and porous border. And, finally, there was Abdul Rashid and the powerful people and entities he represented. He and Mahmud al-Fasal had been very helpful, but Batani realized that their longer term objectives were not necessarily complementary to his and that, eventually, Abdul Rashid could turn his considerable resources against him. Reviewing, Batani realized he had omitted the drug traffickers who, having recovered from the shock of his coup in the poppy growing areas, were dedicated to killing him. Concealed in the back of a van en route to meet the director of the Chinese copper mining project south of Kabul, Batani shrugged and wondered how he might convince the CIA to send Hannah Crossman out to assist him.

The meeting Batani thought was to be a routine get-together with a mining engineer turned out to be much more. The first thing he noticed upon entering the trailer being used as the construction site office was the presence of two additional men, one of whom was Kingsley Yong. The other, unknown to him, was introduced as Mr. Jian from China. Batani learned later that he was a senior member of the Chinese government and Communist Party who had come to Afghanistan covertly, ostensibly as a member of a group of mining consultants. His mission was to have a serious chat with Mir Batani Khan.

"We are pleased with the security services your people are providing us, but we frankly get the impression your resources are strained. I'm sure you understand that our requirements will continue to grow as the mine comes into production and the railroad is extended toward Afghanistan's northern and southern borders. You must assure us that you have the capacity to meet our needs, for which Mr. Yong here has been providing you with generous stipends."

Batani smiled and raised his hands dismissively. "Do not be concerned, Mr. Jian. I am fully aware that I must increase my forces to keep up with the remarkable growth of your enterprises. In fact, I am in the process of doing that right now, while at the same time acting to reduce the threat to your enterprises by gaining the cooperation of certain of my Afghan brothers and their followers. My principal problem---almost my only one---is that your security needs are growing more rapidly than my ability to finance their coverage. I'm afraid that I will need more funds."

Having said that, Batani waited for the expected push back, which encouragingly did not come. Apparently, the Chinese anticipated being held up for more money and, after remarkably little negotiation, Jian told Yong to increase Batani's bimonthly allowance by a half million dollars. It became apparent to the Taliban leader that Jian had come to stir fry much bigger fish.

"My government is very much interested in pursuing additional, far larger projects in your country, which would create tens of thousands of jobs for your citizens and generate large royalties for your government."

Jian pulled a map of Afghanistan from a plastic folder he was carrying. It was obviously taken from the Internet, and marked as having been produced by the Central

Intelligence Agency. He pointed to the long, narrow spit of land that projected eastward from the main body of the country, what Americans would call a panhandle.

"This, as you know, is the Wakhan Corridor, which gives Afghanistan a common border with China. My country wishes to build a railroad through it that will connect the Chinese national rail network with the north-south line that we are now constructing for the copper mining project. When it is in operation, trains originating in China would be able to connect, via this link and Tadjik or Kazakh tracks, to Russian main lines and then to Europe. This would save enormous amounts of time and expense compared to shipping via maritime transport or by rail north into eastern Siberia and then west on the Tran-Siberian Railroad. Equally important, however, is that the tracks would not pass through Pakistan or India and would also service the Hindu Kush where there is a major iron ore deposit in which we are interested."

Batani was extremely impressed by the sweep and audacity of the Chinese aspiration, not to mention the enormous investment it would require. It also occurred to him that the demands on the Afghan government created by such a program would expand enormously, with respect to both creation of domestic infrastructure and dealing effectively with inevitable Pakistani government and Islamist obstructionism. The latter would involve the ISI, Batani recognized, and now he would have a new and unknown chief to deal with.

"Yours is an ambitious and very expensive plan," he told Jian. "There will be security and political issues to make the ones we are now dealing with seem trivial."

His Chinese visitor smiled. "That is why I've come to see you. Although we are willing to invest whatever might be necessary to realize our goals, we will not undertake an out-and-out gamble. Railroads are very difficult to protect from interdiction, particularly where there are many vulnerable bridges and tunnels. We must be assured of a stable and effective government in Afghanistan before committing our resources. While the current government in Kabul may be effective in dealing with the Americans, it does not truly rule the country, certainly not to the extent we require. Our perception is that your country's Taliban, with you at its head, might do what is required, if you are able to eliminate the opposition of your most fanatical extremists. My government is most sensitive to the disruption caused by their imams stirring up not only your people, but also the Muslim minorities living in the west of China."

"I am flattered by China's confidence in me, Mr. Jian," Batani responded with a dazzling smile. "My goals are essentially the same as yours; but although I am making great progress, they are not yet achieved. The unexpected demise of General Orkamzi has made my immediate plans uncertain, since I do not yet know the significance of this development with respect to the intentions of his superiors. I have always operated under the assumption that Pakistan will not willingly allow Afghanistan to go its own way, if that way is to the slightest degree different from Islamabad's. I would welcome China's counsel and assistance in this matter."

"We will carefully consider all of your requests and assist you as we can," Jian replied. "Please remember, however, that China will not be drawn into the political, military or religious conflicts of the Muslim world. Neither will we be a party to a renewal of hostilities between Pakistan and India. Our goals are peace, stability, and economic development, particularly within the borders of China. If the actions of you and your organizations go contrary to these goals, we will terminate our support immediately and, perhaps, take action against you. I hope that is clear."

He stared at Batani until the Taliban leader smiled and showed his palms submissively. Kingsley Yong was highly impressed, both by Jian's determination and Batani's acting.

The facts surrounding the sudden death of General Orkamzi were not exactly congruent to those released by the Pakistani High Command in the days following, nor to those in general circulation without official attribution. The ISI director had, in fact, died when his vehicle left a narrow mountain road in Waziristan at a high rate of speed. But, the rumor that he was running to escape arrest after being summarily relieved of his position was not true. In actuality, his SUV was being chased by a pickup truck with a man in the bed trying to get a clear shot with a rocket propelled grenade launcher as the vehicles careened around hairpin turns. It was not clear to whom the truck belonged or whether the shooter knew who was in the sports utility vehicle, which had darkly tinted windows.

The official report stated that Orkamzi was actually on a high priority, classified mission to contact Mir Batani Khan at his mountain headquarters. The mission was so important that his superiors sent Orkamzi in person rather than trust the matter to a lesser personage. Batani claimed to know nothing about it, although he had heard that the General may have been on the way to find him when he was killed. Observers, particularly those who knew of Orkamzi's multi-layered professional life, doubted the official explanation's accuracy. In actuality, Orkamzi had been urgently dispatched to warn Batani that the Pakistani military was on the verge of taking drastic action against him, if he did not immediately stop his fighters from protecting so well the Chinese mining and railroad construction sites, at least until an acceptable compensation arrangement had been reached with Beijing.

Even without the full details, Batani found the entire Orkamzi matter highly instructive, imagining himself in the place of the deceased ISI chief. He had been so busy scurrying around making deals, mending fences, and gathering funds, both within Afghanistan and abroad, that he was oblivious to his personal vulnerability to even the most inexperienced assassin. However, he also recognized that increasing security precautions would restrict his freedom of movement and action, in addition to saddling him with a considerable entourage. As a compromise, he resolved to be far more careful in the future, but didn't quite know what that actually meant. He would have been far less complacent had he known that the gunmen in the pickup truck that chased Pervez Orkamzi to his death thought that the vehicle they were pursuing contained Mir Batani Khan.

In the General Headquarters compound in Rawalpindi, the unanswered question that kept the Orkamzi matter from being mercifully closed was the selection of his replacement. There were a number of likely candidates, but choosing among them required the leadership to focus on the priorities and objectives by which the selectee would be guided. Orkamzi's great virtue had been that he required little guidance. That virtually eliminated any need to discuss what he was doing to increase the fortunes of those above him. His relationships with foreign agents of influence, such as Abdul Rashid and Mahmud al-Fasal, were well known to his superiors and accepted, as were the rewards that Orkamzi apportioned to himself.

The issue concerning the Chinese railroad construction project in Afghanistan was, however, about more than protection money. The opening of Afghanistan to the outside world through the establishment of a high capacity transportation system that did not begin or end in Pakistan had enormous long-term political significance, insofar as it reduced Islamabad's ability to meddle and to retard the growth of Kabul's relative influence in regional affairs. Currently, the only practical way to move large quantities of cargo was by truck convoy over a largely underdeveloped road system extremely vulnerable to disruption by natural forces and militant interdiction. An instructive example was the necessity to resupply U.S. and allied forces in Afghanistan with beans, bullets, and fuel via a truck route that stretched from the port of Karachi through Pakistan and across Afghanistan, almost all of it intermittently hostile territory.

Whenever the Pakistanis wished to pressure the Americans, for one reason or another, their agents would block the roads, causing hundreds of trucks to back up in holding areas where they could be attacked and burned by insurgent bands. Creation of a high capacity Afghan rail network would not only increase Kabul's ability to absorb foreign investment that Pakistan badly needed as well, but it could seriously tilt regional influence in Afghanistan away from Islamabad.

A rumor of China's interest in building a railroad through the Wakhan Corridor had reached Islamabad and Rawalpindi; Beijing's interest in the Hindu Kush iron ore deposit was already known. The resulting panic was exacerbated by the fact that the Corridor is bordered on the south by India, which was assumed likely to be interested in partnering with Beijing. It was recognized that the key to the entire enterprise was the ability to insure the security of both the railroads' construction and their subsequent operation, lack of confidence in which would discourage the necessary investment. At General Orkamzi's last meeting with his superiors, it was agreed that reconciliation of the contending factions within Afghanistan must be prevented at all costs. Mir Batani Khan was obviously the greatest threat to that objective, and the need for his elimination, if necessary, accepted. The director of the ISI was told to find Batani and to issue a friendly, but final warning.

When Hannah Crossman returned to Washington from the south of France, there were no messages from Paul Rayner on her answering machine, and his home number did not respond. After two days, she tried his office number, to be told only that he was away "on assignment." Since she had not informed Paul of her departure, much less where she was going, Hannah felt embarrassed about being annoyed that he was not there with his usual bemused complaints when she returned. It occurred to her that he might be pretending, in order to give her a taste of her own medicine, but she had no time to ponder the question, because the news of General Orkamzi's death had also reached Washington and her seniors wanted to know what had transpired at al-Fasal's villa after they left. They were disappointed to learn that Abdul Rashid had effectively cancelled the meeting Hannah was to have attended. However, they found a conversation Hannah had with her host just before departing for the States to be intriguing, if also puzzling.

"Al-Fasal told me," Hannah reported, "that Abdul Rashid seemed very disturbed by the news about Orkamzi, which al-Fasal found strange. Other than the travail and inconvenience involved in breaking in his replacement, there was no real reason for Abdul Rashid to be that concerned. Later, it became apparent that it wasn't Orkamzi who Abdul Rashid was so concerned about, but Batani. Why specifically that was, al-Fasal didn't explain, but Abdul Rashid directed him to bring Batani back to France for a meeting as soon as feasible."

"We are all concerned about Batani," Admiral Bergen noted, "although each of us undoubtedly has different reasons. The man is a helluva lot closer to an international dealmaker than an Islamist insurgent, and he's been using a lot of our assets to support his activities. Batani appears to be going in our direction, so we need to protect him, at least while he's on our side. There are people out there who, I'm sure, would like to kill him, many of them the same ones opposing us.."

"President Kitteridge doesn't want to simply pull out of Afghanistan," Bergen continued. "He believes that a nationalist regime, even if it's anti-American, could achieve our primary goal, which is to keep that country from participating in an expansionist Islamic jihad, the goals and policies of which are established in the mosques rather than the seats of government. An acceptable regime could be as fundamentalist as it wished, as long as it focused on the well being of its people and not on what it believed to be the Jihadist commandments of God. The key to that is the presence of opportunity for better, happier lives inherent in economic development. That is now becoming possible in Afghanistan, which needs the will and leadership to grasp it. The President believes that Batani may be able to provide that leadership. In any event, he's all we've got at the moment."

"I have the impression Abdul Rashid believes the same about Batani," Sam Glover volunteered. "But, the future of Afghanistan is greatly dependent on what happens in Pakistan. There is no evidence that either the Pakistani establishment or the various militant tribes in the border areas are prepared to permit Afghanistan to go its own way unimpeded, particularly if they don't get a considerable piece of the action. Should the extremists take over, the outlook would be even worse."

"The President basically agrees with you, Sam," the Admiral acknowledged. "He knows that, however obstructive the people now in power are, our problems would multiply many fold, should we be forced to deal with an Islamist regime, particularly one that had nuclear weapons. So, we will need to walk the fine line: playing the middle against both ends, so to speak. We will need to help Batani succeed, while simultaneously keeping the Pakistani political and military establishment from failing too badly."

"Good luck to us," Sam Glover intoned somberly. The three men turned to look at Hannah, seated against the wall.

"Wherever it is you're thinking of sending me," she reacted, "I can't leave until I've done my laundry."

CHAPTER EIGHTEEN

It was the beginning of high season on the French Riviera, so the increased number of private jets arriving at Cap Ferrat airfield was not noticed, except by the security officials recording aircraft tail numbers to be sent to Paris along with their passengers' passport data. Mahmud al-Fasal had thoughtfully notified his government contacts of what was to occur, they in turn instructing local officials to ignore the convoys of black luxury sedans and their escorts that came to take the newly arrived off to the large, white villa on a bluff overlooking the sea. Its altitude above the surrounding terrain made external surveillance extremely difficult, if not impossible. However, since the French Government knew the individuals involved and, generally, why they had come, its only official manifestation was a uniformed local policeman, in an unmarked car, posted near the driveway entrance to warn off any nosy journalist who might appear.

The men who came, one by one over the course of two days, were senior representatives of Abdul Rashid's sponsors, the sources of the huge sums he dispensed, through Mahmud al-Fasal, to promote the international Islamic jihad. There were ultimately fifteen of them from Muslim countries and those with substantial Muslim minorities. Several wore Arab robes, but the majority looked like conservatively dressed international businessmen, lawyers and bankers, which indeed they were. Interestingly, those from Western countries arrived early, apparently aware that the need to wait until all were present assured them at least a half day by the pool. Those who arrived the latest, already focused on the business at hand, represented donors who considered aiding the jihad a sacred religious duty, most notably Saudi Arabia and the Gulf Emirates. No one but Abdul Rashid and his accountants knew the actual amounts contributed by the individual sponsors over the years, but all assumed that the meeting would not officially come to order until the representative of the Saudi royal family arrived. Sponsors' representatives, and occasionally principals, had met before with Abdul Rashid in Paris on an individual basis, but this would be the first plenary session, convened on orders from Riyadh.

Abdul Rashid's state of mind and health had not benefited greatly from his removal from Paris to the bucolic Riviera. His eyes had adjusted to unaccustomed sunlight, but he could not compensate for his absent legs, and refused to don a bathing suit or shorts to sit on the terrace with the others. Rather, he chose to remain swaddled in the dimness of his host's study. Mahmud al-Fasal, shuttling back and forth between study and terrace, wished they were all back in Paris and he was alone to appreciate the tranquility of the shimmering sea.

The meeting's first session convened around al-Fasal's long dining room table, stripped bare except for bottles of mineral water at each place and small plates of dates, figs, and sweetmeats. Its opening was a bit awkward because Abdul Rashid, the host and chairman, had never before seen most of the attendees. He had been told by his principals who to expect, but it would have been insulting to ask those who actually arrived at the villa to display credentials. Al-Fasal wondered idly whether one or more of the men around the table was also reporting to the CIA or another intelligence service. It occurred to him that Hannah Crossman might as well have been invited to reprise her role at the meeting with Batani in Pakistan. Much of what transpired here would eventually be shared with Bergen, Detwiler and company anyway, and Hannah's ostensible presence on his domestic staff would have enhanced al-Fasal's reputation in the more worldly quarters of the jihad. Seated in an armchair at the head of the table, Abdul Rashid contemplated the task before him with a mixture of concern and bemusement. His sponsors had at last recognized that the circumstances of the venture in which they were engaged were changing and that the relative importance of its three principal influences---religion, politics, and economics---was no longer what it had been.

When they had first come to Abdul Rashid, almost ten years ago now, their dominant motive had been to strengthen and expand the influence of Islam in the world. The funds they volunteered, in increasing amounts over the years, were to be used to provide religious education to the masses of young people who characterized the populations of Muslim countries, as well as to strengthen the cohesion and devoutness of Muslim communities in nations where they were a minority. Inevitably, however, religious movements became dominated by their most fundamentalist elements, aided by the clarity of their us-or-them message now directed against the infidel or non-Muslim. The rise of al-Qaeda reflected the appeal of that message and the ability of its leader, Osama bin-Laden, to organize and fund active operations against Western targets, designed primarily to stimulate punitive reaction that would further inflame the Muslim masses.

"Welcome, gentlemen!" Abdul Rashid greeted them. "I praise God for your safe arrival, and trust that you will be as comfortable here as you would be in Paris. It would be no understatement to say that this is a most opportune time for us to review the status of our joint venture and to chart our future course of action. The context of our undertaking has clearly changed."

The others nodded perfunctorily, but a well-dressed banker from Dubai, who Abdul Rashid knew represented the Saudi royal family, raised his hand.

"As you know, sir, my client is extremely concerned that your efforts are moving us in the wrong direction. The expanding and continuing protest movements in a number of Muslim countries have substantially increased that concern because those countries are left vulnerable to extremists, who will forego no measure or promise that could help them gain power. We accept that the protests are motivated primarily by social and economic rather than religious demands, but we also recognize that there is little prospect that those demands can be quickly satisfied by any kind of government. My client believes, therefore, that our primary focus must be on preventing a state of permanent disorder that would eventually engulf the entire Muslim world and inevitably spread beyond."

The others around the table nodded agreement, in which Abdul Rashid gratefully joined.

"I have been working toward the end you seek for some time, gentlemen," he told them. "We should be directing our money and support to leaders who consider Islam a religion and not a political cause. We need to focus our efforts and support on countries and regions with the best prospects for improving the lives of their people through economic development. Somalia is not one of them and, I'm afraid, neither is Pakistan. This is extremely worrisome because Pakistan is the most vulnerable to the rants of extremists seeking to blame rather than remedy."

"Where then?" several around the table asked simultaneously.

"I think Afghanistan," Abdul Rashid replied, after a momentary pause to build suspense. He was rewarded with a universal look of surprise.

"If the Americans have done only one thing for Afghanistan," he continued, "it was to expose to the world the riches to be found in that country. Already, a Chinese consortium has begun work on a large copper mine and railroad to carry the ore to the Pakistan and Tajik borders. The potential in such projects for lifting the economic status of the Afghan population is enormous, and people who are living better and are optimistic do not shout and wave their guns at evening prayers."

"We know of the mineral deposits in Afghanistan," responded a bearded man representing Kuwaiti petroleum interests, "but also of corruption everywhere in the government and lack of security. Who will invest hundreds of millions in these projects, if their viability cannot be guaranteed? We hear the Chinese have contracted with a private army to protect their mining and railroad works."

"Those are major challenges," Abdul Rashid acknowledged. "But, the private army you've heard about is actually the Taliban, or at least part of it. Mir Batani Khan, its leader, is working very hard to turn Afghanistan into the kind of environment we are seeking, one that emphasizes economic development and keeps Islam in the mosques and off the streets. I recommend we devote our resources and influence to helping him."

"We know of this Batani. He has been very clever and, thus far, successful. But, he is just one man and already the target of a growing number of enemies, who apparently include the generals of the Pakistani ISI and the warlords of many insurgent tribes in his own country. It would be foolhardy to place our faith in him, when he could disappear from the scene at any moment."

"I share your concern," Abdul Rashid responded, "but Batani may be our only option at the moment. I would propose that we hedge our prospects by seeking understandings with the Americans, the Chinese, and perhaps the Russians. If you agree, I will make the necessary proposals. In addition to large sums of money, what Batani appears to need most is personal protection, which would be our most difficult task. I'm told now, for example, that the attackers who caused General Orkamzi's death thought they were chasing Batani."

One by one, the men around the table expressed doubt concerning the viability of their host's proposal, but were unable to provide an alternative. Recognizing that they could not go back to their clients without at least an interim course of action, they hedged by directing Abdul Rashid to study the problem more closely, and to present them with proposals for specific initiatives they might consider. Mahmud al-Fasal smiled inwardly, knowing that Abdul Rashid had already begun to implement his plan. He then frowned, remembering also that he had thus far been unable to locate Batani among his many bases of operation in Afghanistan.

Paul Rayner turned up two days later, leaving a message on Hannah's answering machine. He made no reference to his absence when they met for dinner at a restaurant near her apartment. But, Hannah could tell he was dying to tell her about something; she, of course, contrived to give him no convenient opportunity.

"I called you when I got back almost a week ago," she told him, "but your office told me once again that you were away 'on assignment.' That's what they say on the TV news shows when one of the anchors has a bad hangover or a particularly ugly zit on his or her face."

Rayner laughed. "I really was away doing preliminary work on a great get. Unfortunately, it is so great that I can't tell you what it is, because you spooks cannot be trusted with secrets. Please don't ask."

It was Hannah's turn to laugh. Paul was giving her a taste of her own medicine, and she found herself enjoying it because he was sitting across the table smiling. But she sniffed dismissively.

"Why would I be interested in your little secret when I already know some of the world's great ones?"

Had she known Paul's secret, however, Hannah would have been more than interested. The good reviews from the *American Focus* interview of Alfred Oberling had yielded an additional reward: Roger Norton had decided to introduce Paul Rayner to Reggie Huggins, explaining to Oberling that the connection could prove very useful later in the campaign, should an opportunity arise to publicize the Administration's national security failures. Rayner and *American Focus* enjoyed a much better public reputation than the cable pundits and commentators normally counted upon to support Oberling's positions.

For his part, Reggie Huggins was less than thrilled, his thirty plus years in the CIA having left him permanently wary of both journalists and politicians. He briefed Rayner principally on the capabilities of his own company, Global Security Applications, telling him almost nothing about the foreign contacts he had made or pursued. However, when Rayner intimated to Norton that he thought Huggins was exaggerating the importance of his connections, the former CIA operative was directed to take him to Paris for introduction to Mahmud al-Fasal. That was where Rayner was when Hannah got back to Washington and, although his trip was in vain (al-Fasal was, of course, in the south of France), Rayner was impressed that the staff at al-Fasal's Paris hotel residence apparently recognized Reggie. Most useful to Rayner was that he now knew about al-Fasal and where to contact him for a future get.

CIA's Station Chief in Islamabad had been able to determine, through contacts in the ISI, that interrogation of witnesses had revealed Pervez Orkamzi to have been a victim of mistaken identity: the vehicle in which he was riding was thought to be carrying Mir Batani Khan. If the attack on the vehicle had not been ordered by Pakistani authorities (who presumably would have known that Ork-amzi rather than Batani was aboard), who then, Bergen wondered, was responsible for the intended assassination of the Taliban leader?

The cause of Admiral Bergen's angst was, at that moment, generating a great deal of his own in the town of Khost near the Pakistan border south of Kabul. It was the headquarters of the regional warlord whose forces had been most instrumental in harassing the workers preparing the right-of-way for the railroad the Chinese were building in Logar Province to connect with the Pakistani rail system at the border. Batani's fighters, along with NATO troops and the Afghan National Army, had been providing pro-tection for the project, but as the rail line grew longer and the copper mining works more extensive, the task became more and more demanding of resources. The insurgents could choose their time and place of attack and had be-come adept at simultaneous attacks in different places defended by the same poorly coordinated multinational forces. In addition, the attackers had recently acquired long range mortars that enabled them to lob shells into the work sites from the surrounding hills and then ambush defensive units coming out to find the launch points. Batani recognized that the current circumstances could maintain indefinitely, at severe cost to his credibility with the Chinese and others supplying him with indispensable funds. Through an intermediary with whom both he and his adversaries had friendly relations, Batani arranged the shura in Khost that was now getting underway.

The large meeting room was rapidly filling with men wearing turbans and dusty robes, all carrying small arms of varying description. Batani noted that they appeared identical to the men who appeared at every other meeting he had attended throughout Afghanistan and the Pakistani border areas: young, bearded, hollow-eyed and thin. Their leaders were somewhat older, with longer sometimes graying beards and more evident self-assurance. All contrived to give the impression they were there against their better judgment, and would gladly consider killing Batani as compensation for time spent. He, on the other hand, had come in unescorted, and there was no mass of men and guns surrounding the house. Paradoxically, this had a strong deterrent effect on the men in the room, they believing logically that Batani would not be so stupid as to come unprotected, meaning that he had protection they could not see. The impact of that assumption was terrifying because it signified, they believed, that American drones were circling silently overhead waiting to launch missiles into the house and their vehicles upon signal. The earlier attack by such aircraft on Batani's enemies in Konduz City was well known throughout the country, its ferocity and impact magnified by frequent recounting. Muttering voices faded as the men in the room contented themselves with the rationale that it was important to know your enemy and to look him in the eye.

Batani surprised them, however. They knew he was an Afghan and that he was said to lead the Taliban, but he did not look like them and his speech contained foreign intonations. Batani wore no beard at this meeting; his black hair was cut short in the European style, and his lack of a head covering was itself a mark of estrangement. Were it not for the fear of drones overhead and their missiles, there would be every argument for simply shooting him and getting on with the day. But, his ability to command the support of the Americans, and it was rumored the Russians and Chinese as well, made his guests sit down to listen.

"I've come today to learn from you, my brothers!" Batani began. "I am very much interested in your strategy for dealing with the foreign invaders and your plans for the future of your lands and people. I am facing many of the same challenges, and would like to study how you, in this district, are managing so well to meet them, to the great benefit of your people and yourselves."

There was no reply, his audience fixedly staring at Batani's face as though expecting him to provide the answers to his own queries. Finally, a man in the front row, better fed and more finely dressed than the others, replied in a contemptuous voice:

"We have no need of strategy. This is my district and those who wish to live and work here, even to pass through, must do as I command. The foreigners do not understand this, so they must be made to pay. They speak of the government in Kabul, but we care nothing for its orders and directives? They are all corrupt thieves, who take from my people and give nothing in return. We hold against the Americans only that they believe Kabul should rule, which we cannot allow to happen."

When the speaker fell silent, his people cheered, as was expected of them. Most of the men and boys in the district were fighters in his cohort because there was no other way to earn even a rudimentary living. Their leader, in turn, was under constant pressure to generate income sufficient to both meet his payroll and maintain the relatively more opulent lifestyle of a local chieftain. The rich foreigners who came within reach were fair game, regardless of their motives and missions. If they were infidels, so much the better: it was much easier then to get one's ragged riflemen to loot a NATO supply convoy than to oppose tanks and machine guns in the cause of Islam.

"The American government undertook to build for you a fine, modern road through your district, something that will yield nothing but benefit for you and your people," Batani continued. "Yet, your mujahedin attacked it mercilessly until the construction crews almost packed up and left. What was the sense in that?"

"Of what use to us is a fine road when we have only wagons and mules, and not very many of those," the District Chief responded. "It became of value to us only when the company building it began to pay me to protect its crews and equipment. Once I posted my guards around the construction sites, there were no more attacks...perhaps because the attackers were now the guards."

He could not contain himself and burst out laughing, joined by everyone in the room, including noticeably Batani, who gleefully admitted: "I did the same thing with the Chinese!"

They shared a long and relieved laugh, and tension in the room was broken. When they stopped laughing and sat silently smiling at one another, happy to have found common ground, Batani resumed his inquisition.

"You say that you have no use for the new road because you have no motor vehicles. Is it so then that you are not interested in acquiring such vehicles, since you would need a good road on which to drive, if you were so interested."

The district chieftain hesitated, recognizing the trap. His fighters surrounding him, listening to the exchange with Batani, waited anxiously for his response. They badly wanted pickup trucks and the heavier weapons they could carry, also the utility vehicles that would enable the men to ride where they now had to walk.

"Of course, we would like such things," he finally replied. "But we are not rich, and most of what we have must go to maintaining our families and homes."

"But, must it always be so, my brothers?" Batani asked disbelievingly, now playing to the entire room. "The Americans have discovered that Afghanistan is wealthy in minerals and other resources that can provide jobs for our men, education for our children, and golden trinkets for our women. But, the foreigners whose help and money we need to dig these riches from the ground will not come, if they know we are waiting to kill them. Why should we not avail ourselves of what God has provided? He certainly doesn't wish us to spend our lives fighting one another for scraps."

"What you say is true, Mir Batani Khan, but our weapons are our only protection from the thieves who come from Kabul and elsewhere to take what is ours while pretending to help us. We know no other way to protect what is ours but to fight for it."

Batani tried hard not to show his frustration.

"We have spent our lives, throughout history, fighting against foreign invaders and, when there were none, against one another" he virtually shouted. "It is time we joined together to fight *for* something. If we join together, the invaders will not be able to steal from us and order us about, but will have to give us a fair share of what is taken from our land. We cannot go on forever fighting with everyone we encounter. It is a certain way to end up poor and dead."

The men in the room were becoming excited, but their leaders were more restrained. "What of the government leaders in Kabul? They say that the foreigners who wish to come to Afghanistan must deal with them."

Batani laughed. "The foreigners will deal with whoever can provide them with what they need, and that more and more is us. I already have arrangements with the Americans, the Chinese, and the Russians. If we are united and pursue our affairs correctly, we will soon be the government in Kabul."

The fighters in the room cheered, now almost unanimously, and Batani knew it was time to finish.

"I am planning to convene soon a grand shura in Kandahar City, at which all those who wish to have a place and a voice in our country's future will be represented. I hope you will agree to participate."

The district warlord nodded, while his men cheered. Batani smiled and pulled several sets of keys from a case on the table before him, and handed them to the leader.

"These are but a token of the rewards to come from our venture together. A proper chief must have an appropriate vehicle in which to ride to Kandahar, as must his brave men. These vehicles will be delivered to you tomorrow.   Later, we shall meet to determine the most effective ways to aid the foreigners who have come to make us wealthy."

His listeners again cheered, and Batani knew that Kingsley Yong would be gratified that his employer's funds were being put to such good use.

CHAPTER NINETEEN

"Where do we stand with this man Batani, Admiral," President Kitteridge asked, as he sat down at the Situation Room conference table,

"On the brink of adventure, Mr. President," Bergen replied with a wry smile, which Mason Kitteridge returned. He had just finished reading the file of recent reports dealing with Batani and his activities.

"I agree with you, Admiral." He looked down the table at the other attendees: the Secretaries of the departments dealing with foreign affairs, plus the Secretary of Homeland Security and the Director of National Intelligence. The Directors of the FBI and principal Intelligence Community agencies were seated in the background.

"I've called you here together today because we are at a strategic crunch point in Afghanistan. I want you to know what course I propose to take and to give you an opportunity to talk me out of it, if you believe it would be a mistake. I recognize the risks involved in what I propose to do, but have not been able to see a better way to go, and doing nothing is not an acceptable option."

He nodded to Admiral Bergen, who signaled the projectionist. The lights went out and dual photos of Mir Batani Khan came on the screen. One showed him bearded and in traditional Afghan robes, the other in a well cut business suit with only trimmed mustache. The latter photo had been taken by the French security service during his recent visit to Paris. As Hannah Crossman had noted at the time, Batani looked a lot like the young Omar Sharif.

Bergen began: "The read-ahead on Batani with which you were provided told you of his background, education, and experience. He claims to be leader of the Taliban in Afghanistan. However, Batani is not an ideologue, religious or political; his is an Islam of convenience. If he wasn't who he is and where he is, he would be running for Mayor of New York or Chicago or promoting the world's largest housing development in the Arizona desert. Batani is extremely bright, charismatic, and determined to create an economic miracle in Afghanistan. The tactics he's using are brilliant, considering he has no official position and that all of the resources he's been using belong to us, the Chinese, the Pakistanis, Russians, and international narcotics traffickers. As he has become more successful, however, he is increasingly the target of a broad range of foreign and domestic enemies, including probably the Pakistani ISI and the Afghan government in Kabul. Should he die, all that he's built and accomplished will probably go immediately down the drain, because he's not yet created a permanent organization or infrastructure."

President Kitteridge signaled for the lights to be turned back up and began speaking to the group, after a moment's reflection.

"Batani is important to us because he may represent the only horse we can ride out of Afghanistan that has a chance of winning, and that depends on how you define 'win.' We have been fighting and spending there for more than ten years, but I have little hope that the good we've done will survive very long, once we're gone. Potentially, however, Batani offers the prospect of an Afghanistan too alive to its own potential to permit itself to be exploited by foreigners or homegrown fanatics and criminals. If we can help to realize that prospect, then we will at least prevent Afghanistan from harboring our enemies and allowing them to use its territory as a base for international terrorist operations. To my mind, the possibility of achieving that will make the risks we take on Batani worthwhile."

"Seems to me, Mr. President, that we have nothing to lose for trying," SECDEF Trentwell White ventured. "If Batani doesn't succeed, we'll have risked nothing more than we already have, except perhaps some money."

"Unfortunately, Mr. Secretary, Batani will not be our principal risk: that will be Pakistan. Islamabad cannot allow Afghanistan to slip away, certainly not to become more prosperous and influential in international affairs than is Pakistan. The worst outcome for us would be for failure in Afghanistan to result in Pakistan falling under fundamentalist control, a development that would make our problems in Afghanistan appear inconsequential by comparison. The Pakistani establishment will fight Batani all the way, while we are forced to play on both sides simultaneously. It's a dangerous game, ladies and gentlemen."

"What are we doing to improve our prospects, Mr. President?" the Secretary of Homeland Security asked.

Kitteridge nodded again to Admiral Bergen. "We've been making cooperative arrangements with unaccustomed partners," the Admiral replied, digressing to remind attendees of the high classification and extreme sensitivity of what they were about to be told.

"An agreement was made with the Russians that has given us a base for our unmanned aircraft from which they can cover all of Afghanistan and most of Pakistan without requiring use of Pakistani or Afghan facilities. We've also increased our intelligence collection capabilities so that we are not nearly as dependent upon ISI input as we once were. The Pakistanis now know that they can no longer jerk us around, and we have a hedge against the future possibility President Kitteridge mentioned: that Pakistan will go to the extremists and become a target of our drone operations.

"We have also come to an understanding with the Chinese, for whom Afghanistan is a very big deal from two aspects. First, Beijing has committed a huge sum of money to obtain mining concessions from the government in Kabul for which it needs protection that only Batani seems able to provide. Second, the prospect of extremist regimes in Pakistan and Afghanistan scares Beijing even more than us. As I think you know, the Chinese Government is paranoid about the potential for unrest and rebellion among its many minorities, particularly in its western provinces. We have seen protests of a few hundred people balloon suddenly into thousands, aided by the Internet and mobile phone communications. The Chinese believe that, if they can raise the economy of Afghanistan by spending and investing large sums there, it will discourage religious and political extremism or at least efforts to export it to China."

"We agree," the President interjected, "and I've directed that we support Beijing's initiatives, even though the raw materials they acquire will give them advantage in world markets. I expect to take a lot of flak over our arrangement with the Chinese when word of it leaks out, as it inevitably will. But, if push comes to shove, and we find ourselves opposing an Islamist Pakistan looking to promote the jihad throughout Asia, China will make a fierce and dependable ally, albeit for reasons we don't necessarily share."

"Finally," Bergen continued, "we have been working covertly with some of the more conservative supporters of the jihad to limit the influence and impact of its more fanatical leaders. The governments, companies, and individuals funding their operations over the years have become scared by the effects on international order of terrorism and insurgencies, and have instructed their agents to assist us against the extremists. All of us are now focused on Batani who, clever devil that he is, has been hitting each of us up for aid, usually in the form of large amounts of cash. But, if he can pull off what we hope he can, it will be worth every cent."

"How can our departments help?" the Secretary of State asked, on behalf of everyone at the table. President Kitteridge responded:

"The scope of international cooperation in this matter is very broad and encompasses things not obviously related to what was talked about here today. For example, Beijing wants to build a railroad through the narrow strip of Afghanistan that connects to the Chinese border. We support that, since it reduces the ability of Pakistan to demand a role in everything because its central location has dominated regional lines of communications. But, the price we've exacted from China in return for our support is a limitation on its future role in Afghanistan to trade and commercial operations. All of you may become involved in similar situations and opportunities, about which I want to be immediately informed. Admiral Bergen is my point man on anything to do, directly or indirectly, with Mir Batani Khan and should be kept informed, even where relevance is not yet established."

As meeting attendees departed, the President called his intelligence chiefs to the Oval Office for final instructions.

"We need to do everything in our power to help Batani succeed and to keep him alive. Send people out there to keep watch on him and, in particular, on those he trusts who have ready access to him. But, don't tell him how much we're concerned for his success and welfare. He'd be likely to hold us up for another ten million."

Hannah, who had been in the Watch Center during the meeting, was waiting in the anteroom when her bosses left the President. The three of them spotted her immediately and spoke almost simultaneously.

"Hope you've had time to do your laundry, Hannah!"

General Raheem Malik was not at all certain how happy he should be with his sudden promotion after almost ten years in his current grade and a series of unspectacular staff positions in the army of Pakistan. He had just been called into the Chief-of-Staff's office unexpectedly and told, first, that he was being promoted and, second, that he was going to replace the late Pervez Orkamzi as Director of the Inter-Services Intelligence Directorate. He was then told that the durability of both the promotion and appointment was dependent upon his success in neutralizing Mir Batani Khan in the coming three months. It was to be done in a way that did not implicate the Pakistani government, and certainly not the Army. Malik would be allowed to devise his own plan for accomplishing the mission, and command unlimited resources, as long as it was not known where they came from and for what they were being used.

"We were one of Batani's original sponsors, Malik, and it turned out to have been a big mistake," the Chief-of-Staff told him. "Orkamzi was working with a man in Paris named Abdul Rashid. The idea was to build Batani up as a Taliban leader in order to counter the influence and resources of the Kabul government and the more extremist tribal warlords and potentates who won't follow our lead. However, two things happened instead. First, Batani espoused a strategy for gaining power in Afghanistan that was unacceptable to us. Second, he began to cleverly implement it, taking advantage of the resources and cynicism of the Americans, the Chinese, Russians and anyone else he could find. Batani's success has made willing supporters of our foreign friends, and he now aims at displacing the Kabul government to install a regime acceptable to all countries that believe they have a stake in Afghanistan. All, that is, except Pakistan. We cannot afford an Afghanistan able to function and prosper without our approval and cooperation. With its greater resource potential and more manageable population, Kabul would soon be dictating to us and, God forbid, making deals with India and China at our expense."

By now, the Chief-of-Staff had worked himself into a frenzy, and was pacing his office, staring at Malik to make sure he understood the gravity of what he was being told. The latter could do nothing but nod and be dismissed with a warning to waste no time getting started on his prime task, the first part of which was determining where Batani was to be found.

CHAPTER TWENTY

"I got a call from Batani last night, Mr. President. He has a request for approval and support that absolutely requires your personal sign off." Admiral Bergen, in his excitement, had begun speaking before he was halfway across the Oval Office. President Kitteridge looked up in surprise.

"The Afghan Government has got twelve senior Taliban leaders being held in a special compound on the edge of Kabul," Bergen continued. "Batani wants to mount an operation to free them so that he can enlist them and their followers in his cause. He's talking close to ten thousand men."

"Why does he need our approval?"

"First, because almost all of the Taliban were captured by our forces, some at the cost of substantial casualties. Batani wants to know that we would be okay with having them back on the loose. He can't guarantee they wouldn't be back shooting at us some day.

"Second, because his attack on the compound would normally bring American units in the vicinity in to assist the defenders. Batani doesn't think he can prevail against

American troops, and he doesn't want any of our people to get hurt. But, he needs us to put on a big show so that he can convince his new recruits of the great risk taken to rescue them."

"How do we do that, Admiral, assuming we agree?"

"I'm sure that something could be cooked up with our local commanders. But, the major problem is that there would be no way it could be pulled off without the Afghan Government guessing it was a put up job, and that we were actually helping the Taliban. Do you consider what Batani is trying to do to be worth that cost, sir?"

"Should he succeed in getting all of those leaders and fighters to follow him, Batani will have made substantial progress toward unifying Afghanistan under his banner which, for want of a better alternative, we are making ours. I don't see that we have a choice here but to go all in, Admiral. But, see what you and your associates can do to hedge our bet."

None of the military and civilian officials with whom Bergen consulted in meeting Batani's need favored release of the Taliban captives under any circumstances, all making it clear that they were following orders under protest. It was almost certain that word of the White House role in the matter would leak into the roiling current of political rhetoric rushing toward the next election. However, when Batani's fighters successfully pulled off their raid and rescued the Taliban prisoners, the accusation of American acquiescence in the operation was rejected by the public as incredible. While many people claimed to know what had occurred, there was no hard evidence or unimpeachable witness, so the fiasco was attributed to the corruption and ineptitude of the Kabul government.

Almost two weeks after Batani's raid, the rescued Talibs found themselves in a closely guarded room in what had once been a small warehouse on the outskirts of Kandahar. They had been smuggled individually by various uncomfortable routes and conveyances following their rescue, and were surprised to find one another again, doubly so when their savior turned out to be Mir Batani Khan, who now stood before them on a small platform at one end of the room. He had entered followed by several women in full-veil attire who proceeded to provide the guests with steaming cups of tea and other refreshment.

Only one man in the room, himself an outsider, recognized that one of the women was an imposter. He was Mahmud al-Fasal, wearing a traditional Afghan robe and seated unobtrusively on a low cushion against a wall. The woman was Hannah Crossman, wearing the same burka and headdress she had worn many months earlier at the first meeting with Batani arranged by the late General Orkamzi. Admiral Bergen had demanded, as a condition of American acquiescence in Batani's plan, that his covert representative be present at all meetings with the freed insurgent leaders and that no joint agreements be made without prior U.S. approval. He offered to send Hannah Crossman out under cover to fill that role, and was somewhat surprised when Batani accepted with obvious enthusiasm.

The coincidental presence of Mahmud al-Fasal reflected a similar concern on the part of Abdul Rashid, who had returned to his Paris compound and worry beads. Support for Batani would, perhaps, be his last major opportunity to influence the course of events in Pakistan and Afghanistan.

Mir Batani Khan looked over the members of his congregation, who had been talking excitedly among themselves. They were now looking up at him with varied expressions of dismay or disbelief on their faces.

"Why do you look at me so strangely, my brothers?" he asked jovially. "I have come to welcome you to freedom and a more promising future."

Initially, there was no response. Then, a voice from the rear of the room replied: "We expected that we were being taken to be killed. Now, we are here being fed tea and cakes and listening to you, whom we have been struggling against for almost a year. We do not know what to think."

Batani laughed. "Do you think I would have gone to the trouble of rescuing you, if I wished to have you killed? Where you were, you were already dead, just waiting for the bastards in Kabul to think of a good explanation for your deaths. Had I wanted you dead, I would have left you there."

"What then do you wish of us?" another voice asked.

"I would like you to recognize the futility of the path on which you have been leading your people and the great possibilities that would open for you and them, if you join me in realizing the shining prospects of our country."

Many in his audience laughed. "Those are noble words, Batani Khan, but empty ones," the loud voice responded. "Of what country are you speaking? Here, we have only the invaders, the drug traffickers, the religious fanatics, and the criminals in Kabul taking everything for themselves and their cronies. What is it you ask us to join?"

"I am asking you to join me to resist and defeat these people, just as we joined to defeat the Soviet invader. Should we fail to do so, our future will be infinitely worse than our miserable present. A new era is dawning in Afghanistan bringing the possibility of great wealth, comfortable lives and an end to our isolation from the modern world. The jackals already know this, and are acting to take everything for themselves. We must stop them or you will be doomed to spend the rest of your lives fighting each other over nothing."

Batani's plea was greeted with hoots of derision.

"What is this new dawn nonsense you speak of? The only wealth we have seen is that which the Americans have brought with them, and will take home when they soon go, God willing. We desire only to be left in peace to live and work as we always have."

It was Batani's turn to laugh derisively.

"You will not be asked your preference. Once modernization gets fully underway, it will roll over you like a tsunami. Your only chance is to gain a voice in it now."

"What is this tsunami? Tell us about it!" The question came in a chorus of voices betraying both interest and mounting concern. Batani smiled with relief and signaled one of his men, who brought an easel holding a map of Afghanistan onto the platform.

"The government in Kabul has already let to the Chinese a concession to develop a huge copper deposit in Lugar Province that is already being worked on. It includes creation of a railroad extending from the mines to the Tajik and Pakistan borders. These developments alone will bring much money and a large number of jobs into our country, and connect it to the outside world. I am told the Chinese also wish to construct a railroad through the narrow corridor that connects Afghanistan directly with China, ultimately to provide a rail connection with the markets of Europe. These initiatives are but the beginning and, because they are basically desirable, can be delayed but not stopped. I know that many of you and your fighters have been attacking the camps and people working on these and other projects, often exchanging fire with my own fighters. No one gains from this, and it must stop or we shall all end up dead or working for the Chinese and Pakistanis."

The Talibs talked among themselves, principally to sound one another out to see who would be first to make an overture to Batani. Finally, a number of them asked him, almost in unison, what specific measures needed to be taken.

"First," Batani replied, "we must organize so that we are not wasting strength and resources fighting one another and can present a united front in dealing with the Americans, the jackals in Kabul, and the Pakistani military, in particular the ISI. Second, we must establish cooperative relationships with the organizations bringing desirable improvements to our country and people. Such relationships will require that a substantial portion of the profits and fees flowing from the concessions be paid to us, much of it to be distributed among you. We must make it clear that nothing will progress without our agreement and cooperation."

The reaction of his listeners was noticeably more positive, beginning to border on the enthusiastic. It was not simply the prospect of unanticipated riches coming to them, but also the probable opportunity to strike back at the despised Afghan government. Batani noticed their look of anticipation as he continued:

"Third, my friends, is the inescapable reality that our objectives will be fiercely opposed by Kabul and Islamabad, to the extent that we shall be at war with them, just as we are at war with the Americans now."

"What about the Americans, Batani Khan? Shall we have to continue fighting them as well?"

"I do not believe so. The American goal in Afghanistan has become much less ambitious since their intervention began. They now would be satisfied with evidence that our country will not be ruled by extremists or become a haven for international terrorists, neither being an outcome we shall permit. Given such evidence, they will gladly take their troops and go home. In any event, I do not believe they will hinder our efforts,"

"...And our Pakistani Taliban brothers?"

"That, unfortunately, is another problem entirely," Batani admitted somberly. "They share the same faults that I just accused you of having, but theirs cannot be readily rectified. It is likely that, for reasons of their own, our Taliban brothers in Pakistan will oppose the strategy we agree upon here today, meaning that we shall have to fight them. That will be unfortunate, but it would, in any event, please the Americans and the ISI."

From coming into the room fearing they would soon be killed to leaving it as members of Afghanistan's grand army of the future, the Taliban leaders had come a long way in the blink of an eye, and their seemingly dazed reaction to what had just occurred showed it. When Batani stopped speaking, they stood silently in place, as though waiting for instructions.

"My brothers and (I hope) friends, I believe we have accomplished great things here today, and I plan to convene a grand shura here in Kandahar in the coming weeks to agree on further actions. You are now free to go, with my best wishes!"

The effect in the room was electric, everyone beginning to speak with his neighbor as though just discovering his presence. After a strategic pause, Batani raised his hands to quiet them.

"I know that many of you are a long distance from home, naturally without means of transportation. However, each of you will find outside a new vehicle dedicated to your support, given to you in celebration of our new alliance. Please go with God, and drive carefully."

Standing unobtrusively in the back of the room, Hannah Crossman heard the men cheer and rush to the door. Outside, was a line of shiny black SUVs, each with a driver. She and Batani watched as the Talibs drove off, waving to one another as though departing a family picnic.

"You appear to have been a great success, Mike," she told him and, later, Sam Glover when she gleefully awakened him in the middle of the Washington night. "Hopefully, they will continue to cooperate with you."

"One can only try," he replied, looking weary. "Should some not be helpful, well, I've taken the precaution of having one of your CIA transponders installed in each of the vehicles.

When Hannah arrived in Afghanistan, she was met again by Jed, the Agency's station chief in Pakistan. He had been ordered to meet her plane and brief Hannah on the situation she would find upon joining Batani's entourage. Unlike her last trip to the area, this time Hannah was transported by Agency plane directly to Afghanistan, with only brief stops for fuel. Bergen and Glover did not want her to pass through Pakistan, knowing that the ISI would be immediately informed and likely place her under surveillance. General Malik, Orkamzi's successor, was still a largely unknown quantity, but indications obtained by Jed from friendly sources were alarming. As a new man in a very difficult position, he was apparently under great pressure from his superiors to perform well during a period of increasing danger to Pakistan's relations with the United States and its interests in Afghanistan. Malik would eventually find out about Hannah's presence in Batani's camp, which could prove a threat to her safety, but would certainly send a message to the ISI regarding the ambiguity of its relationship with the CIA.

"We must stop meeting like this, Hannah. People are beginning to talk," Jed laughed, as she came off the plane at Bagram airfield.

"I'm sorry that you had to drag all the way up here from Pakistan, Jed, but the bosses seem to be hyper about my welfare. I wonder whether it would be the same, if I were a man?"

"It's not a problem, Hannah! I'm spending more time in Afghanistan these days than in Islamabad and Karachi, and expect that to continue. Our Station Chief in Kabul has got his hands full just keeping up with who's trying to do what to whom: it's a perpetual game of high stakes musical chairs. I've arranged with the military to fly you to an advanced base near Kandahar where Batani's headquarters are at the moment."

"What do you mean 'at the moment'?"

"Our boy Batani has adopted an interesting tactic of relocating himself and immediate staff to wherever he believes the action is or is going to be, often on the spur of the moment. It is very effective, but extremely dangerous because his security precautions need to be altered each time he moves. When he moves to another part of the country, he makes a point of imposing himself upon the hospitality of the local warlord or district chief rather than setting up his own compound.

Contrary to what you might think, this has enormously beneficial effects. First, his host is honored by having the grand poobah come to stay with him and, second, he knows that the Batani has not come to settle in as permanent competition. Third, if the host himself is being troublesome, a friendly visit of several weeks will convince him that it's best to do what Batani wishes, and to not piss him off. Finally, and perhaps most important, Batani has made a point of not challenging the supremacy of the local chiefs in their domains. On the contrary, the message he constantly conveys is that their present fiefdoms are safe and future prosperity unlimited, if only they remain within the collective under his leadership. These people are continuously being tempted by all manner of propositions that offer an immediate reward for changing sides. So far, Batani has apparently succeeded in stopping that, at least in much of Afghanistan. But the battle is constant and everywhere, so he stays on the move."

"Sounds like I'm in for an interesting time."

"Our people in Kandahar have arranged a covert rendezvous with Batani to transfer you, hopefully unseen. I'm told you will employ your usual cover as a free-lance journalist come to do a profile on Batani. You are likely to be both helped and hindered by Batani's determination to invite other journalists to visit him and, perhaps, to hang around for a while. He believes that providing regular access to the media will help get his message out and legitimize his campaign for power in Afghanistan. I agree with him, but you will need to be careful of your cover around your fellow journalists."

"Thanks, Jed. Is there a contingency escape plan?"

"Unfortunately, with Batani frequently on the move, it's impossible to reliably plan for contingencies. You have your satellite phone. If you need to, call home and we'll try to come get you."

As the Army helicopter in which she was riding descended toward the marked landing pad in the compound at the edge of Kandahar, Hannah looked out over the drab city which, for all the world, looked deserted. Leaving the aircraft, she was hailed by a young Captain who introduced himself as the base's intelligence officer and said he would be her escort to the meeting with Batani's agent. He gave her a camouflage jacket, armored vest and helmet to wear so that she would not stand out from the other people at the base. Embarking in a small convoy of armored Humvees, they left the compound and proceeded slowly into the city, crews closely scanning the roadside ahead for signs of an impending attack or installed explosive devices.

"This is one of our normal patrol routes," the Captain explained. "We vary the time every day to make it more difficult for them to set up an ambush, but we don't want to do anything different for you that might risk alerting the enemy. Your contact will meet us in an abandoned warehouse that we often drive through as part of the patrol route."

They arrived there fifteen minutes later, and entered through a large opening that had once been the main entrance. The sudden blackness made Hannah nervous, the

2

only light being a portal at the other end from which the doors were missing. Now inside, three men stepped out of the darkness, a fold of their robes covering the lower half of their faces.

"How do we know these are the right guys?" Hannah asked, trying not to sound nervous.

"We don't. But, if they were not our contacts, they would have been shooting already."

"Very comforting," Hannah allowed, unconvinced, as one of the men waved them to stop. She and the Captain got out of their vehicle, as the soldiers manning the other Humvees took the three under cover with their weapons.

"Will the soldier with you, Captain, please take off his helmet," the apparent leader ot the three requested. Hannah complied, and the man came immediately forward, removing the cover from his face. It was Mir Batani Khan himself.

"It is good to see you, Hannah"

"Same here, Mike, and a relief as well."

Mahmud al-Fasal felt both physically and mentally weary as he sat quietly listening to Batani enlist his fellow Taliban, relieved when the effort appeared successful. He amused himself watching Hannah Crossman, disguised from head to toe, circulate through the room dispensing refreshments, unable to protect herself from the more than occasional pinch or squeeze. He wondered what her tormentors might say and do, were they to discover her true identity. The two of them had arrived at Batani's compound within days of each other, both given the same basic mission, albeit for different reasons: keep Batani honest and alive. Abdul Rashid's objective was more nuanced. His international backers were opposed to terrorism, but they also wished to support Muslim fundamentalism, just not in their own countries or regions. Afghanistan was sufficiently remote to meet their needs and its future seemed inextricably tied to that of Pakistan, which was also considered a safe home for the true faith.

Abdul Rashid knew that Batani was not a fundamentalist. Victorious, he would turn Afghanistan into a latter-day Turkey, using the secularizing benefits of economic development to keep Islam and its imams in their place. This was what the Americans wished would happen and, truth be told, so did Abdul Rashid and Mahmud al-Fasal. But, should that reality become apparent, their funding would dry up and their international network go out of business. Still, Abdul Rashid instructed al-Fasal to support the Americans in dealing with Batani, at least until something occurred that absolutely precluded it. It had occurred separately to both men that, if all else failed, they could probably become wards of the CIA.

For his part, al-Fasal was happy he didn't have to work at cross-purposes with Hannah, whom he greatly admired for both her beauty and aplomb. Their basic instructions were simple: monitor Batani's plans and operations, providing timely reporting and warning to their superiors, particularly of actions that could prove dangerous and/or counterproductive. The channel was also available to Batani for requesting the assistance of American operational assets, a benefit of which he took frequent advantage. To his credit, he did not attempt to isolate Hannah and al-Fasal from operational matters, but rather made a continuing effort to demonstrate that he was trustworthy as well as smart. Even the real journalists who passed through Batani's headquarters were made to feel that they were truly being given access to the inner workings of his movement. His payoff was increasing testimony in the world press that his was not one of many insurrectionary bands in Afghanistan but an actual alternative government.

In her day-to-day life, Hannah was very careful to act as required to maintain her cover, a practice made difficult by Batani's efforts to have her near him as much as possible. Al-Fasal found this amusing, only slightly less so when he was forced to tell Hannah that gossip among the staff revealed that her cover had, in fact, become skewed: most everyone thought she was Batani's concubine. Hannah was, of course, shocked, but accepted that it was a more useful explanation of her presence, particularly for Batani. Nevertheless, she persevered as a writer, making sure she was seen daily transcribing copious notes on her laptop computer after a session with Batani or one of his lieutenants.

"I am sorry your life has been so complicated, Miss Crossman," al-Fasal told her one day in the room that served as a canteen for the staff. "But, at least your true identity has not been discovered."

"I appreciate your concern, Mr. al-Fasal. It is somewhat strange: I've never had a cover for my cover before. But you never know who is going to show up here to make nice with Batani. The other day, I almost stumbled on a man named Kingsley Yong, who works for the Chinese. He and I have talked on the phone in Washington, although I don't recall that we've ever met. But he knows who I am and where I work. And some of the reporters who are always passing through are bound to have worked in Washington and could have seen me, perhaps on Capitol Hill, when I worked for Admiral Bergen. If I'm exposed, Batani could be accused of being an American stooge, and the big bet we're placing on him go down the drain."

"That thought has occurred to me," al-Fasal admitted somberly. "But, at the moment, I'm more concerned about the pressure on you. I suppose your superiors want you to steer Batani in certain directions in which he may not wish to go."

It occurred to Hannah that al-Fasal might be trying to wheedle classified information from her, but concluded that she was being churlish; they were after all on the same side. Nevertheless, she resolved to be more alert to that possibility, although the necessity annoyed her. Al-Fasal noticed.

"Your face tells me that you are unhappy, Miss Crossman. Is there something I can do?" Surprised, Hannah quickly covered:

"I was just thinking that it is time you started calling me Hannah instead of Miss Crossman. I think we now know each other well enough."

"It would be an honor and a pleasure," he replied. "I'm afraid, however, that I do not have a familiar name that you can use, as does Batani. No one has ever called me Mike or anything similar."

"We can come up with something suitable, if you wish. But, I would be very happy to call you Mahmud." He smiled.

"Now that's settled, Hannah, please tell me what is bothering you. But, please be assured that I am not seeking to learn your government's secrets."

To cover her embarrassment, Hannah got up quickly and went to refill her tea mug. Returning to the table, she decided that she needed to talk with someone and that al-Fasal, whom she liked and admired for his abilities and experience, qualified---despite being (nominally) an agent of the Islamic jihad.

"My principal problem is personal, not professional, and I'm sure that I'm far from the only one who's ever had it. It seems that, in the last couple of years, when I find myself out in the middle of nowhere, not knowing what might happen, I wonder how much longer I can continue to do these things and, above all, why I continue to do them. These doubts never come to me in Washington, where I can act on them, but always when the most useful thing I can do is focus on keeping from getting my butt shot off. Careerwise, I'm doing very well, and could eventually go on to a cushy senior executive job on the seventh floor at CIA Headquarters or, perhaps, even in the White House. But, so what? After it's over, what have I got; who will remember?

Back in Washington, I'm seeing a very attractive and talented man, who knows where I work and its drawbacks, and is trying to accept them. But, I cannot tell him whether I'll be there when he calls and, if not, where I've gone and for how long. When you saw us in Paris, we had come to get away from Washington and the middle-of-the-night phone calls. But, as you know, they caught up with us, and Paul was suddenly left alone, without explanation, while I took off for parts unknown. We managed to survive that, but he doesn't know where I am now, and I haven't the foggiest idea when I'll be able to go home."

"What you are doing for your government and country is very important. Very few get such an opportunity to serve and to do it well," al-Fasal told her softly.

"That's what I tell myself, and I believe it. But, nowadays, it doesn't make me feel much better. I maybe could convince myself to chuck it all, if only I knew what I would like better. This business gets into your blood, but you don't realize it until you find yourself back home, maybe at an endless meeting or bored to death sitting in traffic on the Beltway, thinking how exciting life was when your ship was being sunk from under you in the Indian Ocean, and you were about to be dumped into the sea."

"Well, I know clearly where I prefer to be," al-Fasal told Hannah with certainty. "It is on the terrace of my home on the Riviera, sitting by the pool."

"Amen to that," she responded.

CHAPTER TWENTY-ONE

"Batani is getting ready to move, sir!" the breathless aide announced, bursting into General Malik's office in the senior staff compound in Rawalpindi.

"I've been told that for weeks. Where to, this time?"

"Our people have not told us yet, sir: Batani's security is very tight these days. But, it looks like he will move his headquarters east and north from Kandahar to, perhaps, Khost or Jalalabad. It is said he has a beautiful CIA agent managing his security. "

"I wish I had a beautiful CIA agent to protect me," Malik lamented, "and I know my late predecessor, General Orkamzi, undoubtedly would have wished the same. But, at the moment, I would gladly settle for some reliable information from our informants in Batani's compound. Both Khost and Jalalabad would move him much closer to Kabul, and Jalabad sits directly on the main road from Kabul to Peshawar and Islamabad. That would be my guess, as to his destination. But, what is he up to?"

"Our agents tell us, General, that he is being successful in gathering to him many of the Islamic tribes and councils in the south of Afghanistan and is negotiating a truce and cooperation agreement with the Northern Alliance. They all regard him as a heretic and possibly insane, but his arguments make sense to them and he is being able, thus far, to carry out his plans. The Americans are helping him or at least indulging his initiatives. The CIA's drones are finding his enemies with remarkable regularity, and they are not getting intelligence from us."

"At least not that we know of," General Malik amended. "Batani has also gained the support of our friend Abdul Rashid, which means more money for him and less or none for the Islamists. The man has become a major threat."

Malik was reminded once again of the overarching assignment given him when appointed to replace the dead Orkamzi as Director of the ISI: stop Batani by any means necessary. That imperative had since become infinitely more urgent, as he was being continually reminded by his superiors. They would begin making explicit their implied threats to sack the new ISI chief, if he did not soon succeed. Malik could not let that happen, for he had few resources to fall back on, and could not bear to give up the life and privileges of a senior military officer.

There was yet an additional, perhaps more cogent reason: in the course of his developing military career, Malik had begun accepting favors from a number of Islamist leaders, in both Pakistan and Afghanistan. Now risen to a sensitive position, he was vulnerable to blackmail and the demands of his radical associates, to whom Batani and all he stood for was anathema. Their simple, insistent directive to Malik: Kill him!

Under closer surveillance by his many enemies, Batani had become significantly less adventurous, as concerned his personal movements and activities. He no longer dashed about like a latter-day Lawrence of Arabia,

visiting provincial capitals and tribal headquarters to rally
the fighters he found there to his cause, often accompanied
by little more than a single aide and his driver. At the urg-
ing and instruction of the CIA, he now concealed his intentions and movements by replicating his entourage several
times, sending each copy to a different destination or via
a different route, while waiting until the very last minute
to reveal the one he personally intended to join. Hannah
Crossman appreciated the effectiveness of this tactic, but
it drove her crazy because her orders required her to go
wherever Batani went. Since she could not be replicated,
her whereabouts were a telltale sign of Batani's intentions,
so she was forced to endure, along with him, the same concealment and evasion practices. These involved, among
other things, being squeezed together in the back of loaded trucks and sharing quarters during rest stops enroute.
Batani quite obviously enjoyed this, but Hannah thought it
beyond the call of duty. It was what had given rise to the
widespread view that Hannah was Batani's mistress, which
she was forced to admit was a more realistic cover than the
one she pretended to.

One of the guesses regarding Batani's destination
proved correct. After brief stops in a number of districts,
he ended up in Jalalabad, taking up residence in the palatial (and securable) home of a local potentate who was persuaded by a large bribe to go visiting abroad. Jalalabad was
to be a major stop on the route of the railroad being built
by the Chinese from their copper mine concession southeast of Kabul to the Pakistan border, where it would connect with the existing line running through Peshawar and
Islamabad. With protection provided by Batani's forces,
construction progress had been speeded up and advance
survey and construction crews began appearing in Jalalabad, attracting notice and comdemnation in the mosques.
Recognition that a major test of strength was coming had
prompted Batani's move, that plus the fact that Jalalabad

was a lot closer to Kabul and astride the principal route to Pakistan. He assumed the symbolism would not be lost on his opponents and supporters alike.

Having confirmed Batani's relocation, General Malik decided to journey to Jalalabad to meet his nemesis for the first time. The visit would give him an opportunity to both size up the man and scout his surroundings. It would also demonstrate to his superiors that he was pursuing his primary mission. His reception at Batani's new headquarters, a sturdy stone building encircled by a high wall with a single gate, was reserved but not unfriendly. He was required to pass through a series of gatekeepers who verified his identity and required him to temporarily surrender the pistol holstered on his belt. Carefully observing his surroundings, Malik saw no one he thought could pass as a beautiful CIA agent, in fact no foreigners at all other than several guards at the gate and a European TV journalist and his cameraman waiting expectantly outside the building for a promised interview. Hannah, of course, had been alerted to Malik's visit and departed the compound earlier for a tour of the city with Jed, who had come from Islamabad to keep tabs on General Malik. Other than the expectedly tight security, the ISI director had noted nothing extraordinary before being ushered in to meet with Batani in what had been the homeowner's dining room. Despite his knowledge of Batani's background, Malik was surprised by his host's youthful appearance.

"Welcome, General Malik. I have been looking forward to meeting you since hearing of your appointment to replace our late, lamented friend General Orkamzi. You have large boots to fill: your predecessor was a very active man who spent little time in his office. You have heard, no doubt, that the people who caused his death thought they were pursuing me?"

Malik nodded, as Batani indicated for him to be seated, whereupon an aide entered with refreshments.

"So, in a sense, you are indebted to me for your promotion." Batani laughed at his own joke, but Malik didn't appear to find it funny.

"We have much to discuss," Batani continued, "since I have not had an opportunity to meet with senior representatives of your government for many months. My country has entered a period of rapid change that will only become broader as time passes. As Afghanistan's neighbor and friend, Pakistan will naturally have a great interest in these changes, and will undoubtedly benefit from them greatly."

"Of what changes are you speaking, Mir Batani Khan?"

"To begin with, development of the mineral deposits the Americans have kindly found for us all over the country and the infrastructure that must accompany such development. I'm sure you know of the copper mining concession the thieves in Kabul have let to the Chinese and the new railroad that is soon to come through Jalalabad. They are but the beginning."

"But, these are matters for the government in Kabul, not for you," Malik remonstrated. "My government is very much concerned that these developments proceed properly, with proper recognition of Pakistan's interests and concerns."

"I'm sure it is a matter of concern," Batani laughed. "But, what Pakistan considers her legitimate interests and concerns are not necessarily the same from my country's viewpoint. What differences emerge must be carefully resolved, and peacefully. We have been at war with various invaders for more than thirty years, and it must stop. We cannot fight and build at the same time, and we must build in order that our people prosper."

"A very noble sentiment, Mir Batani Khan, but that is the responsibility of those who rule in Kabul, while you are here in Jalalabad an outlaw."

"Last week, Malik, I was in Kandahar, much further from the capital. Now, I am a great deal closer: in Jalalabad. Soon, I will be in Kabul. I hope you will convey to your leaders that the future course of Afghanistan will be as I chart it."

"And, do the Americans approve of what you are attempting?" Malik asked, disingenuously fishing for intelligence.

"I do not care whether they do or not. But, why should they not approve? My aim is to eliminate ignorance and poverty in Afghanistan, root causes of extremism, which is what the Americans are really fighting. They wish to go home believing their expenditures have been worthwhile, and I intend to help them do that."

"You will not succeed without Pakistan's cooperation."

Batani hesitated, seeing a pointless confrontation at hand.

"That may be true, my friend. But, my failure would also be Pakistan's. Neither of our countries will succeed until we lift our people out of the unrelieved poverty that causes them to believe their only prospect of a better life lies in heaven. We are mullah-ridden, General Malik, driven by the mosques to oppose what is new, to mistrust our fellow Muslims, and to oppose the infidel regardless of who he is. Afghanistan's new possibilities offer an escape from this lunacy, and I propose to take advantage of it. Pakistan may be able to prevent my succeeding, but the final result would be that both countries end up with nothing."

Reporting to his superiors upon returning to Rawalpindi, Malik was surprised to find substantial agreement with Batani's view. Encouraged by his covert connections with fundamentalist imams, and a strict religious upbringing, the new ISI Director strongly believed that the ultimate goal of Pakistan's government and military should be the establishment of a state and society firmly based on Sharia Law. Anyone who was in opposition was to be considered a traitor. However, listening to the discussion among the senior generals following his report, Malik was amazed:

"The heretic Batani is unfortunately correct," the Chief of Staff stated bluntly. "Naïve people believe that the choice is simple, that we either follow the path of God or that of the secular infidel. But, we quickly discover that almost every imam pretending to great religious authority has his own unwavering belief as to what, to him, constitutes true Islam and, therefore, what is heresy. And, they are not reluctant to use their preachings to attack fellow Muslims whom they consider apostate, and even urge that they be killed. A great irony of the modern era is that the only cause that apparently will unite Muslims is resistance to a common invader. But, when that invader is modernization and economic advance rather than a Soviet or American soldier, our unity disintegrates and we fall back on the old strictures instead of dealing with the demands of reality."

He looked around the table for comment, but his fellow officers were largely concentrating on keeping their faces expressionless. This was a highly charged subject, and none wished to be perceived to support a viewpoint that could prove politically risky or incorrect. The COS was judged by many of his colleagues to be indiscreet in expressing his views, his tenure thought to be uncertain, as a result. But, he was also pragmatic and decisive in advancing the interests and beliefs of his political and military superiors, a quality unusual and appreciated. His position was safe, as long as that concurrence continued.

"Pakistan cannot consider a future separate from that of Afghanistan," he resumed. "We must jointly refocus our attention and resources on peaceful economic development in cooperation with international agencies and businesses. There is, at least at the moment, in Afghanistan far more of what would interest prospective development partners than in Pakistan, and it may remain so. Therefore, our strategy and operational tactics must have two priority goals: first, to make sure we share in any benefits---political, economic, social, whatever---derived from Afghanistan's development and, second, to prevent the leadership in that country from becoming powerful and capable enough to challenge our ability to achieve the first goal. Mir Batani Khan is a threat that increases with each passing week. General Malik has been assigned to rid us of this threat, and he must act immediately or forfeit his opportunity.

"Mr. Huggins, this is Kate Bryant of Overseas Security Services calling. We've been told your company, Global Security Applications, has people on its staff with experience in security and personal protection operations overseas. Is that so?"

"Yes, it is. But, why are you asking?

"Our firm has been awarded a State Department contract to provide qualified personnel for security missions in Afghanistan. Some of the people we had lined up when bidding on the contract have now dropped out, and we are looking for replacements, three to be exact, on an emergency basis. We are obligated to deploy these people within three weeks. The pay, as I'm sure you know, is extremely good, and each person signing up will receive a twenty thousand dollar bonus for helping us out."

It was an offer not to be scorned, but it impaled Reggie Huggins squarely on the horns of a dilemma. He had the people: himself and two former CIA Directorate of Operations colleagues, all with actual experience in Soviet-era Afghanistan. The other two, he knew, would be more than willing to go because the remuneration was great and they were bored to death. Their joints were now a bit creaky, but they wouldn't find out how much that mattered until they got to Kabul or wherever.

The problem was much more basic: Global Security Applications was already under contract to *Oberling For America*. Its pay rate was not nearly what it would be in Afghanistan and billable hours had fallen recently while Roger Norton figured out what tack the campaign was going to take in challenging President Kitteridge's bid for re-election. But Huggins had been assured only recently that his company's services were valued and that the contract would be maintained. There was no way he could consider stiffing a man who might be President of the United States within a year.

The Oberling campaign's principal foreign affairs problem was that the Kitteridge Administration had independently adopted as its own the war strategy Roger Norton had hoped to beat the White House to death with: get out of Afghanistan quickly and use the money saved to reduce the national debt. Since Oberling could obviously not support the President on this issue, Norton needed to come up with another angle that could gain traction with the electorate. This dilemma proved fortuitous for Reggie Huggins, who found Roger Norton more than willing to have he and his people go to Afghanistan, and even offered to continue paying for Global Security's services, albeit at a lower consulting rate. Reggie's assignment would be to keep his eyes and ears open while doing his security job, reporting back periodically via email his observations as to how the American mission was proceeding and progress being made toward the goal of getting out of the country as soon as possible. No classified information would be requested or promised.

Huggins' appearance in Jalalabad took Hannah by surprise, as she immediately reported to Sam Glover.

"I came to the guard post at the compound entrance this morning and there he was, looking like he had just come to Tombstone to fight at the OK Corral. He was wearing camo fatigues and an Australian campaign hat, you know, the kind with one side pinned up. The basic difference between Reggie and Wild Bill Hickok was that Reggie was wearing only one .45, but with the holster tied to his leg no less."

"Did you talk with him?"

"He's as happy as a bug: back in the saddle again! Told me he hadn't realized how much he missed the old days in Afghanistan. How in hell did he get here. Sam?"

"I guess I'm responsible for that," Glover admitted. "Reggie and his people were becoming pains in the ass working for Oberling here in Washington, so I arranged for him to be offered a contract over there, knowing he wouldn't be able to refuse. He was actually very good the first time in Afghanistan and should also do the job well this time. What have they got him doing?"

"He's assigned to perimeter security as sort of a supervisor of the guards, all of whom are contract people or Afghan policemen. I don't think he's happy with them."

"Well, don't let him hang around Batani or find out what he's doing. I suspect Reggie is spying for that asshole Norton in addition to playing Wild Bill Hickok. By the way, the word back here is that you are Batani's mistress. Please don't let Huggins find out about that either.

"How is our boy Batani doing?" President Kitteridge asked, as he and Admiral Bergen walked back to the Oval Office after a briefing in the Situation Room.

"He's doing exceedingly well, sir, which means that we're soon going to have a very large problem. Both the Pakistanis and the Kabul government have been waiting for him to overreach and fail, so that they can stop worrying. But, he's showing no sign of doing that. On the contrary, my former assistant, Hannah Crossman, who is attached to his headquarters, reports that he is getting ready to take on what may be, at least symbolically, his greatest challenge: straightening out the perpetual mess in Torkham. Should he succeed at that, his next stop could very well be Kabul."

"What's Torkham?"

"It's a small Afghan town on the border with Pakistan that is the crossing point for most of the supplies brought into Afghanistan to support our troops and those of our allies. Because the country is landlocked and has no railroads, the only way to bring in significant volumes of cargo is by truck through Pakistan from the port at Karachi. Take a look at a map, and you'll see that the route is an absolute bitch and our greatest point of weakness, although we've been making it work---most of the time---since we began serious military operations in Afghanistan. We are running continuous truck convoys, many of 150 vehicles or more, through the territory of two countries that are less than hospitable. A large number of the trucks are tankers carrying fuel, and you can imagine the damage a single grenade or rocket can do. The biggest bottleneck is Torkham, and it is largely unavoidable.

"The convoys need to use the main highway that goes from Karachi, through Islamabad and Peshawar, connecting at Torkham with Afghan National Highway 1 that goes through Jalalabad to Kabul. There is a railroad line to Torkham in Pakistan, but not in Afghanistan. Building that link is a requirement of the contract that Kabul signed with the Chinese to develop the copper deposits in Logar Province. But, we have begun to get intelligence indications that the Chinese are planning to concentrate their resources on building the railroad first north to Tajikistan and east to China rather than south to Pakistan. That will piss the Paks off mightily, and make the Torkham problem even worse."

"Although few Americans have even heard of Torkham, it's like the crossroads of the world. Reportedly, some 20,000 border crossings are made there daily, mostly locals of both nationalities going about their daily business. But, the town is in the Federally Administered Tribal Areas rather than in Pakistan proper, so the extent of central government control and influence is limited. There is no question but that the Taliban use the crossing and roads for their own resupply, and all manner of even less savory traffic goes back and forth across the border. The town itself is a perpetual mob scene.

"But, the really dangerous thing is that the Pakistanis can shut us down completely at any moment they choose by closing the gate at the border crossing. They have actually done it several times for a few days at time to show that they are angry with us about something. When that happens, the trucks pile up on both sides of the border and are sitting ducks for terrorists. There have been instances of more than a thousand vehicles parked, waiting to get through. The two main things that hold the Pakistanis back are (1) they cannot afford to push us too far without serious repercussions for which they are unprepared and (2) that almost all the vehicles are locally contracted, and their owners need the money. But, should Islamabad come to the conclusion that we intend to cut Pakistan loose, for example by supporting Batani's ambitions for Afghanistan at the expense of Pakistan's interests, all bets could be off, and we might have to find another main route in and out, other than through Pakistan."

"What would Batani be trying to do in Torkham?" Kitteridge asked.

"Torkham would be the ultimate test of Batani's strength and strategy for uniting Afghanistan; everyone will be watching. As they say: 'If he can do it there, he can do it anywhere.' The area is a hodge-podge of warring and competing tribes, Islamic sects and criminal enterprises mixed into a huge population of generally poor people just trying to get by. Batani will need to somehow attract as many as possible to his cause, to the extent that they stop fighting one another. This is what he has been able to do successfully elsewhere, but the difference in Torkham will be that the critical elements will be Pakistani rather than Afghan."

"Are we planning to help him, if possible?"

"We have made available a slush fund of ten million for him to spread around. In addition, he will be given priority targeting access to Predator resources. If Batani has trouble with specific tribal leaders or Islamist extremists, we will try to take them out, wherever they are. The Pakistanis profess to be outraged when we hit targets in their hinterlands, but they are, more often than not, happy to be rid of the troublemakers."

"Is this going to work?" the President asked searchingly. "Is it worth the risk to Batani's life, as well as his credibility, not to mention our own plans?"

"I honestly don't know, sir. I had thought to make a quick trip out to speak with Batani face-to-face or to perhaps send Jim Detwiler, but decided it would be too difficult. No senior American official, like Jim or myself, could get quickly in to see Batani without the world finding out about it almost immediately, and that would make Batani appear an American puppet. Ordinarily, we arrange to meet with him covertly in a neutral spot outside the region, but there is not enough time to arrange something like that. So, I have briefed Hannah Crossman by secure telephone, and she will talk with Batani on our behalf."

"Is she the one they are calling 'the beautiful CIA agent who lives with Batani and protects him'?"

"Mr. President, you have been watching obscure cable channels again!"

CHAPTER TWENTY-TWO

The first indication of impending disaster came in the form of an abrupt call to the Chief of Staff's office, the second when General Raheem Malik entered to find the President's private secretary also there. The latter, known in government circles as the Dark Angel, was a saturnine man of high intellect and little humor whom the chief executive of Pakistan dispatched to do necessary dirty work. Where the Angel lurked, someone was usually being sentenced to professional oblivion or worse. The COS did not wait for the door to close to begin shouting at Malik:

"Why have you done nothing about Batani? I told you months ago that the man is a great threat to Pakistan and must be eliminated. But, you have done nothing!" Seeing the look of shock and surprise on Malik's face, the Angel kindly explained:

"We have been reliably informed that Batani is conspiring with the Chinese to divert the huge sum of money they are supposed to spend on the railroad to our border to build the northern extension of the tracks and a direct connection to China through the Wakhan Corridor. Present construction will stop at Jalalabad, which as you know is Batani's current headquarters."

He paused momentarily to let his news percolate before telling the dazed Malik what had already become obvious to him.

"The effect of this change will be to remove Pakistan from the political and economic mainstream of Asia. The Afghans and Chinese will be able to deal directly with each other without consideration of Pakistan's interests and claim to participation. When the line northward to the Tajik border is completed and the tracks connected through to existing systems in Russia and westward, the Afghans and Chinese will have direct access to Europe, and will be able to siphon off much of the freight traffic that now must pass through Karachi. It would be an economic disaster of incalculable magnitude."

Malik was incredulous. "How could Batani do this? He does not control the government or sit in Kabul."

"He has apparently convinced the Chinese that it is only a matter of time, a short time, before he will control the entire country," the COS replied. "They have reason to believe him because he has proven able to develop sufficient power and authority to provide adequate protection to their current construction operations, which were being attacked on almost a daily basis. In addition, there is a significant element of aspirational thinking in Beijing. Successful completion of a reliable rail connection with Europe could prove to be the most significant economic advance China has made since the beginning of Communist rule. Even if the realistic odds of success are not nearly as favorable as believed, it is certain to be considered worth the risk."

"What will the Americans say," Malik asked desperately? They are sure to see the same prospects that you do. It will not help their long term competition with China."

The Dark Angel shrugged. "At this moment, they are much more concerned with stopping Islamic extremism, as is China. Both see Batani as a pragmatist who will place Afghan prosperity well before religious orthodoxy. Prosperity, they believe, will be the most effective alternative to killing oneself and others in the name of God."

"Do you believe that?" the Chief-of-Staff asked. Again the Angel shrugged.

"Whether I do or not, it is not clear that Pakistan will have the opportunity to test the belief. We are a resource poor and population rich country now in danger of being denied any benefit from the great wealth that apparently is to be found in Afghanistan. The irony of it alone makes me furious, and emphasizes the criticality of your mission, General Malik."

Malik was crushed. "What do you wish me to do?"

"We don't care how you do it, but you must stop Batani. We will give you a week. The future of Pakistan depends on you, Malik. Do not disappoint us."

Returning to his own office, Malik called for status updates from the ISI agents mounting round the clock surveillance of Batani's headquarters and his principal fighting units. None of them was in a position to get close to the Taliban leader, who was being guarded by a special force of security agents, mostly foreigners, now being led by Reggie Huggins. However, their reporting was accurate and timely enough to tell Malik that Batani was getting ready again to go on the road, but could not yet provide his destination. In any event, the ISI chief had no idea what he should do. Even had he possessed a plan, a week would not be enough time to put it in motion to a successful conclusion. It occurred wildly to Malik that the people who directed the strike missions of CIA's drones could be provided with the coordinates of Batani's quarters, but he felt certain his ploy would likely be detected by the beautiful female agent guarding Batani at all times.

"Admiral Bergen asked me talk with you, Mike, about what you are intending to do. The word in Washington is that you're planning to try working your magic in Torkham." Batani looked at Hannah in shock and surprise.

"I have not yet convinced myself to go to Torkham, but already the CIA knows about it. I am surprised that American Intelligence does not rule the world."

Hannah smiled modestly. "Some people are more transparent than others. We are just trying to save you from yourself." Batani's jaw dropped, then he burst out laughing.

"Your admiral was very wise to send a woman to keep an eye on me. If you had been a man, just now, I would have had you shot."

"He would be gratified to have your approval," Hannah acknowledged, "but he is concerned for your safety and the success of our joint ventures. What do you hope to gain from a campaign in Torkham? You are likely to be opposed there by the ISI and the Pakistani Taliban, in addition to your own countrymen. There could be a great deal of shooting."

"Admiral Bergen is correct: there could be a great deal of shooting and many casualties. We could surely be among them. But, I am at the stage of my struggle where such risk is unavoidable. I must go, as your gamblers put it, all in. My campaign to unite Afghanistan cannot succeed until I am welcomed in Kabul, and I can come there only as a conqueror or a savior. However, I do not wish to fight my way into the capital or to unite Afghanistan by killing everyone who opposes me. I might succeed, but the hatred would last forever and the plotting would begin the day I became President. My country will rise only by embracing its future, not by constantly rehearsing its past. There remains only the second option: to win the cooperation of the people, so that my way is given a chance. They need not love or trust me, at least not until I've proven to them that I can succeed."

"How do you expect to do that by going to Torkham?"

"Torkham is representative of Afghanistan as a whole. The conflict, confusion and contention that exist between Pakistan and Afghanistan and within our two countries are demonstrated in Torkham on a daily basis. You Americans are also closely involved there. If I can demonstrate in Torkham that I can at least control this dysfunction, it will greatly strengthen my claim to the leadership of Afghanistan."

"And you are prepared to risk your life on such a naïve hope?" Hannah responded incredulously. This would be the first time you will be in direct confrontation with the Pakistanis, who have strong reason to fear your potential success. What makes you think you can get Islamabad and Rawalpindi to cooperate?"

Batani smiled. "You have correctly identified the most critical question, Hannah. I am going to Torkham precisely because it will force the Pakistanis to negotiate with me directly. Otherwise, they will use their agents and proxies to pursue me. They clearly prefer that I simply disappear from the scene, but that is not going to happen."

"But, what have you got to deal with, Mike?   You have nothing Pakistan would need badly enough to give you what you want."

"That's not true, Hannah. I have something they will want very badly, although they may be just beginning to realize it. It is the key to their future."

Hannah was mystified, and it must have showed on her face because Batani began to laugh.

"In 1891, Hannah, the railroad network of its India colony was extended by Great Britain to Torkham, but for political reasons never beyond into Afghanistan. The lack of effective economic communications between Afghanistan and what is now Pakistan has seriously retarded the development of both countries, as is reflected in the Torkham of today which, except for its long lines of trucks, is pretty much unchanged. The government in Kabul has taken action to build the railroad that's been missing for more than a hundred years. Its entry into service will bring Afghanistan into the modern era and make possible radical economic advance. Of course, Pakistan will also benefit, since the rail line will connect with its domestic network at Torkham and provide a medium for transport of both raw materials and finished goods."

Batani paused. "What I have just told you is background for the new developments that made me decide to go to Torkham.

"The country that will benefit most of all from these programs is China, and not just because of the mining operations they will service. The Chinese are proposing to build and largely fund, a railroad through the Wakhan Corridor that directly connects Afghanistan with China. It would connect with the line from Torkham I just told you about. It is a project very much in Afghanistan's interest, and should be approved. When completed, China will be directly connected with Europe. It will be a modern day Silk Road, and be of enormous benefit to international commerce."

He paused again, this time for effect.

"That is, except for Pakistan. The new line from China will go straight into Afghanistan and then northward. It will no longer be necessary for goods and passengers entering or exiting Afghanistan to pass through Pakistan, thus depriving Islamabad of much of the power they exercise currently at Torkham."

Hannah was becoming impatient.

"That will be great for Afghanistan, Mike! But, how does it help you now?"

Batani smiled. "As the CIA knows, I have a mutually beneficial arrangement with the Chinese. I am providing effective protection for their construction projects in Afghanistan and they are providing me with large sums of money with which to pursue my political ambitions. Beijing wishes me to provide the same support to its Wakhan Corridor venture that I am currently rendering elsewhere in Afghanistan, in return for which I will receive an expanded stream of financial support, as well as Chinese political backing for my campaign to gain the Presidency of Afghanistan."

Hannah nodded, wondering how much of this was known in Washington.

"But, the most useful information I gained," Batani continued, "was that the Chinese intend to stop work on the railroad line to south to Torkham in order to concentrate all of their resources and funding on the northward line to the Tajik border and the one to China, the suspension to last indefinitely."

Batani's way forward suddenly became clear to Hannah.

"...And you believe that you have sufficient clout with the Chinese to talk them out of doing that."

Islamabad would be both infuriated and terrified by the prospect of increased isolation and being deprived of both the political influence and monetary rewards that would come from controlling a major transshipping route. Perhaps more important, it would be a sign that Beijing now considered its relations with Afghanistan more important than those with Pakistan. It was probable that rumors of the impending Chinese move had already reached the Pakistani government and military.

Batani nodded. "I cannot afford to push the Chinese too far, but they really have no choice but to give me what I want. It will not cost them very much additional, and slow the projects down only if we can't find more construction workers. My plan is to force what your American westerns call a showdown with the Pakistanis at Torkham. My proposal will be very simple. In return for ISI cooperation in facilitating the efficient and peaceful operation of the border crossing at Torkham, I will assure the continued construction of the railroad southward to Pakistan. It will not be an earthshaking achievement, but it will demonstrate that I have the ability and wherewithal to deal with Pakistan and China, and the capacity to rule Afghanistan."

"What do you think?" Hannah asked Sam Glover, after briefing him on Batani's plan.

"He's right about one thing. The Paks have heard about the Chinese plan and are, in fact, scared silly worrying that the Chinese love them less than they used to. I think Batani's plan could work, and is certainly worth trying. But, either way, the Pakistanis are not going to like it, and he needs to watch his ass more than ever. And so do you, young lady, particularly if you have to go to Torkham with Batani. The tribal areas in Pakistan are completely lawless, and home to a volatile mixture of terrorists and religious extremists. I plan to send Jed up there from Islamabad to work with you, and you can call on Reggie Huggins, if you need to; he owes me. Don't go far from your security back up, and be armed at all times."

"Thanks, Dad, for your advice," Hannah told him. "It really makes me feel better."

After speaking with Hannah, Glover called Admiral Bergen and James Detwiler, and the three met later at the White House. They agreed that Batani's bold initiative was as risky for him as it was worth pursuing. If he could carry it off, he would demonstrate both a mastery of the byzantine affairs of his country and the ability to deal effectively with its two most ambitious neighbors.

"President Kitteridge agrees with our view," Bergen told the others, "but he wants to hedge, if we can, the prospect that Batani will fail. We can't afford to go all in, as Batani has. How do we manage that?"

"Why don't we talk with the Chinese and Pakistanis back channel to get them to see properly the significance of what Batani's trying to do?" Detwiler proposed. "Should he succeed in controlling the anarchy and endless conflict in Afghanistan that Torkham symbolizes, both countries would benefit greatly at little cost to themselves. China would get its new Silk Road more quickly and Pakistan its long-delayed rail connection into Afghanistan. . . and they avoid the mutual recriminations that would ensue, if China implemented its current intention to stop building the line to Torkham."

Bergen pondered for a moment, then nodded. "Let's do it! I'll tell the President."

CHAPTER TWENTY-THREE

The morning was frigid, the early sun rising behind the mountains brightly illuminating the blue sky in which there was no trace of a cloud. Although the shadows of night had not yet left the single street of the small town, it was already filled with people, muffled against the cold, beginning their daily business with an urgency that would fade as the sun warmed the land.

Above the road, like an evil omen, hung a gray haze that seemed occasionally to sparkle in the sun's rays as they caught suspended droplets of unburned fuel produced by the trucks parked on both shoulders of the road as far as the eye could see in both directions. Those that stretched back into the Khyber Pass to the northeast were mostly empty, headed ultimately for Karachi to pick up more supplies and fuel to support the American presence in Afghanistan. The idle trucks pointed in the opposite direction were fully loaded, many of them tankers carrying gasoline and diesel fuel to meet the insatiable demand of a mechanized war machine. Pakistani paramilitary policemen had made an effort to provide spacing between the parked fuel trucks, and had segregated them from those carrying non-volatile cargoes in the hope of limiting the impact of a maliciously thrown grenade or even a careless cooking fire. Such incidents in the past had caused enormous conflagrations, huge monetary losses, and serious resupply delays in the course of threatening to burn down the entire town.

This was Torkham, by far the busiest border crossing between Pakistan and Afghanistan. Its principal reason for existence was the wooden barrier and flanking huts that blocked the road, largely symbolically, requiring passing vehicular and pedestrian traffic to stop to be identified and checked. The road through the town was always filled with people, generally distinguishable only by the weapons they were carrying. Periodically, a patrol of U.S soldiers from a nearby fire support base would pass through, mostly to let everyone know they were still around and to lend a hand at the crossing point when American convoys came through.

Four days earlier, the Pakistani government had ordered the border closed, for reasons unknown in Torkham. The layer of gray smog hanging over the town had been created by the crews of backed-up trucks running their motors all night to keep warm. The men had now wandered into town looking for breakfast, and street vendors were doing brisk business. Hannah Crossman sat at an open window in the center of town watching this scene, breathing the reminiscent aroma of exhaust fumes and cooking food, fantasizing that she was on a corner in Manhattan buying a hot dog or knish from a street vendor's cart. Her party had arrived from Jalalabad in the early hours of the morning, the road en route otherwise empty of moving traffic because, with the border closed, there was no place to go or to be coming from. She drank the last of her tea, and rose to see what had become of Batani.

As the morning progressed, the number of armed men in the main road increased to the point where they had begun crowding the gate manned by members of the Afghan Army. Although the men made no threatening gestures, the border guards were understandably nervous, although not nearly as much as their Pakistani counterparts a short distance down the road. Unable to determine what, if anything, was about to happen, the latter made frantic calls up their chain of command, word of which quickly reached General Malik, who had moved to Peshawar, both to be closer to Torkam and further away from his insistent superiors in Rawalpindi. He requested the rapid movement of an Army mechanized unit to Torkham to back up the border guards and paramilitary forces.

The Afghan fighters newly arrived in Torkham were wearing the usual nondescript robes and turbans, pulled across the lower part of their faces against both the cold and acrid smog. Closer inspection revealed that every man was wearing, pinned somewhere on the front of his garment, a large metal badge showing the flag of Afghanistan with the words "Peace and Prosperity" in the country's most prevalent languages superimposed. Batani had procured a large quantity of them from China, through Kingsley Yong, and had convinced the warlords and tribal chieftains who had agreed to join his movement to have their fighters wear them as a symbol of unity in the cause of a greater Afghanistan. A much smaller quantity had been gold plated, and these Batani gave to leaders as tokens of their importance, to go along with the radio-equipped Land Rover (with driver) he provided each as a mobile command post. He had obtained the vehicles at a discount through a trading company owned by Mahmud al-Fasal, Batani's primary reward being the ability to contact his subordinates and collaborators when requiring their assistance. In Torkham that day, the men had been told to do nothing but make their presence evident.

Batani himself did not appear in the town until midafternoon, by which time the Pakistanis had reinforced the guard at their border crossing and General Malik, still in Peshawar, had nearly driven himself mad trying to decide how to fulfill the do or die mission given him by the Dark Angel. In Rawalpindi, his aide, who had been telling all callers that the General was in the field and could not be reached, reported that he was being queried by personages to whom he could not much longer give No for an answer. Using her satellite mobile phone, Hannah updated Sam Glover, and was told that Jed had attempted in vain to contact Malik to find out whether a showdown at Torkham was in the offing and, if so, whether or not it could be forestalled or at least mitigated.

"What is Batani planning to do, Hannah? He doesn't plan to start shooting, does he?"

"Not if he follows the plan he described to me. He's deliberately creating tension here to provoke a confrontation with a senior representative of the Pakistani government that will bring decisive action, not the usual BS and double dealing. Batani expects his opposite number to be General Malik, who we hear is in Peshawar. But, thus far, there's no sign of him."

"I'm going to send Jed up to Peshawar to see if he can smoke out Malik, after which he'll come your way. He's got orders to cover your back, so be nice to him."

"You're very kind, Sam. But, who's going to cover his?"

"Reggie Huggins."

The standoff at Torkham continued for three more days, during which time the air in the town became more poisonous and the parked trucks began to run out of fuel.

The crews of tankers carrying gasoline began to tap their cargoes and sell them by the bucketful to the less fortunate at grossly inflated prices, which were even more outrageous if the customer was in Afghanistan where all trucks waiting to go South were empty. Eventually, whether by accident or in retribution, a match or lit cigarette was dropped in the wrong place and a serious explosion and conflagration erupted on the Pakistani side of the border. Two more days passed before order and relative safety were restored. In the interim, the local economy of Torkham continued to flourish, as more customers and vendors from both sides of the border joined the bazaar. Hannah, now joined by Jed, wandered through the crowd, which comprised a cosmopolitan admixture of Islamic fighters, American soldiers, Taliban agents, international journalists and videographers, stranded truck drivers, and local entrepreneurs plying their trades. Several times, Hannah had to dodge to avoid being caught on camera, which would not do, since her real self was supposed to be elsewhere in the world.

One afternoon, an Afghan Army officer approached Hannah as she stood watching the maelstrom of people and vehicles backed up at the border-crossing gate.

"We have another American here who would like to meet you. He is just over there in the gatehouse."

Without thinking, Hannah followed him across the road and into the small building that housed the border guards. Inside she found Paul Rayner.

"I won't ask what you're doing here," he told her. "But the Captain told me you are a journalist and that bothers me a great deal. If it's discovered that CIA agents are going around masquerading as journalists, none of us real journalists will be safe. I, for one, resent that, despite my feelings for you."

Hannah had no explanation she could give him without lying. Although he could accurately guess, Paul had no need-to-know why she was in Torkham, carrying a camera bag with markings that identified her as a member of the Press. He noted that she was wearing no makeup and had her hair severely pulled back into a bun, revealing small gold earrings: a concession to femininity that no military uniform could conceal.

"Are you alone?" he asked.

"Only at the moment," she replied evasively. "There are others with me. What about you?"

"I had a bodyguard and an interpreter from the government press office in Kabul, but they seem to have disappeared."

"I'm sorry, but I'm not in a position to stay with you, at the moment," Hannah told him. "I strongly recommend you find your escort immediately. This is one of the most dangerous places in the country, if not the world."

"I know," Paul replied. "That's why I'm here. I was told that what is happening here in Torkham is a microcosm of our entire struggle in Afghanistan. The trucks backed up are sitting ducks for whoever is pissed off at us at the time: the Taliban, the Pakistanis, the Afghans or all of the above. I've got a camera crew waiting in Kabul for me to tell them the coast is clear to come down to shoot a piece for *American Focus*."

"Who told you to come here, of all places? There are many hotspots in Afghanistan and Pakistan where you can get a good story without the high risk of being killed in the process."

"A guy back in Washington name of Roger Norton. He told me that what happens in Torkham in the next couple of weeks will determine our end game in Afghanistan. He recommended that I come here to see whether I can predict what that will be."

"Is this the Roger Norton who works for Alfred Oberling?"

"That's the one. He and Oberling liked the interview we put together for *American Focus* several weeks ago, and told me they want to show their gratitude by tipping me off to some good stories."

"What they want you to do is find out what President Kitteridge plans to do in Afghanistan so that they can scream bloody murder and recommend the opposite."

"You are probably right, Hannah," Rayner smiled. "But, I don't care, if the story is really good. And, judging by what I've seen here today, it is. This place is a nuthouse, with everyone milling around waiting to shoot at one another or blow things up. There may not be much of a story to be written, but the visuals will be fantastic."

They did not pay attention to the three men who entered the room until they came directly to where Hannah and Paul were standing. It registered at that moment that the lower half of their faces were masked and their weapons slung so as to leave their hands free. Before the significance of this observation became apparent, two of the men grabbed Paul's arms and began to drag him toward the door, while the third attempted the same with Hannah. Had they been better informed, they would have reversed assignments, for Hannah's lone attacker immediately hit the floor with a yelp that caused his confederates to turn from their preoccupation with Paul. Afterward, Hannah didn't remember pulling her pistol from the camera bag, much less aiming it, but its report claimed everyone's attention, as did the neat hole that appeared in the forehead of the man securing Paul's right arm. The shot immediately brought Jed and Reggie Huggins running with pistols drawn, and the incident quickly ended. Paul Rayner stood agape, staring at Hannah while absently wiping a spray of the dead man's blood from his face. He said nothing, and Hannah never heard from him again.

On the seventh day, Batani identified himself to the Lieutenant Colonel in charge of the port-of-entry on the Pakistani side and demanded to see General Malik. Given the message, the ISI Chief concluded that it was a signal from God instructing him how to pursue his assigned mission. He donned a fresh uniform, with all of his campaign ribbons and badges, and directed his driver to take him to Torkham.

Hannah was surprised when Reggie Huggins, who had been keeping an eye on the crowd at the border gate, came to tell her that General Malik had appeared. Batani himself, in an inner room of the house taken over for his temporary headquarters, was surprised only that the General had come so quickly. He stood up behind his makeshift desk to greet him, as he came through after surrendering the pistol in the holster on his belt.

"We seem to meet at unpromising moments, General Malik! Hopefully, the next time will be under more pleasant circumstances."

"You have caused me a great deal of trouble, Batani, and it must stop," the General replied forcefully.

"I am sorry you feel that way, General, but it is understandable. However, I am now in a position to do you a great service, with respect to the problem stemming from the Chinese plans to indefinitely defer completion of the railroad that was supposed to extend to Torkham from Kabul and the north. Your government is very much afraid such an action by Beijing would cause great harm to Pakistan. But, I am in a position to intercede with the Chinese on Pakistan's behalf, and would be willing to arrange it so that you personally received major credit."

"What would be your price for such a service?"

"Peace, General Malik, peace. I would require that the kind of impediments to progress and prosperity in Afghanistan, such as those occurring here in Torkham right now, permanently cease so that the people can devote there lives to building a better future rather than simply trying to survive day to day. Pakistan, in particular the ISI, must actively participate in measures to control the activities of the lawless bands that operate in both your country's territory and mine, particularly those committing atrocities in the name of Islam. We will speak of specific targets when your government has agreed to our arrangement. What do you say?"

Malik was confused. This was not what he had come for, but Batani's proposition sounded reasonable and worth considering. If he went back to his superiors to report Batani's proposal rather than his elimination, would they consider him a success or a failure?

"I will take your proposition back to the capital, Mir Batani Khan, and advise you of the result." Batani nodded and smiled.

"I look forward to your return."

Batani filled Hannah in on the details of his meeting with Malik and she, in turn, briefed Jed and Sam Glover. There was little to do now but wait, although the air quality in Torkham had become increasingly toxic and the armed men in the streets had grown bored and restless in the uncomfortable conditions. In the Old West these circumstances would have produced drunkenness, fistfights, and the occasional faceoff. In abstinent Torkham, they produced bursts of AK-47 fire, not always into the air.

Jed returned to Rawalpindi to keep tabs on Malik and his ear to the ground for indications of the Pakistani government's reaction to Batani's proposal. As usual in Pakistan, auguries were mixed and contradictory, as General Malik discovered when he reported again to the Army Chief of Staff and the Dark Angel. Neither professed to be pleased with Batani's offer, although told earlier by their own superiors that Pakistan would accept it after a suitable, face-saving delay. They did not, however, tell Malik that, and allowed him to leave the meeting still believing that the future of Pakistan and his career rested on his shoulders alone, with time rapidly running out.

Batani was wandering the Torkham bazaar with a coterie of international journalists and their camera crews when told that General Malik had returned and wished to see him. Hannah was lurking out of sight to avoid an unwanted appearance on the 11 o'clock news. For Batani, it was a fortuitous opportunity to focus the world's attention on himself and his achievements in Afghanistan. He directed that Malik be brought to the small café in which he and the journalists were sitting, surprising his security escort and Reggie Huggins, who was about to intervene when Batani began explaining to the others why Malik had come.

"For those of you who do not know of General Raheem Malik, he is the new Director of Pakistan's Inter Services Intelligence Directorate, the illustrious ISI, of which I'm sure you all have heard. He has come because we have made an agreement to resolve, once and for all, the problems between our two countries that have been evidenced all too frequently by the kind of chaos you see here in Tork-ham."

His words created an uproar among the experienced correspondents, for whom any access to the head of the shadowy ISI was a major "get." Suddenly, in the dimly lit interior of the café, many camera lights were turned on and focused on Malik. He fell back startled, reaching for the absent pistol he had temporarily surrendered at the border crossing. Not finding it, he turned to leave.

"Where are you going, Malik? It is time to celebrate!"

The General was furious. He believed that he was being made a fool of, both by Batani and his own superiors. Batani would not be so cocksure, if he did not already have reliable word that Islamabad would agree to his deal. Yet, the Dark Angel, who certainly would have known, had assured Malik that the Taliban leader was a grave threat. The General realized then---what he had really always known---that the business with the railroad was a diversion, and his only path to redemption was to kill Batani and hope that his family would benefit from a fallen hero's due reward. He reached into his tunic and pulled out a small automatic pistol held in his waistband (one did not pat down a General in dress uniform) and fired the entire magazine at Batani standing less than eight feet away. The last two shots went awry, as the larger slugs from Reggie Huggins' weapon threw Malik backwards and down to the floor, where the bullets of the other security guards found him. Batani was also on the floor, bleeding profusely from at least four wounds. Hearing the shots, Hannah ran into the room, heedless of the surprised look of recognition on the faces of some of the journalists. The latter stood transfixed until the sound of the shooting had died away, then rushed from the building to see whether their cell phones could flag down a passing satellite.

Heavily bandaged and connected to multiple IVs, Batani was taken by Army helicopter to the American combat medical facility at Bagram air base, where his condition was further stabilized. It was decided there to evacuate him, under an assumed identity, to the large U.S. military hospital in Germany for surgery and postoperative recovery. Jed rode an Agency plane sent up from Islamabad for the transfer mission. He and Hannah stood on the flight line watching Batani's stretcher being moved from an ambulance to the plane.

"Fortunately, he was wearing a flak vest that stopped a couple of shots that would have otherwise been fatal," Hannah reported. "But, Malik was standing so close that he couldn't miss, and he fired a full clip. Batani will survive, but it will be a long time before he's fully restored."

"Have you been able to talk with him?" Jed asked.

"Just briefly. He's conscious, but still in shock. I think it's begun to dawn on him that he's going to miss his moment here in Afghanistan. By the time he gets back, assuming that ever happens, the world will have moved on and everyone here will be fighting different battles with different enemies or maybe the same battles all over again."

"Do you think he could have succeeded, Hannah?"

"Wishful thinking aside, I think he would have had a good shot at it. In addition to being bright and not afraid to take risks, he had the ability to convince people who started out mistrusting him that he could lead them to security and prosperity. I watched him convince local warlords and tribal chieftains that, for example, killing the workers building a new road through their districts was not a smart thing to do. Then, he hired them to protect the very same workers they had been attacking, in essence paying them to prevent what they no longer planned to do."

"But he appears to have been the victim of his own cleverness in this railroad business," Jed concluded, shaking his head. "The whole thing was a sham that all of the players recognized, but participated in because each was getting something out of it. The Chinese never would have screwed the Pakistanis about the railroad, if only because they need each other to help contain India. But, they could afford to imply otherwise for a while to help out Batani, who was their preferred Afghan leader. Knowing he could obtain Chinese agreement, Batani could make the Pakistanis an offer they couldn't refuse that would get them their needed rail connection to Torkham. But, my contacts told me yesterday that the Generals in Rawalpindi learned the truth about this a month ago from Kingsley Yong. Their actual motive in engaging in this kabuki was to lure Batani to Torkham where they could get to him. That's why they created a fuss by suddenly closing the border crossing without announced reason."

Hannah smiled bitterly. "Apparently, no one informed Malik of the setup. His bosses must have told him that Batani was about to screw Pakistan big time, and that it was his duty to prevent disaster. Do you think Orkamzi would have fallen for it?"

They watched as the plane's door was closed and the engines started. As it began to taxi to the runway, they turned back toward the operations office.

"Well, Hannah, what now?"

"I think, Jed, that I'm going to hang up my burqa and go home to do my laundry."

The author is grateful for the views and counsel of the following individuals in the creation and design of The Drone Paradigm:

Clare and Tom Brooks,
Tom Carroll,
Mary Lee Kingsley
DeeAnna Stone.